Ambitions of A Bison
*Copyright © 2015 By Ira Porter*

Published by
Blind Ambition Publishing, LLC
Philadelphia, PA 19144

Printed in the United States of America
Second Edition, 2021

ISBN: 978-0-9793174-2-2

*Cover Design: Verna Porter*
*Book Design: Ira Porter and Verna Porter*

# Ambitions of A Bison

BY IRA PORTER

## Acknowledgements

To Verna and Ari. You two are the main characters in my greatest creation, and you are my sweetest inspiration.

# *Prologue*

It was just Brandon Smith's luck that he would be late on move-in day at Howard University. It was as if bad luck had been passed down to him. Not inherited, but passed down from his mother, the very person responsible for making him late for the 4 p.m. move-in deadline, and freshman orientation.

August 15, 1998, was circled in red ink on the Howard calendar that Brandon had bought from the Howard Bookstore nine months earlier—when he had visited the campus as part of a black college tour. The tour bus stopped at Cheney, Lincoln, Delaware State and Morgan State Universities before they got to Howard, and for Brandon, the bus ride could not have been more torturous. He wanted to go back home after the stop at Howard—after he had a chance to walk across the Yard. That was all he needed: to walk across the famous Yard, the same one that Zora Neale Hurston, Donny Hathaway, Ossie Davis and a slew of other prominent African-American intellectuals had trekked across since 1867. He was applying to Morehouse, Clark and Hampton, but Howard was the best. And on that trip he made up his mind that the Mecca was the family he would join as a National Merit Scholar.

The trip was only halfway complete by the time they got to his future home, and because he couldn't go back, he had to endure endless hours of riding on the back of a commercial bus amongst a group of restless Philadelphia-area high school seniors. Other schools that they visited tried to recruit him, but his mind was made up. He spent $63 at the bookstore on Howard paraphernalia to consummate the relationship. One of the items was a blue and white wall calendar with the Howard logo in the middle of every page and a bison at the bottom right-hand side.

One of several objects hanging on his sky-blue wall (the others being a Michael Jordan NBA Finals print, and album covers for De La Soul *Stakes is High* and The Roots' *Illadelph Halflife*) the calendar served as a reminder that he was leaving Philly for four years, a prospect that excited him greatly.

"Brandon, why are you just standing there looking at that calendar when you got all these boxes to load in the van?" his mom barked, bursting into the backroom of their West Oak Lane rowhouse. He diverted his attention and stared at her. He would have sneered, but she would have then cursed him out and made them later than they already were. It would simply exacerbate the reason he was upset in the first place.

"I didn't know the van was outside. Y'all took so long to get it. I had my stuff ready to go early this morning, because that was when we were supposed to leave."

"Boy, don't start with me. I told you they gave my other rental away last night and I had to wait on standby to get this one. Uncle Harry had to take me down to the airport to rent this one. Now come on. We gotta go," she said before leaving his room.

At least his Uncle Harry was coming for the ride. That way Brandon wouldn't have to carry his TV, computer and stereo up the steps of his dorm all by himself. And like him, his Uncle Harry didn't care for the gospel music his mother liked to play while driving. So, with Uncle Harry being there, she would just tell Brandon and his younger sister, Belinda, how their father wasn't shit, wasn't ever going to be shit, and that it was better that they heard it from her about the piece of shit he was before they got caught up in it. She would end her rant with a rapid prayer for Jesus to give her the strength needed to deal with such heathens.

Brandon and his uncle packed most of his stuff inside the Ford Windstar while his mom reset the answering machine on the phone and yelled at Belinda that she had to clean her room when they got back from Washington D.C. Belinda ignored her and collected CDs to listen to listen to on her Discman during the trip south, just in case her mom played gospel or Brandon or Uncle Harry played music she didn't like.

By 2 p.m. they were done packing and Brandon's mother, much to his dismay, jumped behind the driver's seat, insisting that she take the job of driving down and her brother Harry could drive back. Pearls of sweat gathered on Brandon's forehead — a combination of the August heat and the stress build-up from him ruminating over how late he was going to be. His paranoia got the best of him. In his mind they would be late, he would lose his room assignment in Drew Hall and would have to spend a night in a hotel while his family left D.C. and went back to Philly. What made things worse was when they got to the traffic light at Broad Street and the Roosevelt Expressway—a good three or four miles away from their home—his mother opened her mouth.

"Belinda did you set the alarm?"

Belinda furrowed her brow, stared back into her mother's piercing copper eyes through the rearview mirror and said, "No. I thought you said you were going to set it."

The brakes screeched, the car stopped, and their mother cursed.

"I'll be damned," she said. "I gotta go back and set the alarm."

"Mom, nobody is going to break into the house," Brandon pled. "There's nothing in there for them to take."

She looked at his worried 18-year-old face and rolled her eyes. She turned around and headed north on Broad Street, back home to set the alarm. Harry shook his head and so did Brandon. Move-in day at Howard was going to be a disaster, but hopefully not a premonition of his first semester there.

# *One*

 

Everything in her sight was pleasing to Falu Davis. The plush, new, royal blue rug she ordered from Physical Facilities Management over the summer had been delivered, and she convinced herself that it was just as sophisticated as the one she saw in President Humphries' office last year, when she was first introduced to him. She copied the exact color and fabric as President Humphries' because to her it meant power and success, everything she craved. Powerful people attracted her, and to become one of them—she taught herself—meant that she had to think like them.

She had to read what they read, eat where they ate, socialize with whom they socialized, and situate herself in surroundings that constantly reminded her of the little symbolic power she had gained and the cachet of actual power she coveted for the future. The rug was small in the grand scheme of things, but it was a step forward. It was validation that at 21, she was on the right track and headed for big things if she continued to hustle and be aggressive. These were attributes she possessed that got her elected as the Howard University Student Association president two years in a row. She was the first person, let alone the first female president, to ever do such a thing since HUSA was created in 1961.

The first year when she was elected, as a sophomore going into her junior year, she was the youngest president and only the fourth female to hold the title. Only the fourth female on a campus where women outnumber men two to one, contrary to the more obtuse and incorrect breakdown other people not associated with the school thought. She got the last laugh and the satisfaction of proving wrong all the pessimists who said she couldn't win as a sophomore. All of those people, including some members of the faculty senate, classmates and other student leaders thought that it would be outrageous for the student body to elect an inexperienced, green girl from Chicago to lead a campus with a student population 10,000strong.

She couldn't mobilize the student body, they said, and she couldn't press issues to the president and board of trustees that mattered most to her peers. It shook her confidence at times, but she only acknowledged it in private. Only on the phone to her mother or father, both successful Illinois attorneys and Howard University graduates who were enrolled at the school when HUSA started. They helped Falu stay focused on what she had to do: Win the election.

She won it after a run-off against the D.R.E.A.M Team campaign. She remembered their slogan to the tee. "Developing Howard for the 20th Century, Retaining and recruiting quality students, Enriching the educational experience of every student enrolled at the university, Always aiming to further our standing and serve our community better, and Moving mountains." It was a lot of junk that took the two engineering student candidates, Kamal Brown and Tyrone Pope, all of five minutes to think of, she told herself. But she never attacked them or got into shouting matches at the speak-outs when they tried to egg her on. She never retaliated when they brought up her age or the fact that she was a spoiled girl from the suburbs of Chicago whose parents donated every year to the university, and accused her of feeling entitled to the position.

Oh, she wanted to attack—and she did in private to friends—but she didn't indulge the urge publicly. She hated them and wished the worst things to happen to them, but smiled in their faces while secretly despising them. When she won, she had cleared her first hurdle on the way to world domination.

She smiled looking into the mirror of her office, more than a year later, seemingly an eternity after that heart-wrenching experience almost made her crack from fear and anxiety. Winning a second year straight was easier, cruising to 70 percent of the 3,300 votes cast in total. She rode the coattails of her first successful term as president straight into office, and now everyone suddenly believed in her and wanted to be her friend. Now *The Hilltop*, the student newspaper, thought carefully before they wrote vitriolic editorials about her.

This year—her senior year—the year before she went off to Harvard Law School, hopefully, would be bigger and better. Getting what she wanted and succeeding felt so good. To top it all off, she was blessed to be breathtakingly beautiful. That garnered her more hatred from female coeds on campus than any of her academic and extra-curricular success, was the fact that.

When she stared into that mirror, bone stared back at her. Beautiful bone, structured high and prominently. In fact, her bone structure was so perfect that it looked as if someone purposely closed off every orifice above her neck with the exception of one, and used that one to suck out any fat or excessiveness. Her milk chocolate skin tone was as smooth as a newborn baby's bottom, and contrasted alluringly to her pearlescent teeth, which were white and straight like piano keys. Her hair was natural and curly and thick. Depending on how she wore it, it would flare out in an afro that rivaled Angela Davis's (no relation) or would cascade well below her shoulders onto her back, wavy from wetting it and pulling it back.

Her body was perfect. At five-feet-eleven, her legs practically stopped at her chin. The years of ballet formed chiseled muscles in her calves, her stomach divided into six equally sized squares and her breasts perfectly filled a C-cup. Not too big for her frame, they sat high and perky on her torso, on their own accord.

If it was true that you could tell how a young woman was going to look when she got older by looking at her mother, well, Falu was going to be beautiful all her life. Because her looks, as the saying went, *she got them from her mama.*

It was almost time for her to join President Humphries and other university dignitaries on stage to welcome the freshman class of the Class of 2002.

"Fix your jacket," Maurice Jerome, her second vice president in as many years, instructed her, as he fixed his navy-blue tie in the mirror behind her.

"Oh, thanks. I was about to get up on stage looking raggedy," she said. "I can't have that."

It was 87 degrees outside, late in the afternoon on August 15, 1998, and Falu, Maurice and a few other aides from her office were dressed in business suits. Falu was dressed in a conservative Donna Karan gray pinstripe skirt suit, with a champagne-colored short-sleeve shirt underneath. That was also made by Donna Karan, her and her mother's favorite designer. She couldn't decide on the shiny, black three-inch heels made by Gucci or the sandals that matched her shirt and the stripe in her suit. She went with the sandals and trekked in between the rows of parents assembled in folding chairs. They waved makeshift fans across their faces as they sat sweltering behind the freshman class — their sons and daughters — which totaled almost 1,200 students.

Maurice took the stage with her, and followed suit with a supercilious facial expression that sought to distance them from the other student leaders, Campus Pals and so-called haters in attendance.

President Milton Humphries stood at the podium, beaming at the audience in front of him. Every few seconds, he swept away sweat on his forehead and gave the onlookers a mouthful of teeth. He cleared phlegm from his throat and ran his manicured fingers back through his salt-and-pepper mane, and then replaced them on the podium before he spoke.

"It is with pleasure that I welcome the parents, friends and family to our beautiful campus today. This is my tenth year as president and my tenth pinning ceremony. Well, actually, it's my eleventh if you count my very own as a freshman here more than 34 years ago," he laughed. "It was hot then and it is hot here today. I'll tell you that much."

Some people in the audience laughed with him. Others fanned. The freshmen sat, looking like freshmen, eager to get away from their parents so all the drinking, smoking, and crazy sex could commence. Falu and her team laughed along to the same joke President Humphries had been telling for years. They had to. They had an image to uphold. Falu had even more to gain by staying on his good side.

"I won't keep you too long, but I hope you get a chance to take a look at our beautiful campus and see all the additions that we are making, parents, especially if any of you are alumni. If you have contributed to our capital campaign you will be very pleased to see that your dollars are going toward making Howard University a better place to educate leaders of tomorrow and of the global community. It is because of the generosity of people like you that these students in front of us, almost twelve hundred, I am told—and seventy-six National Merit Scholars at that—will see some of those improvements during their tenure here," he said. The crowd applauded—more so for the fact that there were 76 merit scholars among the freshmen than any improvements that Howard was getting. This moment was as good as any to wipe his face for the seventh or eighth time so far. He calculated in his head that his speech was 10 minutes, and would be followed by speeches from student leaders and a performance by the university marching band. He had to wrap it up.

"Thanks for your applause. Class of 2002," he said pointing a finger at them, moving it along like it was a machine gun wiping out the front line of an enemy regiment. "They are applauding for you, not me. I already have my degree. Or degrees, I should say. The question is will you get yours? Will you handle your business and do what you have to do in order to have your parents come back four years from now and celebrate with you at commencement?" He let that settle for a minute without saying anything. "That is the question, class of 2002. I want every one of you to look at the student sitting to your left. Look at the student sitting to your right. That student won't walk across this Yard with you four years from now," he said.

All the naïve freshmen stared at each other, wondering who it would be who would flunk out, drop out, transfer, or due to some form of tragedy, not make it to graduation day. All the parents and upperclassmen in attendance were quite familiar with the cliché, but quite true saying about college attrition. President Humphries ended his speech there and allowed the current "Ms. Howard" to sing *The Alma Mater*, the song that won her the title, and which was written by J.H. Brooks in 1916.

> *Reared against the eastern sky*
> *Proudly there on hilltop high,*
> *Far above the lake so blue*
> *Stands old Howard firm and true.*
>
> *There she stands for truth and right,*
> *Sending forth her rays of light,*
> *Clad in robes of majesty:*
> *O Howard, we sing of thee.*
>
> *Be thou still our guide and stay*
> *Leading us from day to day:*
> *Make us true and leal and strong,*
> *Ever bold to battle wrong*
>
> *When from thee we've gone away,*
> *May we strive for thee each day*
> *As we sail life's rugged sea,*
> *O Howard, we'll sing of thee.*

Victoria Mourning sat like every other student leader and listened to songs and speeches that she had heard before. She didn't have a speaking part during the pinning ceremony like Falu Davis did, the arrogant bitch from Chicago who stayed on her floor in the Quad, freshman year in Frazier Hall. Victoria didn't even have a seat on the makeshift stage in front of Douglass Hall. But she insisted on being present at the pinning ceremony since she was also a student leader. She came back early from her internship at Goldman Sachs to move into her dorm room and get situated for her senior year. Some of the sisters from the sorority she led as president reminded her of the pinning ceremony at the last minute, so she decided to go.

She hadn't seen anyone during the summer in New York. Working late nights at Goldman, seeing all the beautiful, working women in New York gave her a new attitude toward life, and as a result she came back to school more disciplined than ever. She returned more confident for many reasons, but mainly because over the summer she had amazingly lost 50 pounds. The transformation was especially shocking since no one had seen her during the change—she worked constantly, and spent all her free time working out.

Before, she was five-feet-six and 200 pounds. When she dropped the weight, some of the stretch marks that remained were easy to see in contrast to her peanut butter complexion. Her face no longer looked like a pancake, and her lone dimple was prominent now. She cut her hair into pixie cut. Oh yeah, they would get a kick out of her this year.

Not only was she president of the alpha chapter of her sorority at Howard, but she was also nice looking again, and she hadn't felt that way since freshman year, when guys fought to get her number and take her out. Her freshman year was the best of all her years at Howard, but before she knew it, she gained the so-called Freshman 15, which turned to 30, then 60. She had been dumped by a few guys. She felt the sting in the heart of not getting called the next day after she made the mistake of sleeping with a guy or two. But there were two episodes involving her and a guy at Howard that temporarily broke her spirit. Now she had it back, and she knew he would be at the pinning ceremony.

She sat on the side of the stage with the Campus Pals. Campus Pals was a whole other story when it came to Howard traditions. They were the welcoming party for incoming freshmen. A group of boisterous, outgoing, upperclassmen, they traveled in cliques and initiated new entrants into their organization—one of the most popular student organizations on campus—like they were a fraternity or sorority. In short, they were jokingly like a cult.

Victoria knew many of them from having entered Howard together. Some of them were her sorority sisters, at least one was a guy she slept with freshman year, and many of the other girls were just sorority hopefuls or rejects who would be coming to rush events again this year in an attempt to join before they graduated.

She sat with them on the side of the stage; breaking the continuity of their Campus Pal T-shirts with their nicknames on the back, and their denim or khaki shorts. Vicky, as her friends called her, wore a white linen skirt and a shirt to match. The only thing she wore that wasn't white was the canary yellow flip-flops on her feet from the Gap. She didn't even fit in with the random Panhellenic members sporting their various paraphernalia. It was just too hot for all of that, she said, and today was her day back on campus in her new body, which curved nicely in her skirt, accentuating the attributes her physique had to offer. Yeah, they were looking at her. Some of them could not believe it was her. Not even Falu Davis, whom she caught looking at her from the stage, before Falu got up to address the crowd.

"Vicky is that you?" Tracy Hampton, a Campus Pal from Michigan said to her, beckoning with open arms for a hug.

Vicky smiled and hugged her back. "It's me, girl. I lost some weight over the summer."

"I see. Damn, how much did you lose? You look really good, girl. I need to get on whatever diet you were on," she smiled and sat next to her.

Vicky thanked her and didn't comment on Tracy getting on her diet. She studied her classmate as Tracy spoke to other familiar faces in the crowd, and noticed the hanging skin under her chin, the flab around her arms, and the panties sticking up out of her jeans as she sat on the folding chair. Tracy had the potential to be a cute girl. She was cute freshman year when she first got to Howard, but now she was a little chunky, and being chunky wasn't cute. While Vicky didn't comment on Tracy saying that she needed to adopt whatever diet Vicky was on, she agreed with the sentiment wholeheartedly. Along with the new attitude she adopted over the summer was a severe case of disgust for overweight people—and what she considered the trifling lifestyles they lived that made them overweight.

Situated in the back of the section with all the Campus Pals, Vicky couldn't see many of the faces of the curious freshmen who looked back at them, the student leaders and university officials on stage. Watching them triggered nostalgia for 1995, when she sat where they sat, a freshmen from a suburb of Detroit, and certain she was destined to be a stockbroker and a millionaire by age 30. She hoped to meet her husband at Howard, and go from there to Wall Street.

These freshmen looked just as hopeful as she did. As she sat, looking at her surroundings, she wondered who among them would be Campus Pals one day. Who among them would be the president of HUSA like Falu Davis? Whoever it was, Vicky hoped they wouldn't be as arrogant.

She wondered who among them would want to join her sorority, or if the future president of her sorority was sitting 50 feet away from her and she didn't even know. Lastly, she frowned when she thought about all of the girls who would get their hearts broken at Howard the way she did. Some by the very Campus Pals staring at them on that hot August day, the guys who used their status as upperclassmen and Campus Pals to get first dibs on all the pretty girls just happy to be away from home and have older guys liking them.

Oh, the traps would come. The guys would be charming. As she sat in the back of the rows of Campus Pals, blending in, she stood to stretch. She then saw the cause of her most serious heartache at Howard standing about 100 feet away from her, looking up at the stage. No doubt he did not notice her.


"Which way do you want me to stand when I take the shot, Ben?" Cassie Hebron asked her boss as they stood on the grass next to throngs of students and parents sitting in their chairs.

"Are you serious, Cassie?" he asked back, looking at her incredulously. "You're supposed to be my photo editor and you are asking me where to stand to take a shot. I don't know. Take a bunch of pictures. Get one of the stage, of President Humphries, Falu Davis and everyone else on stage, then get a big one of the new students. You don't really have to get a picture of their parents while they are sitting. I guess you can get one of them after they start pinning each other and hugging each other," he said.

Cassie was making a simple task so difficult, he thought. He hated when she asked stupid questions like that. When they first met a year ago, when he was managing editor of *The Hilltop*, he thought she feigned stupidity because she liked him. But now, a year later, after hiring her to be one of his team of editors, he thought she was really stupid. He had too many other things to worry about besides picking which place she should snap a photo from. He had to spend $200 of his own money to buy the camera she was snapping pictures on and he would have to pay out his pocket for the film to be developed. The university hadn't started paying them their stipends, and Student Activities was taking forever to transfer money from *The Hilltop's* cut of the student activity fee to their account, which he would use to get new equipment. He would get reimbursed in a week or so, but until then he was living off of savings he acquired from his internship during the summer at *The Washington Post*, and CNN's D.C. bureau on the weekends. The *Post* paid. CNN—like many other broadcast operations — didn't.

"You're right," she said, turning from him, flashing a camera light at Falu Davis as the student leader reached the podium to speak. "When you find a freshman to interview, just signal for me to come over so I can get a picture of them for the story," she continued.

"That'll work. Just take the pictures first. I'm not gonna interrupt anyone while Falu is talking, although I should," he sneered at the stage.

Benjamin Bishop stuck his pen on top of his right ear, placed his reporting notepad in the back pocket of his shorts and knelt on the grass to tie his sneaker. Before he grabbed his tattered laces, he mopped the sweat from across his brow. It was a combination of the heat, the East Coast humidity and the fact that he let his hair grow over the summer into a bushy, little nappy afro that caused him to swelter. It was his quiet rebellion from working in two newsrooms where the majority of people were white, and he felt like the blacks were powerless. He figured locs, afros and braids made them uncomfortable. It was the only way he could think of to push the limit. The good thing about his internships was that now they were over, and he could get on with his last year at Howard before he entered the "real world."

He would be the eyes, ears and voice of Howard, as Editor-in-Chief of *The Hilltop*, the student newspaper. This was a job he planned on having since he stepped foot on campus three years earlier, and he had trained himself for it mentally. All the late nights staying up, crafting last-minute stories on HUSA meetings that took forever to be over with, because they started late and had to reach a quorum, had paid off. All the homecoming step shows, Spring Black Art Festival performances, the dignitaries who spoke in chapel, and famous lecturers who came to speak with students had prepared him. He covered them all. His G.P.A. suffered because of it, but he managed to keep it a little above a 3.0. As a broadcast journalism major, it bothered the other print students who felt he should not have been elected EIC, but secretly everyone knew he was the best person for the job. Each summer he maintained broadcast and print internships and had won a Hearst Award for collegiate journalism the previous year, after an internship at *New York Newsday*, one of his hometown papers.

"They got some cute freshmen this year," Cassie said, coming back over to him.

"Whatever," he said. "All I know is I wish Falu would hurry and finish talking her shit so we can get this interview over with and I can get out of this heat. I'm already chocolate enough," he said staring at his arm.

"You and me both," Cassie laughed. "Don't you have other stuff to worry about for the first issue of the paper? Why are you covering this anyway? I would've thought President Humphries would have had you on stage with the rest of the student leaders."

"He didn't ask me to. Go figure. I'm the only reporter the paper has until next week, when the upperclassmen come back."

"Poor you," she smiled.

"Wait, Falu is wrapping up her speech. They're about to pin each other. Make sure you get a shot of that and then come back over here. I wanna interview that kid right there with the Phillies jersey on," Ben said.

"He's cute."

"Yeah, yeah, yeah. Just get the shot," he snapped.

Minutes later, President Humphries, Falu Davis and other student leaders came down from the stage and started pinning new freshmen with the Howard emblem. Ben watched as other freshmen joined in and started pinning each other, shaking hands, and smiling for pictures with their families. Ben and Falu caught glimpses of each other, but didn't gesture to acknowledge each other. They didn't quite hate each other, but they weren't friends either, which was sad because freshmen year they hung out with the same people. Ben even tried to date her, but she rejected him, which was something many other girls at Howard didn't do.

He walked up to a cocoa-complexioned kid a few inches shorter than him, who was sporting a red Philadelphia Phillies jersey, jean shorts and Timberland boots. The freshman didn't notice Ben approach him, and grabbed hold of an older woman who looked like him before they both posed for a picture. Ben let the family have their moment before he introduced himself.

"Hi, my name is Benjamin Bishop. I'm the editor-in-chief of the student newspaper here, and we're doing a story on the pinning ceremony. I was wondering if I could ask you guys a couple of quick questions?" he asked, staring at Brandon Smith. Before Brandon could answer, his mother butted in.

"You sure can, young man," she said, extending her hand for him to shake. "My name is Debbie Smith and this is my son, Brandon. We are from Philadelphia," she smiled.

"Oh Philly, huh? I've only been there once, but I liked it," he said, shaking everyone's hand.

"We love it," Debbie shot back.

"Mom," Brandon snapped, stepping up to where his mother was so he could be interviewed.

"So, you are the editor of the whole paper? That's tight. Do y'all let freshmen write for the paper? I was thinking about trying out for it."

"Of course we do," Ben said. You should be seeing signs up soon, inviting people to come to our budget meetings so they can get stories or bring ideas.

"Oh good, because I have a lot of ideas."

"Well come to our meetings," Ben said, whipping out a card for Brandon to have, "and let us hear them."

Ben asked Brandon a series of questions about why he chose Howard, how he felt about finally being there, and if he thought he would get homesick. He had to scribble in his notepad quickly to accommodate Brandon and his mother, who was determined to be quoted just as much as her son in the story. Much of what she said was not going to be put in the paper, since the whole point of the article was to talk to the incoming student. But she simply talked too much.

He listened and stared into her eyes—beautiful eyes—he thought to himself, until something even more beautiful mixing and mingling with the new students distracted him. It was a face he used to like seeing, the face of a girl whose bed he shared many nights, until his shallow, selfish side and childish personality traits took over and he gave her up. Vicky Mourning was smiling in everyone's face, shaking hands and greeting new students. He couldn't listen to Brandon and his mother talk anymore after seeing Vicky. She was slim and beautiful again, just like she was when he first met her years ago. After what he did to her, it would be so fake and phony to go up and speak to her, but he planned to.

"Look at you. You made the news your first day on campus," Debbie smiled. "Send me a copy of the article when it comes out so I can show everyone at church, okay?"

"Yeah mom, whatever. You took over the interview. I probably won't have any quotes. And then you jumped in front of me when the girl was taking the picture," Brandon complained.

"I did not," his mother shot back.

"You did so, mom."

Brandon was getting sick of his family and he was so happy that they would be leaving him in a short time to go back to Philly. He was happy that although they got to school late, they were still able to move him into Drew Hall. He and his uncle carried his things up the stairs since the freight elevators were being used by students just as late as he was. His mom and sister set up his room while he had to rush to Greene Stadium to take a class picture with the rest of the freshmen.

After he came back from taking the class picture, he knew that Howard was going to be good to him. There were so many pretty girls. His roommate, Tony, a dude from Los Angeles, seemed cool, and he relaxed a lot after walking across the campus. He felt like he was a part of something much bigger than he had first imagined.

The Campus Pals were so friendly and hyper; the band played actual hip-hop music, and fraternity brothers and sorority sisters made noises and hand gestures displaying their school spirit. And although he had decided he wanted to be a political science major, he quickly thought about being a journalist. The editor-in-chief of the student newspaper came up to him and interviewed him for a story. This guy was sharp, too, which automatically inspired Brandon.

Brandon had never met someone who wasn't a working professional who carried themselves so confidently and gave out business cards. He looked at Ben's card in his hand, then spotted Ben shaking President Humphries hand, then the student body president's—who was beautiful—and then the hand of another curvy, pretty girl dressed in all white. He smiled to himself, awestruck by all the potential things that could happen.

# *Two*

November 2, 1998

At least twenty-five hundred students, staff, and administrators milled about the Yard in the twilight, waiting for the show. It was 10 p.m. Sunday, the official day before homecoming week started, and everyone gathered for the fireworks ceremony on the Yard. It was an annual tradition. The athletes came from their comfortable rooms in Cooke Hall, a dormitory dedicated mostly to athletes, nestled close to all the learning halls like Douglass, Locke, Human Ecology, Fine Arts and The School of Business.

You could always tell the athletes because they made the most noise in public, called each other names and dressed in their Howard paraphernalia. And they traveled in packs based on activity: football players, some big and gargantuan, hung with only football players; basketball team members, tall and lanky, followed each other; and the women's volleyball team—some pretty, some average—all hung in unison. The whole athletic department followed suit. This was true even for teams whose season hadn't started, like the baseball and tennis team.

Freshman boys, looking like freshman boys—skinny and awkward—proudly identified themselves as such by either wearing gray and blue Drew Hall dormitory t-shirts with thermal shirts on under them, or shouting "Drew Hall" as they walked across the grass. Only freshman girls thought that that was cute. Upperclassmen just stared and remembered when it was them doing the yelling.

Freshman boys from Carver Hall, a satellite dorm about six or seven blocks away from campus in the Ledroit Park area, never yelled their dorm's name. One reason was because it wasn't strictly a freshman dorm like Drew, and the other was because they didn't want everyone to know they were freshmen.

And the freshman girls came to the Yard in droves from the Quadrangle, consisting of Truth, Crandall, Baldwin and Frazier Hall dormitories. They also came from the Bethune Annex, the most recently constructed dorm with state-of-the-art amenities and their own cafeteria. It wasn't strictly a freshman dorm, but many of them stayed there, waging a silent battle against the quad girls. As the notion went, girls from Bethune thought they were better than quad girls. Bethune Annex was a dorm that had opened less than 10 years earlier, and at one point allowed male residents. But that policy suddenly changed, in a seemingly cruel twist for males—who as the university put it, had low retention rates. It would seem that a school dedicated to keeping male retention rates high would try to accommodate them in the simplest ways.

But the freshman girls came, and many of them dressed for the runway instead of a night of leisure. All of that pageantry to watch fireworks shoot from down in the valley hundreds of feet in the sky, and then explode in rainbow colors. Some of the girls wore the regular sweatshirt and sweat pants getup, with their heads wrapped and sneakers on their feet; but others wore heels, designer jeans and leather jackets. You just never knew who you would see on Howard's campus. Colin Powell was on the Board of Trustees, and for homecoming many celebrities and entertainers walked across the Yard. Some were looking to discover new talent. For a student population where the majority of the coeds were nice-looking, it never hurt to be seen looking your best.

Greg Harris always looked his best. Even if he wore a white t-shirt and jeans, it had to be presentable. The jeans were crisp and wrinkle free, and so was the t-shirt, as if it was made on his body. White to match the smile that twinkled whenever he spread his perfect valentine lips in someone's face showing off his dimple. His smile, curly hair, light skin and green eyes drove girls who were caught up on complexion crazy. He was an even six-feet tall, 200-pound mass of muscle. Greg, originally from Los Angeles, was what people called a "super senior." Although no one knew, they guessed he was 23 or 24.

He knew many professors, and all if not most of the upper-classmen knew him, because they had probably all gone to at least one of the parties he threw over the years. Many girls on campus threw themselves at him—a good number of whom he'd caught and sexed in his off-campus apartment. He was many things to people on Howard's campus: the number-one weed and ecstasy supplier, fake ID maker, party promoter, money maker, and well connected, entrepreneur.

He openly displayed how fat his pockets were, from the jewelry he wore, to the cash he flashed, to the 1999 Black Lincoln Navigator he pumped around campus in. Greg made more money as a college student than some new faculty members. He wasn't in a rush to graduate from Howard.

Only administrators were supposed to have access to drive past the metal gates on campus for parking to see the fireworks, but Greg knew Harold, one of the university police officers—the one guarding the gate that night—so he let Greg in.

"Harold, what's up, baby?" he said, rolling down his window to shake Harold's hand.

"You tell me, young," Harold said, speaking in his D.C. slang. "The party can get started now that you here. All the girls are out here for you. When you gon' put me on one these Howard jaunts, young?" It was more D.C. slang that made Greg smile. He looked to his left and saw the fraternity and sorority members stepping on the Yard, and throngs of people surrounding the flagpole watching them.

"I'll see what I can do for you, Harold," Greg said, peeling a $10 bill from the knot he carried in his pocket and offered it to Harold.

"Nah, young. Just get me in touch with one of them Howard girls and we cool. You know I'll look out for you," Harold said, pushing Greg's hand back. "That last girl you hooked me up with was nice, but she was a "urea" (area) jaunt. I want me a lil' Howard chumpy," he smiled.

"Oh, I see. Let me see what I can do. I'll be in touch."

Greg pulled up to the first empty spot he saw, which was next to the Andrew Rankin Memorial Chapel, a two-story, red brick building with stained glass windows. Throughout the school year, different preachers and guest speakers would speak there on Sundays. It was one of the few buildings Greg never stepped foot into when he got to Howard. He killed the fog lights on his truck, closed the moonroof, and hopped out, clicking the alarm for the sound effect, which caused people to stare. Sometimes he just loved the attention.

Today he smelled like CK B and was dressed in black Polo jeans, black and red, throwback elephant-skin Air Jordans, and a gray zip-up hoodie, with a white Polo shirt underneath. He rarely wore hats because the girls always commented on how nice his curly hair looked and wanted to run their fingers through it. As soon as he stepped foot on the cement, the calls came. Handshakes by Kappas, Alphas, Omegas and Sigmas commenced, and hugs and kisses on the cheek from bubbly girls followed.

He had just made it in time for the fireworks to start. He walked around the Yard speaking to various people during the 30-minute show, which displayed mini-rockets, M-80s and fireballs that made loud noises and danced across the November skyline, above the clock tower of Founder's Library. As Greg suspected, one of his admirers—a freshman from Philly who wrote for the student newspaper—was out on the Yard getting quotes for a story about the show.

Greg liked the hustle Brandon showed. From the first time Brandon introduced himself, asking Greg if he could interview him for a story about the number of students turning to alternative forms of income besides work study, Greg took a liking to him. The young journalist was looking at activities such as party promoting and doing hair. The story had already been done many times over the years that Greg had been at Howard, and Greg had been quoted in *The Hilltop* before, but this kid was serious about his craft. He had come all the way downtown to The Ritz, a popular nightclub for freshmen and the under-21 crowd, along with those who hadn't discovered fake IDs.

The Ritz was one of the clubs that Greg promoted parties at sometimes. Freshmen were eager to party and had lots of money to throw away—namely because their parents replenished their First Union and Bank of America accounts frequently.

The group of guys Brandon came with were busy dancing with girls, getting phone numbers, while Brandon worked before getting down to fun. He interviewed people, danced in-between interviews, and ended when he caught up with Greg, the main person he had gone to the club to speak with.

Greg took him in the bathroom, answered his questions and admonished him to never come to a club with a pen and a pad ready to do stories again … although, he also complimented him on his determination. From there, Greg gradually took Brandon under his wing and paid him top dollar to write term papers for him. That work expanded to include short biographies for a group of models Greg recruited for a new website he was running. Brandon gladly went along because he liked all the amenities of being a friend of Greg's.

"Clark Kent, what's going on?" Greg said, punching Brandon on the arm as he was blindly about to walk by him.

"Greg, what's up man? I didn't even see you," Brandon said beaming. He tucked his notepad into his back pocket, slipped his pen behind his ear, and gave Greg a handshake and a hug. Next, he gave out handshakes to all of the people around Greg.

"I know you didn't see me. You're too busy filling your little notepad up with quotes from everybody and their momma on campus," he laughed. "I bet you won't even use half of them," Greg teased.

"You're right. I won't, but it's better to have too much than too little," Brandon shrugged, and looked around at the crowd on the Yard.

"This my little protégé right here," Greg told the crowd around him. "He told me he wanna write for *The New York Times* or *The Washington Post*, but I might let him in on how to get some major paper," Greg smiled. So did Brandon.

"Let me talk to you for a minute," Greg said, tapping Brandon on the arm for them to walk away from the crowd. They walked over to the walkway between Founders and Rankin Chapel. Greg looked around at the crowd to see if anyone was watching them.

"How many stories they got you writing a week at that paper, man?"

"About two. Sometimes more. This week I got a lot to do because it's homecoming."

"That's right. It's homecoming. Your first homecoming at Howard. Don't spend all your time working on that paper. You better get out there and meet some of these little girls. Don't always think I'ma set something up for you," Greg snapped.

"I am. I got a number already tonight. What do you think I use this reporter stuff for? I've been getting numbers."

"Oh, for real," Greg smiled like a proud parent. He gave him a pound next. "That's a good thing. Keep that up, man. You gotta do more than just schoolwork here. You gotta balance that with a little fun."

"I know."

"Make sure you call me on Friday, because I got those passes for you for all the parties this weekend. And good looking out on that paper the other day for history class. I wish you could take my midterm for me on Wednesday, but I should be alright. I actually studied," Greg said.

"No doubt, man. I appreciate the tickets, too. I'll probably see you on the Yard for Yardfest so I'll get the ticket from you then," Brandon said. "What did you want to talk to me about?"

"I was just checking to see how hard they were working you. I need to ask you, have you heard anything about Ben or anybody else at the paper working on a story about me for this week's paper?"

"Nah, I haven't. Why? What's the story?" Brandon asked.

"You telling me the truth?"

"Yeah. Why? What's up?"

"I just heard a thing or two about that pussy-ass editor you work for, Ben. Heard he might be running on a bogus-ass story about me. I need you to find out if he is and get a copy of it for me." Greg's face was serious now. He was holding on to Brandon's shoulder, looking him in the eyes.

"Okay. I'll do that, but damn, what kind of story is this? It sounds like something big."

"Well, if he blows it up bigger than it is, it might be a big story, and you might be a part of it, too."

"Me? How am I a part of it?" Brandon asked, thinking about the two term papers he had written for Greg. He started to regret doing them.

"Just find out what Ben is up to. I'll tell you later. If he's not up to anything, then you don't have anything to worry about," Greg said. He and Brandon walked back into the circle of people, where they ran into Katrina Armstrong—an acquaintance of them both. She hugged Greg before he walked back toward the middle of the Yard and put her arms around Brandon.

"What's up, Mr. Reporter. Whatchu workin' on now? I know you working on something."

"I'm doing a little sumthin' sumthin'. It's for Friday's home-coming paper."

"Uh-huh."

"You are hard to get in touch with," he said. She took her hands from around his neck.

"Told you that from the beginning," she shrugged.

"Well, when can I see you again?"

She smiled and shrugged again. "I don't know. I'll call you. I'm trying to do a lot of things this semester," she said, "But I'll call you."

Katrina was sort of telling Brandon the truth. She would call him if she had the time or felt like being bothered with him, or needed to use him for anything, but only if it was for one of those reasons. It wouldn't be for what he was thinking.

Katrina was Brandon's first piece of action at Howard. Greg set it up for him one night when they were at his apartment in Columbia Heights, watching the Redskins play the Eagles. Katrina was an average-looking upperclassman, a junior from Atlanta.

She was also a closet weed addict who loved to party. She hung around Greg and his crew sometimes, and had sex with Greg occasionally, but only when he ran out of other options. Her body was her saving grace. She had an ass like Jennifer Lopez, except it looked better, and when she wore Parasuco Jeans she could make a blind man stare. Her chest filled a D-cup and her stomach was flat as an ironing board. She wore her hair straight, down to her shoulders, and had a slight acne problem that ruined her caramel complexion. To a nice guy on campus, she would have been a catch, but Katrina liked to get high and have sex. Many guys knew her, and if not from personal experience, than by word of mouth.

Brandon was just a freshman that she let have a taste and he turned out to be greedy, constantly wanting more. So she had to create distance. But him being a freshman, he didn't always catch on. When Brandon had sex with her, he told all his freshmen friends, in true boy fashion, and got much applause for it.

Not only was she his first at Howard, she was his first period. Eighteen years he had waited to have sex, and now he was addicted. Since Katrina, he added two freshmen girls to his numbers and was working on more. Those were the perks of hanging around Greg: girls, drugs, and money. If Greg came to the cafeteria or the popular student restaurant, The Punchout, while Brandon was eating, he sat at Greg's table and got noticed by all of Greg's female admirers. They remembered Brandon's face and got really friendly with him. His first semester at Howard was turning out great.

"Drew Hall!" Tyrone Hall, a dorm mate who stayed on the third floor along with Brandon, screamed in his ear walking up to him. "Yo B, what up? I saw you talking to your upperclassman shorty with the fat ass. What, you 'bout to tap that tonight?"

Brandon smiled and thought of lying just to get the congratulatory punch on the arm. "Nah, I was just saying hi. I ain't pressed over that. I already had it," he boasted. "I got two numbers tonight," he said, pulling out his notepad to show Tyrone.

Tyrone smiled and shook his hand. "I got one too," he said. They started to walk back toward Drew Hall when Brandon heard a familiar voice call him.

"Brandon. A yo, Brandon, let me talk to you for a second." Brandon was poplar tonight.

Brandon turned around and looked at the second reason why he was gaining so much popularity on campus. Ben Bishop, the editor-in-chief of *The Hilltop*, was calling his name on campus. Just like Greg, everyone knew Ben. Professors and administrators even knew Ben. Where Greg usually dressed in the most expensive urban wear, Ben pumped across campus in suits, shoes, sweaters, and sometimes Timberlands and jeans. Like Greg, girls flocked to him, but these were the more serious, scholarly girls who moved toward Ben.

Ben spoke at Brandon's freshmen orientation class, freelanced for *The Washington Post*, and was interviewed on CNN along with three other college newspaper editors about the need for independent college newspapers, so university administrators would not have a say-so in the collegiate free press. Ben was someone Brandon's mother wanted him to be inspired by. Not Greg Harris.

"What's up, Ben?" Brandon said, shaking his hand and hugging him.

"You tell me. I saw you talking to your boy Greg. You got him in this story, too?"

"Nah, I was just talking to him."

"Good. You've been quoting him in too many stories. I don't want to see him in any more stories you turn in. We already give that drug dealer too much free advertising, and that's about to stop."

Brandon looked at Ben's chocolate face, thinking about the tip he was supposed to inquire about for Greg. He could either try to be sneaky, which would be futile because he was not smarter than Ben, or he could fake being dumb and ask him about it innocently.

"No problem," Brandon said. "Are we working on a story about Greg or something?"

"Why? Did he ask you about it?"

Brandon didn't answer him.

"Did he ask you about it?" Ben snapped.

"Yeah, but I told him no, because I didn't know about it."

Ben smiled. "Ha. He's scared now, and he should be. Let him keep asking you. The less you know, the less you can tell him. All I know is you better keep your distance from him, Brandon. You have too much to lose to be caught up in the shit he's caught up in."

"What shit is he caught up in? Why can't you just tell me? I'm not involved in anything," Brandon said, knowing that that was not true. Ben shot him a look that suggested he also knew it was not true.

"Please, Brandon. Do you think you're the only impressionable freshman he's gotten over on? What did he do, get you girls or something? Does he give you free weed for putting his name in the paper? Does he give you a little bit of money every now and then? I know what we pay at the paper isn't a lot, but it's all legal," Ben said.

Brandon didn't respond to Ben's accusations— all of which were true. Greg gave him money, notoriety, girls, and drugs. Brandon had done a good number of dumb things for Greg so far, from setting up drug deals for other freshman guys from his dorm who wanted to buy weed, to letting Greg bag up two ounces of weed in his dorm room, to writing term papers for him.

"Well, all I know is if he did something illegal, I didn't have anything to do with it," Brandon said. To that, all Ben said before he walked off was, "I hope so."

"I can't believe you came on the Yard with him, Vicky. I can't believe you even talk to him after your history with him," Vicky's closest friend, and line sister, Stephanie Drake, said, standing with Vicky and about a dozen other sorority sisters on the Yard.

"I know, right. Girl, you need to leave Ben alone. I hope you're not even trying to go down that path with him again. I mean he is cute and all, but please, you can do better, Vicky. We will be done with Howard at the end of this school year and there are so many men out there for us," her other friend Michelle offered.

Vicky knew they were telling her the truth— well, all except the last thing Michelle said about all these available black men to date once you get out of college. Vicky had friends who graduated before her who could not find a man, and who complained how the good ones were all either taken, gay or unfaithful dogs. She worried about that more than she let her friends know, but in the back of her mind, she was thinking about marriage. And Ben Bishop, if he had grown up any since when they dated, would be husband material one day.

At the moment, she wouldn't take him seriously after how he had hurt her. She was just entertaining him because it gave her satisfaction to have him and every other guy on campus chasing her again. She was only going to get a quick bite to eat with Ben after they left the Yard, but it was her second date of the weekend. The night before she went to a movie and Uno's Pizzeria with Sean Burks, a senior finance major who had a 4.0 and interned on Wall Street with her the past summer. She had no plans whatsoever of getting back with Ben. He broached the subject a few times during several of the conversations and dinner dates they had since he approached her during the pinning ceremony a few months back. Each time she changed the subject and just tried to enjoy the attention and company.

He was still a tall drink of water. He was still funny and smart and now he had more notoriety on campus. If she believed everything he said, he had given up his desultory lifestyle with Howard girls and decided that he needed to start thinking about the future.

"Puleeze. Y'all think I'm taking Ben seriously? Ain't no way," she said, half lying, half telling the truth. "We are just going to get something to eat, but I probably won't be eating because it's way too late for me to be eating now," she said, and lightly rubbed her stomach.

"Oh yeah, we forgot Miss 'lose fifty pounds over the summer, stop eating red meat and pork,' girl," Stephanie teased.

"Hey, I know what it's like to be fat, and I don't want to feel that way anymore. Stop hatin' bitch," she said playfully.

"Well, if all it is is a quick grub, order something really expensive and make him pay for it," Michelle said, staring off into the distance in Ben's direction. He was talking to one of his staff reporters. Vicky felt bad for Ben from the supercilious looks her friends gave him when they walked up on the Yard together. They barely spoke back when he did, and they sucked their teeth when he walked off. Now Michelle was telling her to order an expensive dish and leave him with the bill. It was so Michelle to think and do something like that.

Vicky couldn't believe how her friend always got guys to do stuff for her like that. She secretly believed Michelle was a ho, and that was how she got so much stuff from guys, but she also believed Michelle had a warped idea of the relationship between a man and a woman, and that was why none of her relationships ever lasted more than a few months. Vicky suspected the fact that Michelle rebounded so quickly after every breakup was where she got the idea that there was a line of college-educated, money-making brothas out there for them to date when they left Howard. Michelle would be wrong.

Vicky's mother always told her that it was hard to find a man after college, and that a lot of people meet their spouses in school. Although she would deny it, that was what Vicky wanted. She couldn't afford to take the chance of not interviewing possible mates. So yeah, she would wait while Ben Bishop had to go to talk to one of his freshman reporters. She would go get something to eat with him, and she would ultimately decide how far she would go with him. The ball was back in her court.

In the meantime, while she waited, she had to put up with an endless stream of girls coming up to her, speaking in their most polite voices. They stood in a circle and watched her and her sorors step and make hand and finger gestures. All the sorority wannabes who wanted to join her outfit knew who she was. She knew they would all be there for Rush and were trying to gain brownie points. Some were genuinely polite. She remembered their faces. Some were fake. She remembered theirs, too.

"So how long are you going to be with him tonight? You know we got step practice at 1 a.m. We gotta win first place this year," Michelle said to Vicky.

"I know. We probably won't go anywhere far. After that, I gotta finish writing these last two pages for my international marketing midterm and then I'll be right over to practice," Vicky said.

Vicky was excited about step practice and the upcoming step show. It was one of the biggest, if not the biggest event during the week of homecoming before the game. She and her sorors had been practicing literally since the first week of school. They timed themselves, practiced, rearranged things and replaced girls who would be a better fit. They had to win.

They had alumni coming back from across the country to see them perform. They knew that they were alpha chapter and that a lot was riding on their performance, and they knew that two of the other three sororities were alpha chapters, too, so they would be practicing just as hard.

Ben didn't leave her waiting too long. She noticed him before he got back over to where he was and said goodbye to her friends, just so he wouldn't have to put up with their glares. They walked down the hill to Georgia Avenue, across from Banneker Field. They crossed at the traffic light where Wonder Plaza began, and squeezed by the crowd of people coming from McDonalds and those leaving from and going to the Yard. She had to stop in her room at the East Towers to get a jacket. He had to go into *The Hilltop* office to check and see if a phone call he was waiting on had come. Ten minutes later, they met out front and proceeded to walk to their destination.

Ben's Chili Bowl was one of the most famous eateries in D.C. It was a hotdog and burger shop that dated back to the 1950's and it served the best half-smokes and chili in all of D.C. Many celebrities frequented Ben's when in town, including people like Bill Cosby and Denzel Washington, both of whom had pictures on the wall.

The line inside Ben's was long, as usual. Most people waited near the grill and watched their burgers sizzle and the fresh chili being spread across them, but Vicky and Ben got a booth in the back and placed their order. She grimaced when she heard Ben order: a half-smoke with chili, extra onions, and mustard. He ordered chili fries and a large banana milk shake. Vicky used to eat like that. It was how she got fat, which was one of the reasons that led to Ben hurting her once.

"I'll just have a bowl of veggie chili and a Diet Coke," she said to the waitress taking their order.

"Is that all you're gonna eat? I thought you said you were hungry?" Ben asked.

"I'm not that hungry. Besides I shouldn't even be eating that. It's after 10 p.m. and that is too late for me to be eating like this."

"If you say so. I remember you used to love Ben's," he smiled.

"Yeah, Ben's is still the spot. I just gotta watch how I eat now. I don't want to be a pig again," she said staring into his eyes.

"Well, you look good. You always did. Good luck with your new diet and everything."

"Thanks."

"So, I know step practice must have you running around like crazy this week."

"Yes it does, but you must be running around a lot, too. You got a paper to put out on Friday. And aren't you guys supposed to be running a special edition on Monday to wrap up homecoming festivities?"

"Yeah, we are. I'm definitely busy this week. With that and midterms, I got a lot on my plate, but not enough to stop me from trying to steal some of your time," he said smiling. She smiled too, but didn't say anything.

"So, can you tell me anything y'all might be working on? We got a bet in the office on who is going to win the step show this year, and based off what you tell me, I might be able to make my pick," he said.

"Well, you should already know who's going to win the step show," she said, popping her collar, "but tell you what we're doing? Yeah right, like I'm that crazy. You don't see me asking you what kind of exclusives y'all got going on at the paper, or what was so important that you had to talk to your little reporter friend about on the Yard today."

Ben's facial expression changed to perplexed. "Don't get me started on that. That's just one of my potentially really good reporters, and he is hanging out with the wrong crowd," Ben said.

"Well, you know how freshmen are. They have so much to prove. We used to be freshmen," she laughed.

"Yeah, I just hope he stays out of trouble."

"Dag, what kind of trouble is he in?"

"I don't know, but he might be caught up with Greg," Ben said. He didn't even have to say his last name and Vicky knew who he was talking about. Her facial expression changed to a worried look.

"Are you serious? Does he know about Greg and the kind of people Greg hangs with? Does he know about what happened with you and Greg sophomore year?"

"No," Ben snapped and twisted his lips. He hadn't told Brandon about how Greg— well he didn't see Greg— but suspected him, and his friends jumped him sophomore year. Ben had gone snooping around into a case where a girl on the cheerleading team who partied with Greg's crew one night wound up hospitalized. She had taken some GHB and had to be rushed to the Washington Medical Center because she kept throwing up and hallucinating. Greg was selling GHB, also known as liquid E, the date rape drug, and had given her some. When Greg found out that Ben was snooping around with campus police, to whom it had not been reported, he and his friends jumped Ben one night and threatened worse if he published a story. That ass whipping stayed with Ben. It lingered in his heart like a stubborn piece of fetid fecal matter refusing to be flushed. This time, Ben wasn't backing down from Greg.

"I didn't tell him about Greg, but I might. But Greg is up to his same shit."

"What happened?"

"Well, most people don't know about it yet, but he has a web-site for models. You gotta pay to join, or you can only see the pictures of some of the girls playing in bathing suits on the web page. I paid and saw that there are Howard girls on the site posing, topless, and some of them are in their rooms in the Towers. It's porn basically, but you can't take pictures for porn in a campus dormitory. And, a few of those girls are teenagers."

"Why am I not surprised?" Vicky asked. "So, are you going to do the story?"

Ben looked around to see if anyone was listening to him, and nodded his head yes.

"But Vicky, this has to stay between me and you. I haven't even told some people on my staff yet."

"I won't say anything. I can't believe this. How did you find out about this?"

"His dumb ass shorted one of the models on some money and she came running to me. I didn't even know about the site until she told me."

"Wow this is major news. I promise I won't say anything," Vicky said. "I'll just look forward to reading the story on Friday. But you better be careful, because Greg is crazy and I heard that he has a gun."

He ruminated over her comment without responding. They ate, and he eventually tried to hold her hands, but she pulled them away.

# *Three*

After the fireworks ended, Greg met up with his friends Poncho and Neeko, two D.C. area drug peddlers who supplied him. They were partners in all of Greg's business interests. Poncho was a Puerto Rican Greg met from his neighborhood in Columbia Heights. Poncho's family used illegal money he made to open and run a laundromat off of 11th Street. Neeko was a proud West Indian who mastered both Patois and English. All three were hungry when they met that night, so they cruised in Greg's truck searching for food.

Negril, the only campus Caribbean eatery, was closed. Because of Neeko's ongoing beef with the proprietors of Tropicana, another Howard student favorite Caribbean food stop off of Florida Avenue, they couldn't eat there. Two other options came to mind. Ben's Chili Bowl or Trio's Pizza in Adam's Morgan.

"I'm sick of chili. I had Ben's the other day. Let's do Trio's," Poncho said from the back seat.

They cruised U Street, past the African-American War memorial, Seven-Eleven, and a hole in the ground where new condominiums were being built. The last landmark was a sure sign of oncoming change to the area where great black musicians like Duke Ellington once frequented clubs. They even passed construction where developers were building a new restaurant and jazz club called the Ellington.

"Ain't that ya boy right dere," Neeko said, as the car slowed in traffic near 13th and U. They cruised in front of Ben's Chili Bowl and Greg watched Ben and Vicky leave the restaurant laughing and looking happy.

"Look at him," Greg said. "Laughing like a little bitch." Looking at the couple made Greg think of the rumors about him that he heard Ben was chasing. It temporarily made him want to get out of the truck and beat the snot out of Ben yet again—the way he, Poncho and Neeko did a few years back, after the nosy journalist posed a risk to their operation.

"So, you really think he is gonna print something in the paper about you on Friday?" Poncho asked. "I think he learned his lesson from the last time. Schoolboy don't want any more trouble," Poncho said and smiled, remembering that he dealt the last blow to Ben's head, just as Ben was trying to pick himself up off the ground. Poncho's right hand connected to the side of Ben's head with such fury that it made him collapse.

"Fuck dat. Let the little batty boy know we see 'im," Neeko said, reaching over the steering wheel to pound the horn. He hit it twice and rolled down the passenger side window, raising both of his hands in the air.

"Don't act like you don't see me, batty boy. I know you remember me," Neeko smiled.

Ben's temporary bliss with Vicky was disrupted by fear after he saw the sinister faces grinning at him from the black truck. He grabbed Vicky's hand and walked more briskly down U Street. Greg laughed at Neeko and at Ben.

"Dat pretty boy don't wan' get hurt in front of his little girlfriend. He better leave a crazy man like me alone, den," Neeko said. "I can't even front. His girl did have a fat ass," Neeko laughed smacking his knee.

"I know, right. I swear a year ago she was fat," Greg said, pulling off. Traffic was moving again.

Falu Davis exited her communications law class fretting over unsure answers she gave on a 50-question multiple choice midterm that she just took. The one-page analytical essay she had to write about whether governmental agencies like the FCC could regulate what record companies offered to the public in terms of gangsta rap was a piece of cake. Falu disliked much of the misogynistic lyricism most of the rappers used, calling women bitches and whores. And, although she thought it promoted violence by way of glorifying gun battles and the proliferation of crack cocaine on inner-city streets, she argued that those rappers had a right to talk about whatever they wanted. And if there was a market for it, record companies, as disgustingly greedy as they were, could profit from it.

Falu went further in her essay to attack black leaders who espoused the belief that certain rappers should be censored. Black people created gangsta rap, along with just plain old rap itself, Falu wrote. And at one point in time, the United States Constitution only considered blacks three-fifths of a human being. Black people had to die fighting for the right to vote and the right to enjoy all citizenship privileges for a country that they built. Censoring rappers would be an about-face to all of that progress. It would be limiting someone's freedom of speech. And that, Falu ended her essay with, was unacceptable—for one black person to try to take away another black person's free speech.

She knew she would get a perfect score on that part of the exam, but she was unsure about some of her other answers. Was the current FCC chairman in favor of regulating the number of media outlets companies could operate in the same geographic area or was he not? She wasn't sure and it bothered her that she could have gotten it wrong. She had to get all A's this year to bring her G.P.A. as high as it could be. If she maintained her personal status quo, she would graduate magna cum laude, but Harvard Law School would look more favorably on her application if it read that she finished summa cum laude—top honors.

"Ms. Student Government President, how do you think you did on my midterm? It wasn't too hard, was it?"

Falu smiled as she always did around this particular instructor. "I guess we'll have to see won't we, Dr. Hurst," she said, looking into one of her favorite professor's eyes. Dr. Hurst was one of the professors she planned on asking for a recommendation. He smiled back at her and said, "I'm sure you did just fine. It was only a midterm, but the final will be much more difficult. I am under the impression that I have been going too easy on my students, and that collectively, you all have gotten a little presumptuous as to how easy it is to pass my class," he continued.

"Well, I don't know if that is a fair assessment," Falu retorted. "Why not look at it as people liking you and your class so much that they actually study for it and come to class prepared to engage in battle to defend their opinions."

Her words brought a smile to the old man's face.

"Madam President, this school has prepared you well. I know some law school out there this time next year will be glad to call you a student there," he patted her shoulder.

"I hope so," she said, offering the last words she could to him before the chair of the legal communications department distracted him.

Falu walked from the far end of the C.B. Powell building, the current home of the School of Communications (formerly known as Freedman's Hospital), to the middle stairway across from 211-C. From inside that classroom, she heard one of her former professors, Dr. Harriet Ross, preparing to lecture her fundamentals of journalism class. Dr. Ross was a favorite professor, too, but Falu wasn't going to ask her for a recommendation. She just admired the confidence with which the instructor carried herself, and the fact that once Dr. Harris retired as a local reporter for the ABC affiliate in D.C., she pursued her Ph.D. and dedicated herself to teaching Howard students.

Falu descended the stairs on the second floor one flight and came out into a dead hallway, silent with paintings of important communications alumni and clean white walls and floors. She walked down the hall to her left and waved at a few familiar faces before she knocked on a white door. It was the office of the School of Communications Student President, Marshall Hayes. Marshall opened the door, chewing on potato wedges from KFC.

"Hey Falu," he said, turning around to go back to his desk. He was in his office alone, doing homework, from what Falu could tell. Falu didn't like Marshall that much, and thought that he should not have been elected School of C president. The previous school year during her first term as president of HUSA, Marshall barely showed an interest in student government. He frequently missed general assembly meetings, which sometimes meant that HUSA could not hold meetings because they could not reach a quorum. And yet, he had somehow persuaded almost 800 communications majors to vote him in as president the following year.

"Hey Marshall," she said, "I was just stopping by to remind you about the general assembly meeting on Wednesday. I know it's homecoming week, and that everyone has so many things planned, but I'm hoping we can reach a quorum so we can keep our momentum going and won't have to have an extra-long meeting next time to catch up on things. I mean, I know you're not a part of the general assembly anymore, but usually when you come to meetings, Kamila comes to," Falu said, throwing in a cheap shot.

As School of C president, Marshall indeed did not hold any official seat on the general assembly, the broad body of student leaders who voted on actual measure. Rather, he was a member of the HUSA policy board, which interpreted the HUSA constitution and oversaw the organization's annual budget. Kamila Robinson was one of his flunkies, a rubber stamp for him on the general assembly. She was a member of the Undergraduate Student Assembly, or UGSA, in the position Marshall formerly had. And just like Marshall, Kamila was proving to be a thorn in Falu's side, due to her apathy.

"Well, you said it right, Falu. It's homecoming and no one wants to be stuck in meetings all night. Wednesday is the night of the step show and you know Kamila is Greek. I know she's not stepping, but I know she is going to be there to support her sorority," Marshall said. He was attracted to Falu and disliked her haughty attitude at the same time. She took her job way too seriously, and who the hell was she to remind him of meetings? He knew when they were and he made the final decision on if he came. "And as far as her only coming to meetings when I go, come on now Falu, this is only November. I think Kamila needs to be judged on her attendance at the end of the school year," he said.

Falu could have insulted him more. She could have argued with him, but she had other things to worry about. It was fine if Kamila didn't come to the meeting. She would just pursue a campaign to get her kicked out of UGSA like she did last year with Marshall. But she would be successful this year, she thought to herself.

She said goodbye and left the C.B. Powell building. She walked out the front door, which led to a sprawling grass yard and a semi-circle concrete walkway with senior faculty and staff cars parked in front of the building. The gray sky complemented the cool November air. Fall was her favorite season. Thick sweaters, knee boots and leather jackets. She gushed thinking about how good life seemed to be.

Next, she headed East on Bryant Street toward her dorm, The Bethune Annex. She click-clacked in her chocolate Dolce and Gabbana three-inch heels, which blended perfectly with the gold slacks and blazer that she wore. A hunter green Donna Karan blouse hid behind her blazer and her curly afro bounced on top her head whichever way the wind told it to.

"Goddamn shawty, those pants look like they painted on your ass. Can I talk to you for a minute, please?" a guy in an old-model maroon Cadillac said, hanging out of his window. She gave him a quick glance, but didn't respond. He wasn't bad looking, but for any man to yell at her from a car was unacceptable. It was such a non-charming vulgarity that screamed terrible manners. He probably sold drugs and had different children by different women, Falu thought.

"Excuse me, sexy chocolate. I had to say hi to you 'cause you 'bout the prettiest thing I seen around here. If I pull over, can I talk to you? You got a man?" he asked slowing traffic.

To that she smiled and said, "yes." That was another reason she wouldn't stop for him. Falu was in love with a real man, not a loser who tried to lull college-aged women from the driver's seat of his car. Even if he had approached her with respect, she would not have given him the time of day, because Eric Baldwin was all she thought about. He was a 26-year-old aspiring lawyer, just like she wanted to be. Eric had been accepted to Yale Law School, but had deferred enrollment for two years so he could pursue work abroad. And although he was thousands of miles away doing peace work, they talked whenever they could and fired emails off to each other frequently. Eric was marriage material. He wanted to be a Supreme Court Justice one day, and she believed he could be. She practically melted in his hands when she met him a year and a half earlier, while she volunteered in Cape Town, South Africa.

Her mother's law firm was sending volunteers to work in the small towns, helping lawyers set up shop during the summer, so Falu went. She stayed with a host family during the summer and took classes at Cape Town College that she transferred to Howard and received credit for. That was the summer of 1997, the year she started her first term as HUSA president.

Eric was working for the Peace Corps, teaching English and other subjects to grade school students there, and they met through mutual friends who worked for the law firm. Eric had gone to school at Northwestern and worked as a paralegal for her mother's law firm one year in college.

He had everything she was looking for in a mate—after having spent years at Howard and feeling like she would never meet anyone. She had gotten plenty of offers, but never felt a connection to college boys … except that time when she was a freshman, and an upper-classman who was an Alpha stepped to her. He was the only person at Howard she slept with. Other boys begged to give her cunnilingus, and she obliged, but never let them penetrate her. They often thought giving oral was a guaranteed precursor to dipping their wicks in the pink, but she always left them sorely disappointed. Eric offered a refreshing contrast— tall, caramel, confident, funny, dangerously ambitious, and, like her, from a good family. He was older, too. No one else could compare.

"Well okay then, little lady. I mean, if you want a friend, we can still swap numbers. How about that?" the pest in the car asked. Having a boyfriend was not good enough to scare '90s men away.

"Uh, I'm okay. I have enough friends, but you have a good day," she said, walking in the street while he waited at the red light at 4th and Bryant Streets. The light gave her just enough time to make it to the basement door of the Annex, and inside before he followed her some more.

She heard music coming from her room as she walked down the hall of the fifth floor of the west tower of the Annex. Why on earth did they give her a room in a suite full of silly freshman girls, girls who giggled all the time, took too long taking showers, had their freshmen boyfriends over too frequently, and were now playing their Master P, I'm Bout it too loud in their suite? Thank God she had a single room all to herself. Falu didn't bother to say anything to the silly girls when she walked in. They didn't like her, either, and one of them was just as tall as she was. This one was the main antago-nist, and Falu knew that, freshmen being freshmen, they would want to prove themselves at any moment by fighting or loud talking—so Falu had to pick her battles. She was only dropping off her briefcase before she headed to the Blackburn Center, where the HUSA office was.

She dipped in and out of her room, checked the messages on her phone, grabbed her purse, and used the bathroom. Monday, Wednes-day and Friday she got out of class at 4 p.m., so by the time she got back to the Annex, did all that she did there, and came back out, the city was in a transition phase from day to night. The clouds were gray, mixed with dark blue. She walked past the bookstore, which was located in the quad, up to the "booty wall." The booty wall was a place where freshman girls sat outside when the weather permitted and got hit on by freshman guys, upperclassmen and D.C. locals. She crossed at the wall and entered the wrought-iron gates on 4th Street that divided the Undergraduate Library and Human Ecology buildings. Her feet hurt walking up the short hill, as they did most days walking on Howard's campus. Everything was a hill. To get to any building on campus from Georgia Avenue there was a hill. From the Valley or the School of C to the Yard a hill, and from the Quad to the Yard the same thing.

Falu listened to pebbles pop under passing car tires and watch Panhellenic members step on the Yard as she walked. A crowd gathered outside of Locke Hall, a three-story edifice that housed the School of Arts and Sciences, Howard's largest school. It was a building dedicated to former Rhodes Scholar and Howard professor, the notable Dr. Alain Locke. He represented everything Falu wanted to be, a standout personality in the black community, an example of everything good that Howard offered. She did a term paper on him for an African-American studies class, after she listened to President Humphries speak glowingly about Dr. Locke's influence on him. The man's impact was so great, President Humphries said, that he restored the very mahogany desk that Dr. Locke used while at Howard and today used it in his own office.

She smiled at the students walking by who spoke to her, and walked to the side entrance of Blackburn, the university center. Before she could turn left in Power Hall, a name given to a hallway in Blackburn to offices run by students, including HUSA, Campus Pals and the Election Committee, she saw Claudette Pearl, the secretary for the Dean of Student Activities.

"Falu, hey girl," Claudette said. "Come here for a second."

"Hey Mrs. Pearl. What's going on?"

"The Dean wants to meet with you asap, but she's booked in meeting with the homecoming committee and her staff, then she has the school pageant tonight."

"Asap? Is everything alright?" Falu asked perplexed.

"I don't know. You have to talk it over with her. That's all I can say." Claudette stared at her with a worried face.

"Uh, okay, Mrs. Pearl. I guess if you can't tell me I will just have to meet with her when I can. I'm a judge tonight for the Mr. And Miss. Howard pageant, too, so if she can't meet before that, I'll just see her there," Falu said.

"I'll let her know."

Falu turned toward Power Hall and shook her head in disbelief. Mrs. Pearl just acted really weird, but it made her wonder what the problem could be.

It was 4:45 p.m. and she had called an office meeting at 5. Most of her staff was already waiting on her. She and Maurice had an office separate from the general office area.

"The Dean wants to meet with me," she said. "Do you know what it's about, Maurice?"

"I didn't know she wanted to meet. She might need some of the homecoming tickets back. They gave us like seven extra tickets to all the events this year."

"That's probably it. I don't care. She can have them back. As long as everyone on staff has their tickets for each event, and you and I have our two apiece for each event, we don't need the extra tickets. I wonder why Mrs. Pearl was acting all weird because of that. I'm not gonna be upset if they need their tickets back."

Maurice shrugged, shuffled papers and left the room. Falu dug in the bottom drawer of her desk and grabbed her black flip-flops that she used around the office. Her toes ached from pumping around campus in heels all day. She slipped them off and rubbed her feet before she slipped the flip-flops on. She grabbed the notes for everything she wanted to touch on in the meeting and met her staff.

"Okay you guys," she said looking at the faces sitting down, staring back at her. She had all their attention, which was the way she liked it. "I'm not going to talk long because I'm hungry. I know you guys are too, and this is homecoming week and we all want to enjoy the festivities. First of all, I just want to say good work so far this year. I know the school year only started a couple of months ago, but I see you guys working hard. I've been in touch with some of the members on the general assembly, but Tracy, I need you to call all of them and remind them of the meeting on Wednesday. Tell them it's a short meeting. We need them there. Also, is the agenda finished for this week's meeting? We have to email that out to them tonight or tomorrow morning by the latest. It should have already been emailed out. Make sure *The Hilltop* has a copy, too," she said.

Her staff wrote down everything she said. "And Alexis, I want you to open the meeting up on Wednesday with a report about our trip last year to Philadelphia for The Million Woman March. Be sure to mention the possibility of Jada Pinkett Smith and Sista Souljah being part of a symposium here in the spring, possibly during Spring Black Arts Festival. Also, I know Maurice had some things he wanted to see on the agenda, but make sure you have your call for a vote on the technology committee. That is really important, and other members of the general assembly are interested in that. I'll let Maurice talk after this, but you guys know that he has all of your tickets for all of the homecoming events this week, so you can get them from him after the meeting," she finished.

Maurice spoke for a few minutes and then handed out homecoming tickets. Altogether, the meeting lasted about 40 minutes. Falu went to the Dean's office to see if she was finally out of the meeting. Falu hoped to tell her that she could have the homecoming tickets back, but the Dean was still occupied, and Mrs. Pearl was gone for the day. Falu went downstairs to beat the crowd of students rushing to Blackburn for dinner. The cafeteria was a place where the student body could see her, but the Punchout, which served traditional fast food, was quicker, so that's where she got her food. A grilled chicken sandwich, fries and bottled water comprised her typical go-to meal there. She had to stop eating that way, she told herself privately, but the food came fast, giving her precious time. She would have to type up a few things, return phone calls, and respond to emails before she headed to Cramton Auditorium, where she would be a judge for the annual homecoming pageant.

After five months of living in Japan, Charlene Jones still got lost when riding the subway there. It was partially her fault sometimes when she did, seeing as how she could read a little Japanese. But she was still learning so much. She could speak Spanish, which she learned in high school, but Japanese was so much more difficult to learn, starting from the characters in their writing system. Unlike the Roman-derived letters of English and Spanish, Japanese kanji looked like drawings to her. They were abstractly and meticulously drawn and looked like figures to her. Some looked like letters and others, scenes from a flipbook. English numbers were printed on subway signs; thank God.

Every night in her 300-square foot apartment in Kawasaki, a city about 12 miles outside of Tokyo, she practiced what she had learned earlier in the day at her Japanese class. She would unfold the black futon provided by the Japanese Association of Teachers Teaching English (JATTE) program and lay on it reading at night. That was on nights when she wasn't eating and drinking with other expatriates at unknown bars and clubs, talking about the U.S., what colleges they came from and the states they were from.

Other nights she spent at the gym, running nervously on the treadmill as Japanese people, mostly older to middle age ones, moved out of her way, whispered and watched her. It was a scene she knew all too well after arriving in June to teach English as a second language. Whenever she got on the subway, older Japanese people would stare and admonish the younger ones who sparked conversations with her—the ones who could speak English.

They would rap popular American rap songs to her and she would smile and nod when she recognized the artist they quoted. The kids would touch her hair, which she wore in twists, since she knew she would have to do it herself. She knew she wouldn't be able to find a beauty salon that could do her hair the way girls did it in D.C., where she had just graduated from Howard University, or in Cleveland where she was originally from. They were fascinated with her hair. Three weeks after school began, she was the subject of an exhibit at one of the JATTE cultural museums. A Japanese photographer snapped an array of shots of her deep dark skin, her bright smile and natural hair, and she was showcased to crowds as part of the traveling art show that toured Tokyo, Osaka, Nagoya and Okayama.

She got a chance to visit all of the museums where her pictures were shown and interacted with audiences—mostly Japanese students who were learning English as part of the JATTE program. Like the students in the classes she taught and the ones she interacted with on the subways and buses, these ones patted her hair and posed for pictures with her. Any of her friends back home would have clowned her for thinking that she was someone important, the way she posed and snapped shots with them, speaking English and broken Japanese.

All Japanese students had to take English at some point in their educational career, so lots of the young people had a working understanding of the language. That made it easier for Charlene to find subway stations, grocery stores and bus stops. And that was only when there were no English signs. In Japan, the government was strict about letting foreigners into the country, let alone letting them work for longer than a year without renewing their work visas. Yet, the powers in charge were quite English-friendly, placing signs that read "McDonalds," "Gap" and "Supermarket," for the convenience of any *gaijin*—foreigners—that happened to be passing through.

On Tuesday November 4, 1998, Charlene missed the subway stop for her station in Tokyo. It was 10 a.m., and she was supposed to begin teaching at 10:15. But in Japan, being on time for work meant getting there 15 minutes early, especially for teachers, because they had to prepare for work. She got off three stops after the Nittochi Nishi-Shinjuku Building, which was the JATTE East Japan Tokyo headquarters. Since her supervisors had taken a liking to her and gave her good reviews on her three-month evaluation, they asked her to substitute more frequently and travel the country teaching at remote schools.

She was called a "rover," and this week she would be teaching in Tokyo, her first time doing so since she had been in Japan. She taught in the North, far South and even to the West, where she toured the coast of the Sea of Japan, which was just across the water from Korea. The cold temperature there reminded her of Cleveland or winters in D.C.

Charlene was excited about teaching in Tokyo because the assignment was reserved mostly for Japanese teachers who were fluent in English and Japanese. When JATTE first hired her, they said her chances of teaching Tokyo were slim to none. Tokyo was too expensive to let their transplants teach there. Since the organization only paid their teachers the annual equivalent of $35,000 USD in yen, said teachers could never afford life in the ultra-expensive capital. Even with the fact that in Japan, only 11 percent of their paychecks were withheld for taxes, it would still be too big a stretch . JATTE could not afford to house its army of educators in the city—the world's largest — because space was more coveted there than in heaven or hell.

The fact that she had to take a short ferry ride and connect to a train to get there every day would be part of her excuse for being late, not because she couldn't read the signs.

She climbed to another train station she could not and did not recognize the name of and called Motoko Ooka, her supervisor for the week, to tell her what happened. Motoko gave her directions to get to the school and she finally arrived 45-minutes later. Like most buildings in Tokyo, it was a skyscraper and she had to go to the 18th floor. The short, pale security guard at the door did not speak English well and called for Motoko to come down and sign Charlene in after he saw her employee badge. Charlene patted her hair into a perfect ball and fixed her conservative blue slacks and blazer in the mirrored walls of the lobby. She checked to make sure there was no lipstick on her teeth and smelled her breath to make sure it didn't stink. Motoko came down with the quickness to get her.

"Charlene?"

"Motoko?"

"Hi yes, I'm sorry you got mixed up on the trains. This is your first time working in Tokyo?"

"Yes," Charlene said, following Motoko into the elevator.

"Don't worry about it. You are not the first person to get lost on the subway and you will not be the last," Motoko joked. I have been doing this for twelve years, and if I had yen for every time someone got lost, I could start my own school," she joked.

Motoko took Charlene's tardiness well. That was a good sign, seeing as how Charlene sweated bullets on her way there, thinking that she had blown a great opportunity. She would remember the stop on tomorrow's train ride, and leave a half an hour earlier just to make sure.

"I'm so sorry about that. Were you able to get a fill-in for the class?"

"Yes, I taught the class. It was a boring crowd, so you didn't miss much. A class of stockbrokers from the Tokyo Stock Exchange. They take the course because their job pays for it, so their interest is minimal. Most of them took English in school at some point here, but believe it or not, every Japanese isn't breaking their neck to learn the language," she joked.

Charlene mustered a smile.

"I guess it's a good thing you did teach that class, although the next class will probably be just as eager to learn," she joked, using her fingers for air quotes.

"But you will not be teaching any of the early morning classes."

"I won't?" Charlene asked.

"No, we got a filler at the last minute for them, otherwise I was going to have to teach them and I have other things to do. We have you down for all late-afternoon classes, and today you have grade school children, so be thankful. With the children, as you know, you will have a Japanese instructor in the class, too, just in case they run into trouble," Motoko said.

Charlene tried to conceal her joy. Teaching colorblind children was much better than a room full of arrogant stock brokers, all of whom she was probably taller than.

"Aww. I love the children. This will be fun. I have a lesson plan that I taught in Osaka."

"Good, you can use it here," Motoko said.

Charlene followed Motoko to the teachers' lounge, a colorful box where other teachers would periodically come for coffee, tea or to watch BBC news on the television. It was a familiar setup to the other schools at which she'd taught. So, when she walked in she was not surprised to see a tall, skinny, blond-haired and blue-eyed white guy watching the news. He waved a shy wave to Charlene and kept watching TV, so instead of going over and introducing herself to him like she should have—something Motoko should have done for them, actually—Charlene flopped in front of a computer and logged into the system. She had to check emails from family and friends in the States. She had friends having babies, working in the real world, and many heading back to her alma mater this week for homecoming, which she was sour about missing. She knew they would brag and try to rub it in her face that it was the best homecoming ever, so she wasn't surprised when her inbox had seven emails in it with the subject line, "HU, here I come."

What did surprise her was an email from Howard University's Dean of Student Activities, Deborah Thomas. Dean Thomas was a like a mentor to Charlene. She and Charlene joined the same sorority, went to the same D.C. hair stylist and both hailed from the Midwest. When Charlene was vice president of HUSA her senior year, Dean Thomas helped her and the student president she worked for, Falu Davis, get through a rough year—a year in which the two friends waged a silent battle against each other, trying to outdo each other and take credit for every good thing that HUSA did.

They were once good friends, but their year working together killed the friendship. Dean Thomas kept them from ripping out each other's hearts while at school. She was also one of the people who gave Charlene a recommendation for the JATTE program, as well as one for the London School of Economics. She was going to study international economics there after her year of teaching was over. Charlene wondered, *what could Dean Thomas want?*

Five minutes after she had re-read Dean Thomas's email several times, she sat at the computer filled with anger. The Dean, in a nice way, was asking her if she had anything to do with fleecing the university for a staggering amount of money. The answer, she fumed silently, was a resounding no. It wasn't her, but she knew who it was, and she had no qualms with snitching. *Especially* since she would not be in D.C. to defend herself to the professors, students and administrators who respected her.

She detailed her innocence in a two-page email to Dean Thomas and added her name to the carbon copy section. Before she clicked send, she tried to think of anyone else she needed to let know about this, so she could cover her ass. Benjamin Bishop was one of the first people who came to mind. Charlene knew that Benjamin was the editor of *The Hilltop* this year and that he would handle the story responsibly. She had worked up a relationship with him the year before when he was managing editor, and he let her, as vice president of HUSA, write a bi-weekly column in the paper. Yes, she thought. Ben needed to get a copy of this email, too.

# *Four*

It was amazing what a few hours of respite for the feet could do. Falu rubbed a callous on her right big toe and slipped on her brown heels that she kept in a drawer at her HUSA office. If she could have worn the Old Navy flip-flops she wore around the office to the Mr. And Miss. Howard Pageant, she would have, but that would have been tacky. She was ambassador for Howard University, after all.

Plus, there would be celebrities in attendance and they would all see her, since she was one of the five judges. One of the other judges, Dean Thomas, had just walked out of the Blackburn Center as Maurice and Falu were locking up the HUSA office.

"I'm gonna lock it for the night, Falu. I don't think anyone is coming back in here tonight," Maurice said.

"Oh shoot. I just saw the dean. Where did you put those tickets? She's judging the pageant tonight, too, so I can just give them back to her," Falu said, turning around to reach the door before he locked it. "Go ahead without me. I'll lock up," she continued.

"Okay. I put them in the first drawer in my desk. They're in a white envelope."

"Thanks. I'll see you at the pageant."

"You aren't gonna see me at the pageant. Something else came up," Maurice smiled. "I gave my ticket away."

Falu shook her head and smiled back at him. "It's like that, huh? Who is she?"

"Why you gotta be all up in my business? I don't ask any questions when you checking to see if Eric called all the way from Africa."

"Eric is my man, and you already knew about him. I didn't know you had a girl, unless you think you're a little playa," she joked.

"Well, what can I say? You trying to make me late. I gotta go. Don't forget to lock up, Falu."

She turned the lights back on and hit her knee on her secretary's desk, which was located just outside of her and Maurice's office."

"Ouch!" she stopped and knelt rubbing her knee. The bone was just sore. Nothing broken.

She searched Maurice's sloppy drawer and found the white envelope with the tickets inside, stuffed them in her pocketbook, and killed the lights. Dean Thomas was probably already in Cramton by now.

Falu smiled at the cleanup crew that passed her as she walked briskly down Power Hall. She made a sharp right at the corner to exit the building. The cool air smacked her in the face as a reminder that she had to start wearing a coat, even if it was still fall and her dorm was a hop, skip and a jump from campus.

She hated having colds. She passed a boisterous crowd of students walking past the water fountain in front of Blackburn. They looked and sounded like freshmen, giggling heartily, and if they were, Falu thought, they were the only freshmen that would not be in attendance at the pageant. How stupid of them, she thought. Freshman year was the year to experience it all. Go to every homecoming event even if you are broke by the end of the week; all the parties, the step show, fashion show, concert, everything. She did it, and over all the years, her freshman year homecoming remained her favorite. Of course, she had more friends then, she thought, as she walked past the flag squad practicing their routine for Saturday's game against Morehouse.

Freshman year everything and everyone was new, so when she fell out with one girl, there was always another to befriend. Many girls thought she was stuck up, but others didn't mind her bougie attitude because they were equally so. And when there were no girls around for her to hang with, there was a slew of guys lined up to get some of her time. Now, many of the same girls she used to be cool with—all seniors now—barely spoke when they saw her. The causes were numerous: Petty jealousies over guys they liked who instead liked Falu; her embarrassment after two years straight of trying to pledge the same sorority that some of them did; her elevated status as HUSA president (not to mention being the daughter of prominent alums). There was no shortage of reasons for the rifts, but the outcome was all the same: Relationships were forever squandered.

Falu could hear music blasting from inside Cramton as she climbed the two steps in front of the Ira Aldridge Theater. Security guards blocked the side entrance of the auditorium to stop students who didn't pay the $10 door charge from sneaking inside. As she stepped through the glass doors in front of the building and slipped an overweight usher her ticket, she heard the sound of one of the biggest hits of the fall. Jay-Z's *Hard Knock Life* echoed from inside.

She stepped inside and saw a few hundred heads in seats bobbing back and forth, dancing and talking. Dean Thomas was up front talking.

"I know what you are going to say, so before you say it, we don't need the extra tickets," Falu said, raising the envelope from her bag to give to the dean.

Dean Thomas looked perplexed, but took the envelope anyway. "Uh, Falu, who told you I wanted the tickets back? I don't need the tickets back, unless we have alumni who are coming at the last minute who might need access," Dean Thomas said.

"Oh," Falu said, contorting her face. "Mrs. Pearl said you wanted to talk to me, but she didn't say what about. Maurice said that you wanted the tickets back."

"I'll hold on to these just in case, Falu, but that was not what I wanted to talk to you about. And unfortunately, this is not the right place to talk about it fully."

"Well, what is the big secret? Mrs. Pearl had me thinking it was something serious."

Dean Thomas's face changed when Falu said that.

"Falu, this is no fault of yours that we are late in squaring all of our bills from last year and the summer, but we got an invoice from AT&T that does not put a smile on my face," Dean Thomas said. "It just seemed too outrageous, so I asked them to run the numbers and get back to me. But if their figures are accurate, you have a lot of answering to do for HUSA's phone activity and illegal use of university phone codes," Dean Thomas said, searching Falu's face for guilt.

Charlene confirmed in her email that the numbers were accurate, and that they pointed not to her own phone usage, but to that of Falu. *Falu* was the abuser of her power as HUSA president and had fleeced the university for tens of thousands of dollars.

A knot formed in Falu's neck. She knew what Dean Thomas was talking about before she even said it. How the hell did she find out about the stolen pass codes? Only one other person knew: Charlene. That bitch!

"Uh, okay. I'm not sure I know what you are talking about, but if it has something to do with HUSA we need to look into it." Her throat was dry and the fear of God overtook her spirit.

"Well this is very serious," the Dean said over N.O.R.E.'s hit *What, What, What*, and the patter of the show's emcee, as he introduced the judges.

"I need to see you in my office first thing tomorrow morning," she said, turning, smiling and waving to the applauding crowd as light beamed in her face.

The next judge to be introduced was Falu, who tried her best to emulate the Dean. But she was jolted by the thought that she could be found out and her semester, presidency and aspirations might be altered drastically. After being introduced, Falu rushed to the bathroom on the basement floor of Cramton before the show officially began.

She stood in a stall with her hands resting on top of her head. What was she going to do? She was guilty. She could explain the calls on the HUSA phone card and try to pay the balance or forfeit part of her salary to cover it. But what about the three codes she obtained illegally?

She hated Charlene more than ever at that moment. It was such a mistake to confide in her. Better yet, it was a mistake to have picked her as her vice president. Charlene was another one of those friends who fell by the wayside over the years. They started out on a good note and at one point were best collegiate friends. Then they ran HUSA together. Charlene accused Falu of getting a big head after she won the "president" title. Falu accused her of petty jealousy and had to cut her pay once for what she perceived to be a slacking work ethic. By the end of the school season, they had avoided coming to blows with each other on three different occasions. Two were in the presence of Dean Thomas, after they argued over how a surplus would be spent on student programming.

To think, when they first decided to run together and met with Dean Thomas, they heaped bombastic praise upon one another. Now, on opposite sides of the earth, they were archenemies, and Falu was having a potential career deathblow dealt to her by Charlene Jones. *That fucking backstabbing bitch!*


Brandon and his roommate Frank said that they would never go back to Howard China. Hochi, as they called it, was a Chinese takeout spot at the corner of Gresham Place and Georgia Avenue. A few weeks back, a group of guys from his dorm got robbed outside the place by local Hobart Street thugs.

But Brandon and Frank were hungry, so they chanced it that night. Because they were fooling around playing Nintendo 64, they missed the cafeteria before it closed at 7 p.m. Thus, they had to settle for fried wings and rice, with salt pepper, and mambo sauce—a mixture that tasted like ketchup, hot sauce and a sweet element that was new to both of them.

Brandon was from Philly and Frank, North Carolina, both places where mambo sauce didn't exist. They sucked the sauce off the wings, then tore through the breaded skin into the flesh, pulling until it was completely off of the bone and leaving their cold fingers warm and oozing with grease. By the time they cut across the Burr Gymnasium lot and past Greene Stadium, the wings were gone and they had to wait outside of Cramton to finish their sodas before they could be let inside.

"Man, B, I wish you hurry up and finish your drink. It's chilly out here," Frank said.

"What's the hurry? Look at all the people out here," Brandon said, spinning in a circle, looking at the line waiting to get into Cramton. As usual at homecoming time, every established and wanting-to-be-established record label crowded the streets of campus and stalked potential customers. They offered CDS, gave out party invite flyers, and taped album release posters on trees, doors, and car windows.

WHUR—Howard University Radio—had a satellite van parked out from, and so did local stations WPGC-95.5 and 93.9 FM. The Mr. and Miss. Howard Pageant was the first event during the week to see which students would represent Howard for the next year at away football games, between the pages of magazines like Ebony and Jet, and on homecoming game day with the president on the field.

"I'm glad I know you, dude. I won't have to pay for any homecoming tickets this year," Frank said, watching Brandon guzzle his soda.

"Don't get your hopes up high, man. If Kelly can come with me to the step show on Wednesday, I'm sorry to have to do it, but I can't take you. And I don't know about the Outkast tickets on Friday. The paper might only give me one ticket for that, if they decide to let me cover it at all."

"I should start writing for the paper. Y'all get all the hookups."

"Man not really, but if you're serious, I gotta go over to the office after the pageant to type this story. You should come," Brandon said, finishing his drink. He made a failed attempt at shooting it into a trash can near where he stood outside of Cramton. He walked over to the trash can, picked up the plastic bottle and dumped it into the trash. When he looked up, Greg was pulling over in his truck and flashed his flashers. They saw each other immediately and Greg waved Brandon to the truck.

"What's up Greg?" Brandon asked leaning on the passenger door of the truck.

"B, what's up man? You covering this for the paper?"

"You know it," Brandon said, pulling his notepad out of his back pocket.

"Always hard at work. I hear that. What about that thing I asked you to look into the other day? Did you hear anything about that?"

Brandon immediately thought about how Ben said he hoped he was not involved in any illegal stuff Greg was doing. "Nah. If he is working on something I don't know about it. "

"You sure about that?"

"I'm sure. He could be, but I just want to keep my hands clean," Brandon said.

Greg stared at him for a second before he spoke.

"Keep your hands clean? When did they get dirty?"

"They're not. I'm just saying. I think you and Ben must have a beef going on, and I don't want to be caught up in it."

"Oh, he must've been running his mouth, trying to scare you or something. Look at the way you talking, B. Ain't no trouble coming your way man, so calm down. Besides, I know you like money in your pocket. I know you like the love you getting from these shorties, don't you? If not, say so, and I'll wash my hands," Greg threatened, slightly agitated.

"I ain't say all that. Everything is good with you and me. But I just don't know. You come to me acting all weird about a story that Ben is supposed to be doing and then when I ask him if he's doing a story on you, he gets all serious and tells me to watch my back around you. What's really going on?"

"Nothing. That's why I was trying to stop Ben before he started spreading lies. Look, I think he's lying to you. Shit, ask him again. Ask somebody else who works under him," Greg said, the desperation in his voice evident. "I know he thinks he knows something, and I need you to give me a read on him and what it is. Come on, baby, don't let me down. I'm the one that's been looking out for you," he smiled.

Brandon reached over and gave him a pound before they said goodbye. The show was about to start.

He and Frank sat in the middle section of three clusters of seats. They watched for two and half hours as performers sang, rapped, flipped and recited poetry before a sophomore from Tennessee named Audra Keith and a junior from Seattle named Robert White were crowned Mr. And Miss Howard. Afterward, Brandon had to rush to interview them and pageant judges, like the HUSA president who was very short with him and clearly distracted during their interview.

Frank ditched going to *The Hilltop* with Brandon, since he caught up with a girl from one of his classes who asked him to walk her back to The Quad. Following the crowd, Brandon trekked Sixth Street, passing Minor Hall— one of the oldest buildings on campus and the spot where many of the fraternities and sororities on Howard's campus were founded. He was past the Administration building, behind the very mansion that General Otis Howard, the school's founder, lived in while serving as president. Brandon trekked down the red brick walkway to Georgia Avenue and passed another crowd outside of McDonalds. Cute girls occupied the block, but he had work to do, and Ben had told him to come straight to *The Hilltop* after the event.

*The Hilltop*—the student voice of Howard—was housed in the basement floor of the West Howard Plaza Towers, the most coveted dorm for undergraduates because of the apartment-style living quarters. Living in the Towers meant that you didn't have to get the meal plan and you had a bathroom in your suite instead of sharing it with the whole floor. Every college had a Towers-like dormitory. Howard had the West and East.

Brandon waited in the cold foyer of the building for someone from the paper to come sign him in. The old one-eyed security guard who took Brandon's card was suspicious of every student who walked up to him, even those who lived in the building. The Towers might have been a coveted dorm, but security clamped down on visitors at times, out of fear that local D.C. residents would begin walking into them unchecked and cause trouble.

A staff writer on her way out of the dorm signed Brandon in. He traded a glance with the Resident Assistant sitting behind a desk up front and made a series of rights, walking down brown-carpeted hallways until he came to the office. On the outside of the door was a masthead with the name Benjamin Bishop, Editor-in-Chief. Each time Brandon looked at the sign it made him want to become editor by the time he was a senior.

"What's up, my people," he said enthusiastically as he walked through the door. It was empty except for a few editors, re-working stories along the back wall that had all the computers. He threw his jacket on the secretary's desk, checked his mailbox and knocked on Ben's door. Before he could write the story, he needed a word count from Ben so he'd know how long to make it.

A turkey and cheese sandwich on toasted wheat bread, with sour cream and onion potato chips, would have to suffice for Ben's dinner that night. He had finished his last pot pie the night before, and he scrambled his last two eggs and ate them with three slices of turkey bacon that morning. Lunchmeat was the only option he had left until he either caught a ride from a car-owning friend to the supermarket, or took the bus.

He munched on his dinner while he looked over the finishing

touches on a five-page midterm for History Since 1792, a class which he was forced to take as a senior because he skipped it as a freshman. He spent Tuesday morning arguing with freshmen about whether the Emancipation Proclamation really meant anything, and if Lincoln really freed the slaves.

The silence in his room was interrupted by moans coming through the wall, and the sounds of wood knocking against the sheet-rock as a result of furtive movements on the other side.

"Oh yeah, oh yeah, oh yeah. Go deeper. Go deeper, baby, deeper. Like that. Oh, like that. Yeah, oh yeah!"

Ben smiled listening to the sounds. One of his roommates, Anthony, was going at it again with his girlfriend, Stephanie. Stephanie was a screamer, and every time they had sex, anyone in the suite could hear them. It was about 8 p.m., a little early in the night for them to be having sex, but it was better than the usual middle-of-the-night sessions that distracted Ben from doing homework. The late study hour was his usual designated time to hit the books after he left *The Hilltop* office. It was usually Bruce, his other roommate, who made noise during the day.

The Office of Residence Life really stuck it to Ben his senior year, pairing him with two of the nastiest roommates he ever had. They shared a triple on the 9th floor of the West Towers, and already in the first three months of the semester, it was shaping up to be a long school year.

Anthony, a sophomore from Virginia, had two girlfriends he liked to have sex with frequently. One of them went to Howard, and the other visited once a month from his hometown of Richmond. They were both screamers during sex. And they were just as nasty as he was. One Saturday, Ben had to wake up Anthony and Stephanie because she left her panties on the shower rail. And Ben once heard Ashley, Anthony's other girl, giggle after she asked Anthony what were all the stains on his bed and he answered, "Cum." Just nasty.

Bruce, also a sophomore, was nasty in the kitchen. He never cleaned his dishes and left pots uncovered in the refrigerator. In the beginning of the semester, Ben cleaned up after them, but by November he grew sick of them and worked around their mess. He wasn't cleaning after two grown men.

Every time Ben got into an argument or one of his roommates did something stupid, he tortured himself thinking about the fact that he gave up the chance to have his own one-bedroom apartment off-campus to live in the Towers. He tore the lease up at the last minute, because as editor of the paper, he thought it would be better to stay in the Towers. The newspaper office was located there, and he knew he would have to put in many long nights. But overall, dorm life had its perks—mainly girls for Ben.

Although he was seriously chasing Vicky Mourning, his one time girlfriend, they were merely rekindling a friendship, which left him guilt-free to run through Howard women. He was having sex regularly with a beautiful sophomore girl from New Orleans and another cutie he met over the summer. He kept his numbers down just in case Vicky finally came around, so he could dump them and dedicate himself fully to her.

"I'm not giving up yet," he said to himself, sitting at his desk looking at an old picture of him and Vicky. They had taken it together first semester of sophomore year. She was dressed in a jean skirt and fitted army T-shirt, and her long and thick hair hung past her shoulders. They were hugging each other, smiling for the camera. Vicky looked beautiful in the picture, which was taken before she had gotten fat and a little sloppy; it reminded him of good times they had.

When he saw her at the pinning ceremony, she looked even better than in the picture, because she rocked a new hairstyle and her face radiated confidence, unlike before. Four years at Howard had seen them mature in ways they never would have guessed when they first met at the Campus Pals-sponsored ice cream social freshman year. Back then, Vicky and a group of girls she came with laughed and shook their heads at the boys grinding on all the fast girls at the party.

Quickly, she and Ben got together and spent lots of time with each other, although other girls liked Ben. He wanted Vicky. Now, as he sat in his room with the shades closed, he thought about how stupid he was to act so childishly and force their breakup.

During their sophomore year, the year Vicky pledged, Ben couldn't take the fact that she spent more time on line than she did with him. He got jealous, so he broke it off and started seeing other girls. Worse yet, the following year, they tried to rekindle what they had, but Ben really wasn't serious about it. He had actually become a selfish, self-centered, shallow womanizer. Vicky had gained much weight, making her unattractive in his eyes, and behind her back he would dog her to friends when they asked what happened to her.

Their short-lived attempt at getting back together was killed one night when he walked her back to her dorm from his, and a group of his friends approached, shaking their heads and making faces. He snatched his hand away from hers and walked at a slower pace than she did to create distance.

"So that's how it is, Benjamin? You care about what your friends think? You should go with them, because I don't need you to walk me home," Vicky turned to him and said—her voice cracking. They hadn't spoken the rest of the school year after that. Now he had a glimmer of a chance of getting her back and he was not going to let anything get in his way.

"It's about time you decided to show up. You haven't been down here all day," Forrest Hunter, Ben's managing editor, said to him as he came through *The Hilltop* office doors.

"You know Mondays are my long days. Plus, I got mid-terms due just like you and everyone else. This paper gets enough of my time," Ben said.

"Look, we need to finalize a few things for the front on Friday. Of course, we'll have a pre-game roundup for homecoming. Sports was mad that we had to take it from them. We'll have the results from the pageant tonight with a dominant photo of the winners, the HUSA general assembly meeting on Wednesday can go below the fold, and I was thinking about a preview of the R&B concert," Forrest said.

Ben smiled and said, "You got everything covered. That's why I pay you the big bucks. Why are you upset with me for being gone all day when you have everything thought out?"

Ben was grateful for Forrest. He was one of the few pupils in the journalism department who Ben felt was as equally talented as him, so it was a no-brainer who he would pick when he needed a right-hand man to help him fill the two-section, 24-page broadsheet newspaper for thirty-five issues.

"That's only four stories, Ben. We need something else. As you know we usually run with five or six. We have all the artwork we need, but we need another story. A juicy one if we can get it, seeing as how everyone is going to be on campus this week."

"Leave a space open above the fold," Ben said, thinking about the story he planned on writing about Greg Harris, which he had not told Forrest about yet.

"You got something in mind?" Forrest asked.

"Yeah, I do; maybe a column, maybe a story. We'll see."

"You holding out on some major shit, huh?" Forrest smiled. "I know when you holding out, man. You gotta tell me at some point. It's either now or later, but before Friday. Who else are you going to get to edit it?"

"I'll tell you about it when I need it edited, until then I gotta keep this under wraps. I can't afford for it to get out, you know?"

"Whatever. Anyway, check your mailbox. I think the payroll slips are in for you to sign, and a brotha needs to get his check on Friday so I can party."

Ben grabbed the mounds of paper from his mailbox and unlocked the door to his office. He flicked the fluorescent light on and tossed the paper on his desk. In his office was a brown wooden desk, an office chair that looked like it was about to fall apart, a trash can, back issues of the paper on the floor, a chalkboard with reporters' names and phone numbers on it, and a small radio. It was the smallest office in the history of offices, but he made the most of it.

Paperwork would come first, then he would check his email,

then he'd call all his section editors to make sure they were checking up on their staff writers. Blowing deadlines was costly.

He checked to make sure he wasn't paying anyone more than they should have gotten, and docked pay for staff writers who didn't turn in stories. Then he booted up his computer, the main server to all the computers in the office. From his office he could see files on every computer and see who was working on what.

He checked his email account and deleted all the junk mail. Ben smiled when he saw a familiar name in his inbox. Charlene Jones. Charlene was the former vice president of HUSA, the one person of that duo whom he could stand. She was a star student in the economics department, and shocked everyone when, instead of going straight to grad school, she decided to teach English abroad for a year. The last he had heard, she was in China, or Japan, or some other faraway place where there weren't many black people. His pupils dilated after reading her message.

"Oh shit!" he said, placing both hands on top of his head. He got up and opened his office door.

"Forrest, come here!"

"What's up?"

"Look at this email. Charlene Jones sent it."

Forrest walked over, grabbed a seat, and scanned the allegations on Ben's screen.

"Oh shit, is this the front-page story you were holding out on? This is the biggest story of the year, if it's true." Forrest said.

"This wasn't what I had in mind, but it might be the story we need to fill the hole in the front. It would take longer than Thursday to turn this around. Falu would never admit to it. I gotta email Charlene back and ask her some more questions. Keep this between you and me for now."

A knock interrupted Forrest and Ben as they closed down the email.

"Who is it?" Ben asked.

"It's Brandon. I just came from the pageant."

"Come in."

Brandon took the empty chair that Forrest left unattended, pulled out his notepad and dropped it on Ben's desk. "A sophomore and a junior won. It was a clean sweep for Arts and Sciences. I know we have good art, but I wasn't sure how long you wanted the story to be," Brandon said.

"You know this is front page," Ben said. To that Brandon simply smiled and replied,

"I know. My first one."

"I know. So don't mess it up. I'm counting on you, the first freshman to make the front page this year. Stay on your shit and more chances will come."

"Really? Look, Ben I want to thank you. Thanks for looking out for me. I can finish this story in a minute. How many words do you need?"

"Give me six hundred," Ben said, extending his hand for Brandon to shake.

Brandon got up from the chair, walked into the main office and started typing at a computer. He was proud that Ben was taking notice of his hard work and had given him a front-page story during homecoming week. This one he would have to save and send home as well. He sat in front of the PC and felt the guilt of holding out on Ben the other day when he asked him about his involvement with Greg. If he got caught up with anything that Greg was into illegally, all his dreams would be squashed. He couldn't tell his mom, because she would try to intervene. Ben was the only person whose advice he thought he could trust. Brandon got up from his seat and knocked on Ben's door again."

"Who is it?"

"Brandon. I gotta tell you something."

"Come in. What's up?" Ben asked.

"Remember the other day when you said you hoped I wasn't involved with anything involving Greg?"

Ben immediately thought about Greg and his boys trying to

scare him the other night at Ben's Chili Bowl. Just what was Brandon about to tell him?

"I remember. Why? What's up?"

"I might be in some trouble," Brandon said.

# *Five*

"Fifty-seven thousand dollars is a lot money being spent on phone conversations, Falu. The work that HUSA does, and did last year, just does not justify talking on the phone that much. *The Hilltop* usually spends the most money on long distance calls, and we expect that, so we budget accordingly. As a news organization, it makes sense that sometimes they have to reach people who live far away ... but HUSA, Africa? Who are we calling in Africa, Falu?" Dean Thomas asked, sitting behind her cluttered, cherry oak desk.

On top of it were sheets of paper with phone numbers listed and red circles around a number that Falu knew all too well. It was the number to Eric's one-room apartment in Cape Town, the one she called feverishly, abusing university phone privileges to do so. All of her fond memories of lovemaking on his run-down mattress, all the rice and mashed-up potatoes they ate from bowls while holding each other—planning on how they were going to be a black legal power couple—couldn't make Falu any less afraid now. She shifted in her chair and reached for a page with a half-dozen red circles on it. Maybe if she hid her face and didn't respond to the dean's question, this bad dream would all be over with. She would wake up and it would be graduation day; her last day as a student, after her recommendation letters had been sent and she had been accepted to Harvard Law.

The thought of getting caught, and her world imploding almost made her cry, but she steadied herself on the notion of denying everything until she got caught. She had too much to lose, and just because some ugly bitch in Japan felt sour grapes over a friendship gone bad, she wouldn't falter.

"Falu, did you hear me?" Dean Thomas asked.

"Oh yes, I apologize, Dean. I was looking at some of these calls. Didn't you say you asked the phone company to double check? I'm guessing they are charging us multiple times for the same calls," Falu said.

"Yes, I spoke with someone earlier today and they are checking. We should know the official numbers by Thursday, but even if they have charged us twice, that would mean that we spent almost thirty-thousand dollars on phone charges. You realize that HUSA only has a phone budget of six thousand dollars, which is more than the normal amount for most student organizations. And we know that at least seven of the thirty-thousand traces back to your university-issued cell phone. That number is correct, Falu, and all of the foreign calls are to Africa. And then there are some calls to Japan. I'm guessing that was Charlene, since she is in Asia, but there are calls all over on these invoices."

"I see. Well, Dean, I have to be honest about that. Some of those calls to Africa were made by me, and I am prepared to pay the money either out of my pocket or from my HUSA stipend, but I cannot account for the other calls," Falu said, hoping that Mrs. Pearl would interrupt the dean with an important phone call so she could leave.

Dean Thomas chuckled, eased back in her chair and said, "You can't account for the other phone calls even though they were made to the same number?"

"Let me see the invoice again," Falu demanded.

"Ha! Falu, I have more than one hundred pieces of paper, which one do you want to see?" she laughed.

Falu grabbed a handful and stuffed them in her face, so she

could hide it from the dean. Every number she saw was one she talked to Eric on, either at his office, his apartment or a satellite office.

"I would like to see the charges again on Thursday, so I can
make sense of this. I know I did not make all of these calls," Falu said
lying. "Where do we go from here?"

"Excuse me?"

"I mean, it looks like we are going to be over the limit for allotted phone charges, and I know that account has to be squared away
with the university, so where do we stand when we get the official
numbers back?" Falu asked.

"This is a drastic measure, and I am going to have to fight a
drastic measure with a measure just as drastic, Falu. If I get those invoices back on Thursday and the numbers come close to fifty-seven
thousand dollars, we are going to have to call an emergency general
assembly and HUSA policy board meeting. Falu, HUSA will have to
pay all of that money back, and if I have to get that money by cutting
programming money that HUSA earmarked for other student organizations, and if I have to cut from the HUSA executive account, I will.
That bill has to be paid, and it won't fall on the university," Dean
Thomas said confidently.

Damn! Falu thought to herself. There was no way to get out
of this without the whole campus finding out about it. Her parents
could help her cover a $7,000 cell phone bill—they would be upset,
but they would help—but tens of thousands of dollars would be too
much, even for them.

HUSA's programming budget, totaling $55,000, could knock
out the charges, but why should every student suffer for her staff's
abuses? Her staff might quit on her if the executive account—the account that paid their salaries and secured office supplies for them—
was depleted. And how dare Charlene snitch on her, knowing she
made calls to Japan in advance of her year-long teaching stint, as
well as long-distance calls to her family? Why did they need to have
an emergency HUSA policy board meeting? The policy board dealt
with HUSA and the constitution and punishment. Would they fire

her?

"Why do we need to have an emergency policy board meeting?" Falu asked.

Dean Thomas straightened out the papers strewn across her desk. She sipped her black coffee, and placed the mug back on her Howard coaster.

"I told you about the stolen phone cards. I need to know how HUSA got a hold of those cards. The policy board will have to form a committee to look into this, unless you know something that you want to tell me," Dean Thomas said, looking as if Falu had already been convicted.

Falu swallowed, looked back at her, and shrugged her shoulders.

"If I knew, I would tell you. If someone from HUSA got a hold of any identification cards, we would not have been able to track them, because we never see the bills," Falu said, trying to shift some of the blame back onto the dean.

"It would be nice if we could have seen our monthly bills, so we could have caught this problem before it got out of hand. And now this invoice surfaces a whole school year later," she shook her head.

"Well, now it is our responsibility to right a wrong. We could point fingers all day for who is responsible for this lapse, Falu. This should not have taken as long as it did to come to the attention of my office, since I am the one who oversees all financial matters dealing with HUSA. But there is certainly no way I could have known and controlled stolen ID cards. The policy board will definitely have to take action concerning this," the Dean said, throwing the blame right back at Falu.

"So, what are you telling me, Dean? Is the policy board going to take action against me?"

"Well," she folded her hands, "I think you are at fault to a degree, and that is only because of the egregious cell phone behavior. Who knows about the other matters?"

The stinging sensation in Falu's heart felt like it came from a knife. This could not be happening to her now, not when her mother was running for the Board of Trustees. Not when she was preparing to take the LSAT and had already gotten verbal confirmation from President Humphries that he would write her a recommendation letter for law school. Punishment from the policy board, or being publicly blamed for neglecting ten thousand students' programming for the whole school year was something that she might not be able to recover from.

Perhaps the worst aspect of this brewing scandal was that all of her detractors on campus—all the girls she fell out with over the years because of their jealousy, the embittered guys who dismissed her as "stuck up" because they couldn't have her—would be able to point their fingers at her , shake their heads, and indulge in some good old-fashioned *schadenfreude*.

Just as Falu was about to return fire, the interruption from Mrs. Pearl came about the vice president for student affairs needing to speak to the dean. Too bad it came too late.

Footsteps. The more Vicky took, the more she left behind. Her first hike of the day came less than 10 minutes before her 9:40 a.m. volleyball class at Burr Gymnasium. And from the East Towers, Burr was a cute little hike past Banneker, up Georgia Avenue, on a hill that led to main campus. She turned right on Howard Place and climbed another short hill before turning left on Sixth Street. She passed all the truck vendors who flirted with the girls and sold snacks, sandwiches, coco bread and beef patties, as well as bootleg CDs.

After making the long walk to campus, she then had to run, sweat and attempt to knock a ball across a net for more than an hour, before she went back to her dorm and changed for her afternoon classes. She only had two classes on Tuesdays and Thursdays, but they were an hour and 20 minutes, an agonizing 30 minutes longer than the typical course.

After racing home to get a bowl of cereal and take a shower, she ironed her clothes and dressed. Starting again from the East Towers, she had to walk back to the School of Business, where she was completing the last course in her major.

It was 1:45 by the time she met Jasmine and Stephanie on the Yard, standing in front of Douglas Hall. They gathered and looked, and shook their heads at people. Some guys watched them, while ones they knew came over and joked with them. Girls, mostly sorority wannabes, stared too, until they were caught staring and had to avert their gaze. Vicky liked the attention she garnered as sorority president from all the girls who had to suck up to her because of who she was. She had something that they wanted. It was the power. Like most women, she reveled in it.

"I hurt my foot last night in practice. I gotta go home and ice it before practice tonight," Stephanie said. "Are y'all going to the comedy show tonight? I don't have the money right now. My rent is due and the rest of the money I need to buy an outfit for the club this weekend. Homecoming is getting more expensive every year," she added.

"I know, right," Jasmine added. "I might go to the comedy show if my date comes through. I don't really feel like it, since we gotta meet for step practice afterwards, but it's free. You goin', Vicky?"

"Girl, I got too many other things to do besides the comedy show. I still have a take-home midterm due tomorrow, and like you said, I need some rest for step practice. Since y'all hussies don't come correct with your steps, I know I'm gonna be in there all night," she laughed.

"Bitch please," Stephanie retorted. "The only reason I was a little off last night was because I hurt my ankle. Wait 'til I put some ice on," she said, and snapped her fingers in a zigzag motion in the air. "Bitches ain't gon' know what to do with me," she laughed. "I'm surprised Vicky isn't going with Mr. Editor. I know he gets free tickets to all the events from the paper."

"He asked me to go, actually," Vicky said, not wanting to talk about Ben, "but I told him I couldn't go. I might go to the concert with him on Friday if he asks me to, or the fashion show on Thursday. Don't be mad because I don't have to pay to go to anything. He owes me!"

"He owes you an apology, too. I wonder if you got that from him yet?" Stephanie said.

"Don't go there. It's not that deep with us, and yes he did apologize."

Vicky was about to say something else when a troubling sight interrupted her. "Eww! Will you look at her nasty ass?"

"Who?" Jasmine and Stephanie asked in unison.

"Courtney Hall, over there eating those nasty-ass fries and had the nerve to take her gum out and put it on her forehand. Nasty bitch," Vicky said.

On a bench in front of the fine arts building on campus, Courtney Hall, a sorority hopeful, sat eating cheese fries with ketchup, out of a plastic container from the Punch Out.

"What? She's eating lunch, Vicky. What's wrong with that?" Jasmine asked.

"Yeah, but did she have to put that nasty chewed gum on her hand? Couldn't she just throw it away? And those nasty-ass cheese fries with all that ketchup on them; they make me sick just looking at them. And she has the nerve to be all up in my face."

"Vicky, you used to like cheese fries," Stephanie said.

"Used to. Key words are *used to*. And if I knew I looked like that eating in public, I would not have allowed everyone to see me."

Courtney Hall was a sophomore from Kentucky who brown-nosed Vicky whenever she saw her, because she wanted to join the sorority. She complimented Vicky on whatever she wore, waved from across campus and even yelled out her name when speaking, if the distance was not too far. She was not fat, but she wasn't skinny either, which reminded Vicky of herself when she was that size, eating everything that wasn't nailed down. Eating indiscriminately, or more accurately, eating such unhealthy food, was a weakness for Vicky. If she had continued eating that way, she would have never lost the weight over the summer. And she feared, more than anything else, gaining it back, so she gave up stuff like cheese fries.

It didn't help that the night before, she watched a program on television about taste buds. Watching Courtney triggered images from the program. There were about 10,000 taste buds inside of everyone's mouth. Older peoples' tastebuds lose sensitivity as they age. Some taste buds could be damaged by extreme heat or cold, but in most cases, they could be repaired.

The majority of taste buds sat on raised protrusions on the tongue called papillae. The fungiform papillae looked like mushrooms and were present mostly at the tip of the tongue. Filiform papillae were long and thin, and they stood up like hair follicles. They didn't contain taste buds, but they were the most numerous. The circumvallate papillae were in the minority, with each mouth having only 3-14. They were found in the back of the mouth. Foliate papillae were ridges and grooves found at the posterior of the tongue.

Most people enjoyed all five of the taste senses, which were sweet, bitter, sour, salty and umami. The sweets obviously were activated by any kinds of sugar, or simple carbohydrates, while the bitter was triggered by most alkaloids. Black licorice was bitter. Salt taste buds alerted the brain to most sodium products, and the sour taste bud detected mostly acids. Tarts and lemons were sour. And umami was a Japanese term for savoriness. It was found in meat and other delicious foods, along with fermented and aged food. In China they called this xian wei. Parmesan cheese was an example, so were walnuts, broccoli and tomatoes.

What was most interesting was how taste buds can send signals to the brain, but be totally incorrect. Such was the case with other sensations of taste buds, such as that triggered by spicy foods. Spices were an example of false heat, when the somatosensory system misinterpreted an ingredient for an increase in temperature. Capsaicin and ethanol triggered this and could be found in Mexican, Indian,

Tex-Mex and Thai cuisines, causing a burning *sensation* but not an actual increase in temperature. In essence, people who liked spicy foods were gluttons for pain, the report said, because the pain sensors were triggered in the brain when spicy food was consumed. It was somewhat masochistic.

Needless to say, Vicky learned a lot, and it was additional information she used to affirm her discipline in staying away from certain foods. She had trouble understanding how people could not see how their own behavior caused them to gain weight and be unhealthy. They would only turn around and look at themselves in the mirror and feel ugly—the same way she used to—especially when the guys stopped showing her love and Ben Bishop dismissed her because of it.

She hated the stretch marks, the double chin, and the pouch on her stomach. She hated having to shop at Ashley Stewart, Lane Bryant or the Avenue. She wanted to wear Donna Karan and Seven jeans, but weight discrimination was a bitch, and it had made her feel very low at times. Vicky felt embarrassed those nights she didn't want to go out to the club with her girlfriends because she felt fat. And she remembered being intimidated by skinny girls who dressed sexy and stole the attention she once garnered. Standing on the Yard, looking at Courtney, made her think of her old self. It made her feel sympathetic to what she thought Courtney was going through during quiet moments alone, but it also angered her. Luckily for her, she had a little power to change it.

"Vicky where are you going?" Jasmine asked.

"I'll be right back," she said, staring at Courtney with a determined look. She passed a group of guys in a circle freestyling and beat boxing, fixed her black leather jacket to make sure it looked presentable and patted her hair down. She stood in front of Courtney, who was with another girl—another sorority wannabe whose name escaped Vicky.

"Hi, Vicky!" Courtney said.

"Hi, Vicky!" the other girl exclaimed.

"Ladies," Vicky sneered. She grabbed a tissue from inside of her purse. "Real ladies do not place chewed gum on their hands and stick it back in their mouths after they eat cheese fries. After eating cheese fries while sitting out on the Yard, nonetheless."

She stared into Courtney's frightened and embarrassed eyes and stuck out the tissue. Courtney wiped her hands and looked at her friend first. She didn't know if she should throw the fries away or not, but she could not disrespect Vicky, not if she wanted to pledge. It took everything in her not to say something back to Vicky. She could feel the tears bubble at the corners of her eyes. Finally, she took the chewed piece of double mint from her hand and placed it in the tissue.

"Thank you, Vicky," was all she could say. Her friend just stared.

"Do you really think those taste good?" Vicky asked incredulously. She started to admonish her some more, but felt bad and backed off. She had to remember that she was once in Courtney's shoes. "Stuff like that adds weight that is hard to get rid of, ladies. Think about that next time," she said.

"Thanks Vicky," they said in unison, but she had already turned around and started walking back to Jasmine and Stephanie. She had dozens of sets of eyes on her.

"What was that all about girl? What did you say to that girl? She is wiping her eyes, leaving campus?" Jasmine asked.

"I told her how unbecoming it was for her to be saving a piece of already chewed gum and I told her she should rethink her eating habits. These girls don't realize that they are their own worst enemies."

Her friends looked at her with furrowed brows.

"Vicky, I get the gum part, but don't you think that was a little too harsh about the fries? Like I said, you used to love cheese fries from the Punch Out, if I recall. I mean, I'm glad that you lost weight over the summer, and it looks good on you, but you're taking it too far. If I want to eat a cheeseburger and fries, are you gonna talk shit about me and call me nasty behind my back?" Stephanie said.

"Stephanie you are a size two. Who the hell is going to say something to you about eating a cheeseburger and fries? You need to eat more cheeseburgers and fries. I'm trying to help girls like her," she said. Her voice turned serious, but stayed low so people outside of their circle could not hear it. "Y'all don't know what it's like to be the fat girl. Skinny bitches never know, but always have something to say," she began crying.

"I wasn't trying to be mean. I didn't approach her in a mean way, but if I can help her, I will," Vicky said, wiping her eyes. Her tears instigated yet more from Stephanie and Jasmine.

"I'm sorry girl. Stop all that crying. I'm happy you lost the weight, you just need to lighten up a little," Stephanie said while sniffling.


A Tribe Called Quest's *Electric Relaxation* bumped from the speakers in Greg's furniture-devoid living room, which doubled as his photo studio. Neeko, Poncho, and a group of other people surrounded Tamika as she stood on the hardwood floor posing in front of the makeshift beach background. A bright stage light illuminated her caramel complexion and the oil that covered it. She stood in the middle of the floor; slightly bending so Greg could catch the inside of her bikini top.

"Good, Tamika. Just like that. Now stick your tongue out a little," Greg instructed. "Stick it out like you ready to lick on something," he instructed, smiling. His Leica snapped, lights flashed and she switched her position.

Next was a back shot of the cherry red bikini thong in the crack of her ass as she bent over and touched the tip of the red stilettos Greg provided for her. She had thighs for days, and a bubble butt that made any man look twice and silently wish he could penetrate it.

"Goddamn baby girl. We gon' make a killin' off of you," Poncho admired from the back. Another light flashed. Another position changed. Greg took the pictures, Neeko helped them pick out their clothes, and Poncho did whatever, whenever. This was a part of their enterprise. They were preparing for a new web page with three new models that they had just recruited. Tamika went to George Mason University in Virginia, and said she needed the $300 they offered to pay her to keep up with the bills. Tori attended American University and so did Stacy, the lone white girl of the trio. They stood dressed in robes provided by Greg and waited to be photographed.

And while they waited, they either smoked reefer, popped ecstasy pills or drank cognac, all offerings within the vice component of Greg, Poncho and Neeko's conglomerate. Selling drugs and liquor to college students was how they funded online projects such as this, and it would be seed money for the X-rated movies they wanted to do, too. It was all a hustle for the trio, who dubbed themselves the Stacks Family—"stacks" accounting for the thousands of dollars they made and split with each other.

"I want a shot with all three girls in it, real quick. Y'all two get over here," Greg commanded. His cell phone rang while he loaded more film into the camera. "Argh! This better not be somebody from school tryna buy one bag of weed!"

"Hello!" he yelled.

"You got my money, Greg?"

"Money? Who the fuck is this playing on my phone? I don't have time to play. I'm busy right now," he said, pulling the cell phone back to look at the 301-area code number that he did not recognize.

"You busy now, huh? And now all of a sudden you don't recognize my voice," the girl on the phone said.

"Yo, Poncho, take the camera. I gotta take this call in my room," Greg said, handing him the camera. He trekked the hardwood kitchen floors, past the bathroom, and pushed open the bedroom door. In the private lair of his bedroom, he looked out the back window. He recognized the voice, but was just checking to make sure no one was creeping.

"Bitch, why the fuck you callin' my phone? Didn't I tell you that I don't fuck with you anymore?"

"That's fine if you don't fuck with me, nigga. Just give me my money, and I'll stop calling!" Latoya shot back. Latoya was talking about the $150 Greg shorted her on for a photo shoot. They agreed on $400 for one topless and one naked photo, but she was an hour late, so he docked her pay.

"You ain't gettin' shit from me. You fucked up when you messed me over. And I'm warning you, before some shit happens to you that you might regret, don't call my phone anymore!" Greg threatened.

To his threat, she laughed. "So, I'm not getting shit? We'll see about that. I bet you'll regret it when I'm through with ya ass."

"Regret it? What you gon' get your brother on me? You know where I be. Come and get me if you a badass!" He punched the end button on his phone and looked out the window once more. While the view was dim and crummy, he could see enough to know that no one was back there—just an empty alley that divided his apartment building from another one around the corner.

Greg stood on his bed and unscrewed the light cover in his bedroom, and there it was. His nickel-plated 9 millimeter, fully loaded and ready to end the life of anyone who tried to end his. He had money to make, and some ghetto-ass D.C.-area bitch wasn't going to get in his way. If she recruited anyone to try take his money, he would deal with them with hot lead.

Just as he screwed the light cover back on, his phone rang again. His product was needed on campus, and in large quantities. It was enough to make him commit to coming right over. And since he was going on campus, he called another associate he had business with. Poncho and Neeko could take over the photo shoot while he was gone.

Less than 20-minutes later, he was parked on Gresham Road, up the street from Drew Hall, exchanging Ziploc bags full of weed for dollars. Ounces of hydro went for $125, and if someone bought two, he gave them a deal at $225 and threw in two boxes of Dutch's to smoke it in.

Greg made a killing from Drew Hall freshmen. It was homecoming week and they wanted to party. The comedy show, which Greg decided not to attend because he had business to take care of, had just ended, and the clubs were about to start jumping. Freshmen short on cash put in together and bought ounces of weed from him. It was Tuesday night and he had already moved one pound of weed and would probably move one or two more by the end of Homecoming.

For a while, Greg had cut Drew boys off because they were calling him at random hours trying to buy just a bag or two, and expecting him to drop what he was doing to deliver it. Brandon was too nervous to move the product for him inside the dorm, and he didn't trust anyone else. They didn't have the smarts Brandon had. In a way it was a good thing Brandon didn't hustle for Greg, Greg thought, because he liked Brandon. But if the Philly kid got caught up in the fast money and women completely, he would end up like Greg: a bright-eyed freshman who came to Howard from California, with dreams of being a movie director bigger than Spike Lee or Steven Spielberg … but who instead turned into a campus drug lord.

He went from a 3.0 his first semester at Howard to a 2.1, two semesters of academic probation, a slew of W's from classes he had dropped, F's and at least one semester where he took off from school completely. He was staring age 25 in the face within the first three months of the next semester and was only classified as a junior. His dreams of cinematic supremacy morphed into get-rich-quick schemes including drug dealing, low-budget party promoting, dealing bootleg CDs and hustling fake name-brand clothes.

When he learned about web pages and the Internet, his dreams ballooned in size and he conjured plans of selling sex to millions. His family in L.A. barely heard from him, he sparsely attended class and got girls and flunkies to do term papers for him. To top it off, his closest friends, Neeko and Poncho, were two D.C. locals ruthless enough to be the muscle he needed for his enterprises. But deep down, they were gullible followers whom he knew he would never reach his full potential with. But what was instant felt good, kept money in his pockets, and was too hard to turn from after he had dug a whole so deep. The least he could do was stop Brandon from succumbing to the same traps.

Greg turned the music back on in his truck after his customers left. He sat staring at the cars that drove by, headed toward Georgia Avenue, and at the girls and boys on foot who followed them. Homecoming was simply the best time of the year. Parties ran late every night, celebrities flooded the campus, and sex was had, too. He smiled thinking about it, until a knock on the passenger side window interrupted his thoughts.

"Come in," he said, unlocking the door.

"What's up, Greg?" Brandon said hopping into the seat.

"You got Polo on from head to toe, smelling like you been smoking that killa," Greg smiled.

"It's homecoming. I want to enjoy myself," Brandon said. "I had to get fresh for this party at the Ritz tonight. You coming through?"

"The Ritz? Nah. I'm not behind that party. I think D.C. dudes are promoting that one. All my big parties are this weekend, but unless you got a fake ID you won't be able to get in."

"I'm waiting on you to come through for me on that," Brandon said.

"I did say I would get you one, didn't I? I'll call my man in Georgetown tomorrow. So, what's up? What's up with the shorties?" Greg asked, faking interest in hearing the answer. He and Brandon had to talk about specific business, but he could shoot the shit with him to break the ice.

"Oh, they can't get enough of me," Brandon smiled. "It's not even that hard to pull 'em anymore like it was when I first got here. This week I'ma come up on even more girls," he smiled.

Greg smiled back and gave him a pound. "Slow down, man. Just make sure you ain't trickin' none of your dough on 'em and always strap up."

"Oh, no doubt. You don't even have to tell me that. My room-mate Frank, now that's another question, man. I think he's down here going raw."

"Going raw? Stupid freshman. He won't be happy until he got a kid on the way or his dick is burning," Greg snapped.

They sat quietly for a few minutes watching the bodies pass. Greg turned the music down again and looked over at Brandon.

"So, you got something to tell me or not?" he asked.

"Nothing much. He mentioned the website and how you used the Towers sometimes in the background and how that was illegal. I mean, he was talking about you hustling weed and stuff like that, but I don't think he would put any of that in the paper."

"Nah, Ben ain't crazy," Greg said, looking at himself in the mirror. "Is that all he got: me taking pictures in the Towers? Shit, I'm more upset about the whole campus finding out about all of my business like that than being worried about some pictures in the Towers. I can take those pictures down tonight," he said.

"That's about it, Greg. I told you it was nothing serious. I told him I wrote a few bios for you, but that everything you did was legit."

"Aww shit, B! You shouldn't have said anything about it. Now he definitely is gonna write some shit. Yo, I know you ain't gon' do no punk shit and write the story, and be quoted in it, are you?" he asked.

"Nah, nah. It's not even like that. I told him it wasn't that serious, man. He just had me scared, telling me that he hoped I wasn't involved in anything illegal. So I told"

"That nigga is a faggot, I swear!" Greg pounded his steering wheel. "I should go over to the Towers right now and fuck his shit up," he said. "I see he didn't get enough last time."

"Huh?" Brandon asked. He had no idea about Ben and Greg's past.

# *Six*

The one thing being in Japan definitely impressed upon Charlene was the importance of being on time. If she missed her ferry she would miss her train, which would make her late. If she showed up less than 15 minutes early for work, she was late. And Wednesday, November 4th, she had to be into work even earlier for a conference of JATTE teachers in the Tokyo regional office.

The first meeting started at 6 a.m. and she still had classes to prepare for in the morning. She guzzled down warm coffee in Styrofoam cups every 20 to 30 minutes to stay awake. Once the two-hour meeting was over, she fixed her face in the bathroom and went to the teachers' lounge to finish her lesson plan for the day. She would have jumped right on it, but other expatriates who reminisced about the States distracted her. One of them was Eric Lumb.

Eric Lumb was a loser, as far as she was concerned. By mainstream standards he was attractive: Tall, thin and fair-skinned with hazel eyes. His teeth were immaculate, and as white people often said about black people who were surprisingly bright, "He spoke so well." But to Charlene he was repulsive. Charlene secretly hated light-skinned black guys, because they had teased her all throughout school and in her experience were superficial pretty boys. Instead, she liked them big, black and rough-looking. It turned her on to see rough guys. She equated their chocolate complexions with strength and struggle. They didn't bitch like pretty boys, they made her have multiple orgasms when having sex, and they made her feel like she was living on the edge. Safe, conservative, pretty, politically correct guys like Eric turned her off.

Charlene first met Eric in Osaka, along with all the new entrants who started their training there. He turned her off right away, the way he pronounced words, laughed like white people, and made a conscious effort to bond with them instead of the black teachers. There were only a handful of them, and they were supposed to stick together, Charlene thought.

Eric was an assimilator. He was awkward for a 28-year old. The first time the group of teachers went to Tokyo together, they went to a hip-hop club, and Eric admitted to the group that he had never been to one before. Charlene could tell. He came dressed in khaki pants with cuffs at the bottom, brown loafers and a sky-blue oxford. Dancing with the white guys was better than dancing with him. And during another group outing at a bar once, Eric bragged about how he hadn't dated a black girl in 10 years. To Charlene that had to be a conscious decision for anyone to not date a black girl in 10 years. She had already pegged him as a white-girl lover; one who would gain great success in life and not share it with a sister, but hearing him confirm it sickened her. Her dislike for him from that moment on became palpable.

Wednesday morning in the teachers' lounge, as he commented on BBC sports highlights with Timothy Harris —a white male teacher—every word that rolled off of his tongue touched a nerve like rocks pelting Charlene's body; she had to break the silence between her and Eric.

"Eric, look at the clip from the Ultimate Fighting Championship last night. I told you we should've gone, but you wanted get blasted drinking *sake*," Timothy said.

Eric replied with gusto, "Holy shit, that is that the guy who won? What's his name? The Beast. Look at how big and black he is;

91

of course he was going to win. We should've gone and bet money on his black ass," Eric joked. Timothy stared at Charlene without laughing and didn't say a word.

Eric laughed and said, "He reminds me of a saying I heard this black kid say about this movie Oprah Winfrey and Whoopi Goldberg were in. One of my friends from school who saw it told me that Whoopi Goldberg plays the main character and she looks like a fucking troll. She's married to this old black guy who is in love with another woman, and one night he brings the other woman home to his house, where the troll is, and as the other woman walks in she stops dead in her tracks, looks at Whoopi's black ass and says, 'You sho is ugly!'"

Eric couldn't stop laughing after he told Timothy the story. Timothy looked at Charlene again, but apparently the Celie joke from *The Color Purple* was too funny for him to hold in his laughter long, so he joined in.

"The movie is called *The Color Purple*, Eric and I can't believe you haven't seen it. What black person alive has not seen *The Color Purple*?" she asked in disgust.

"Guess I'm the only one," he laughed. "Besides, people always say that. It wasn't even a black movie. Stephen Spielberg directed it."

"And?"

"If he directed it, it's not a black movie." He was getting more serious.

"He directed it, but a black woman, Alice Walker, wrote it and won the Pulitzer Prize for the book, which the movie was based on."

"Uh, oh, excuse me, Charlene. I guess now you're gonna give me a black history lesson," he said holding his hands out as if to keep her back. "Didn't you go to one of those black schools? Guess that's what they taught you there," he said.

"Are you kidding me? 'Didn't I go to one of those black schools? I guess that's what they taught you.' How ignorant do you sound? And is that what you really think they teach at black colleges, HBCU's—historically black colleges and universities, just so you would know."

"Uh, I don't know. I just figured that since it was a black school, they taught about everything black."

"Well, you thought wrong, Eric, and apparently the white school you went to didn't teach you that," Charlene said. By this time, they had attracted an audience and Charlene was the only other black person in the room besides Eric, who may as well have been white.

"I don't want to get into a shouting match about what my school taught me versus yours. I just know that at Tufts University, I was prepared for the real world. My mother wanted me to apply to a black school, but there was no way I was going to do that. That is not the real world," he said, looking around expecting to get support from his white colleagues. But they were just interested in hearing the debate.

They probably subscribed to his beliefs, but it was better if it came from a black person instead of them, and plus, they tiptoed around Charlene, because she was outspoken and they thought she embodied the "angry black woman" stereotype.

"The real world? How is Tufts the real world? That is such a tired excuse, Eric. Going to an all-white school is not the real world, either. If that's the case, then you are a long way away from the real world, being in Japan with one hundred and twenty million Japanese people. And why would you not want to go to college and be around other intelligent, ambitious black students, especially when you have the rest of your life to work around white people? If I lived in a bubble and didn't interact with white teachers, white colleagues and everyday people, then yes, going to an HBCU would have been a detriment, but your logic is flawed and you have been drinking a little too much of the Kool-Aid," she said.

"Look around," she pointed to the other white people in the room. "Did any of you go to black schools?" she asked. None of them answered. "Exactly. When white people go to college, they go to have fun. They don't have to deal with being the minority and putting up with racist professors and fighting against hate crimes on campus. I can't believe you would come out of your mouth and say something like that," she ended.

After she spoke, Eric was speechless. She waited to trade more jabs with him, but he diverted his attention back to television as the room fell silent. Tension inside the room was so thick you could cut it. The fact that Charlene had to defend going to a black school to another black person in front of a group of white people was confirmation enough to her that she made the right decision when choosing a college.

Eric was so caught up in assimilating that he probably didn't understand what she said, but he shut up just so he wouldn't have to listen to her anymore. People like him never got it until they got into the "real world" and realized that white people could turn on them, or until white people innocently and subconsciously made them feel like pariahs.

Charlene was happy for every black person who broke the ranks at majority white schools. Her older sister graduated from Princeton and was now a professor there, but she never bought the logic given to her by people that going to a black school put students at a disadvantage. She had the rest of her life to deal with white people, and at least at a black school, her professors knew her and she wasn't just a number. Best of all, going to Howard afforded her the opportunity to see so many attractive black men, a benefit her sister advised her to relish. It was a benefit that required her to be thousands of miles away in Japan to fully appreciate.

She went back to her desk and completed her lesson plan for the day. She drank another cup of coffee and checked her email before her first class. Two junk emails, one from her sister and another that she was expecting sat in her mailbox. She opened the last one with a sinister smile on her face.

*Dear Charlene,*

*I hope this letter finds you in good spirits and good health in Asia, as you continue to pursue your career goals. You and every other Howard alumnus making their mark on the world gives us the pleasure to brag and say that you once walked across this yard.*

*Here at Howard, things are well. Our student body is enjoying the homecoming season as I write this email, and the first semester of this academic school year is halfway over. As you know, I am serving in my second consecutive term as President of the Howard University Student Association, an office that you are quite familiar with, as you worked as one of my assistants last year.*

*It has come to my attention that you have incorrectly informed our Dean of Student Life and Activities of phone usage irregularities from the last academic school year, and you have done so at my expense. I must ask that you rectify this situation as soon as possible, and by rectifying the situation I mean take responsibility for phone calls that you made to the foreign country that you are now in, using the HUSA identification number.*

*It has also come to my attention that there are numerous calls unaccounted for to states across this country, including Ohio, where you are from. If you could do those things for me, I would appreciate it greatly. If you would like to speak to me via telephone, I can arrange for that to happen and I will cover the expense of the call once you provide adequate contact information.*

*In closing, be brave, fellow Bison. Watch your back in this world. As you probably already know, there are sharks out there, and if you are not always on top of your game, you could get caught up in something way over your head.*

*Regards,*

*Ms. Falu M. Davis*
*HUSA President*

*Bachelor of The Arts Candidate May 1999*
*202-635-9700*


Charlene burst out laughing after she read the email, and covered her mouth when people started staring. She couldn't believe how fake and phony Falu sounded in the email, and how she tried to belittle Charlene's role working under her, only crediting her as an assistant. And then she had the nerve to accuse her of making calls across the country, which though it was true, paled in comparison to the bill Falu racked up calling Africa.

Charlene had already confessed to the dean about calling Japan, which the dean brushed off in an email. The most shocking thing about Falu's email was the way in which she tried to threaten her former subordinate— politely—at the end. Charlene fought the urge to immediately respond to the email, because she felt it was immature and sophomoric. But she couldn't get past the email's threatening tone and fake veneer of sisterhood. Besides, Falu was the one in trouble. Charlene was thousands of miles away. She clicked "reply," and as with the last email she sent to the dean, she copied Ben Bishop's email in the blind carbon copy section.


*Dear Ms. Falu M. Davis,*


*President of HUSA, bachelor's degree candidate, university spokeswoman, fellow Bison, Indian chief, and whatever else you are calling yourselves these days. First of all, it has come to my attention that you must not have availed yourself of all the facts in speaking with the Dean. Because if you had, you would know that she was informed about my calls to Japan while at Howard.*

*Yes, I made the calls. I did so from the HUSA phone card. What I did not do, like some other people, is illegally attain student codes and use them to call Africa. What I did not do was run up an outra-*

*geous cell phone bill and leave it for the students at Howard to have to pay. There is no need for us to talk. Although I look back with fondness, I have moved on from the politics of Howard, which I hope you will, too, depending on where you land. I am completing my year as a teaching fellow here before I enroll full-time at The London School of Economics, where I have already been accepted. Good luck to you in all of your endeavors. I hope the university gets to the bottom of the stolen cards and punishes whoever is responsible.*

*All the best,*

*Charlene Jones*
*Howard Alumnus*
*Class of 1998*


It amazed Ben how drastically D.C.'s cultural landscape varied by geographical area. Northwest D.C. gave you downtown, home to most of the federal buildings; Ledroit Park and Columbia Heights, the neighborhoods closest to Howard which were traditionally black and neither all that safe nor chic to live in; it also gave you Georgetown, the trendy neighborhood where congressmen, senators, and diplomats lived.

Places like Georgetown were mostly white, and up until recently, white people had thought twice about living in other areas of the city. Northeast was more residential: abundant with row homes and apartment buildings. Southwest was by the waterfront and home to more office buildings, apartment buildings, theaters and restaurants.

Southeast Washington, D.C., was another world. On one end there were plush Capitol Hill homes, close to everything important like Union Station, The Supreme Court, the Library of Congress and the Capitol building. Trendy, affluent white people lived in row

homes that cost almost $1 million easily. They dined at sidewalk ca-
fes, jogged freely and walked their dogs in the neighborhood.

But Southeast looked like night and day once you crossed the
Anacostia Bridge. The other side of the bridge was home to some
of the city's most notorious killers and criminals. Dilapidated row
homes, housing projects, drugs and thugs permeated the area. When
D.C. led the country in homicides just years before, they had Southeast to thank for that. It was an area where police tried to isolate
crime, like a cordoned-off battle zone. It was home to the city's only
jail and to D.C. General, one of the city's busiest trauma units. The
Metro, D.C.'s subway network, had not completed its metro stop
there by 1998. Thus, to get there you had to catch a bus, walk or take
a cab after you got off the next-closest sub stop, but cabs rarely came.

On this afternoon, Ben caught the bus. He kept quiet and tried
not to look at the group of teenage boys with their hair in braids and
their loose-fitting clothes. Two older black ladies sat up front, behind
the driver, and clutched their pocketbooks. Ben had to admit, it was
a terrible stereotype to play into, but sometimes looking at groups of
boys like them made him nervous, too, especially as a bougie Howard
student. So he understood why the ladies held their bags so tightly.

"A yo Gary, there's the nuthouse hospital for crazy-ass bamas
like you, Jo," one of the boys standing near the back of the bus said,
as they passed St. Mary's Asylum on Martin Luther King Boulevard.

"Get the fuck outta here with dat, Young. I ain't that fuckin'
crazy. Those niggas they be puttin' up in there don't even be doin'
normal crimes and shit, Jo. I mean I understand stabbing or shootin'
a nigga, but they be on some ovah shit. You ain't gon' never find me
up that motherfucker," Gary responded.

Ben sat quietly until his stop, and feared for his life when the
boys got off the back of the bus at the same stop. Four of them and
one of him, they were all headed toward the projects. All of this for
a story, Ben thought as he walked briskly down the street. What the
hell had he been thinking?

He walked through the crowds onto a quiet street that was sort of like a cul-de-sac dotted with tiny brick buildings. The sun was hiding behind trees and man-made, brick tenements obscuring the beauty of nature. The threat of violence and crime was all ever-present.

Cars blasted loud music on their way down the street. No children played in the street, but a few of their sneakers hung tied over electric wires. A group of dope boys in FUBU jackets blasted GoGo music from a small gray radio that sat on top of a car hood. Ben was nervous as he walked close to them, because the apartment that he had to go to was right in front of where they congregated. He gave a nod to them, but didn't get one back. Instead, as he was about to ring the bell, one of them said, "A yo, whatchu knockin' on my door for? We don't wanna buy shit."

"Oh you live here? I'm lookin' for Latoya."

"Fuck you lookin' for my sister for, Jo?" The man said, staring at Ben.

"Rashaun stop tryna scare my company away," a voice came from behind them. Latoya was staring at Ben from the second floor window. "The door should be open, Ben. Come in," she said.

Ben smiled, looked at her brother and nodded, then went inside. He felt for sure that he was going to get his ass beat after he left. There was limited space in Latoya's house. A tattered black leather sofa was positioned on top of a cheap, two-toned auburn rug with crumbs on it. A television fed snowy images back to them and family pictures hung on dirty white walls. Weed smoke filled the air. Latoya Henry came downstairs wearing navy blue Parasuco jeans and a white T-shirt that her chest stretched to its capacity. She was cute, but he could tell she had lived a hard life by the fact that she looked at least 28 or 29—whereas she told him over the phone that she had just turned 22. She wore her hair in braids and acrylic nails tipped her fingers.

"You drove over here, or you caught the bus?" she asked, coming down the steps.

"I caught the bus. Well, actually, I caught the Green Line, then transferred to the bus and walked the rest of the way."

"I'm surprised. You know y'all Howard people don't be catching no bus to Southeast."

"Well, it sounded like you had something that made it worth coming here," Ben responded. She smiled, assuring him that she did.

"Oh, and I do. I called Greg last night and tried to get the rest of my money from his ass, but he think I'm playing with him. I told him he would regret it. His bitch ass thought I was talking about getting' my brother Rashaun on him, but my brother just got out of jail. I ain't tryna send him back. I want y'all to embarrass Greg on campus."

"Well, what do you have for me?" Ben asked.

"Hold on," she said turning toward the steps, "Sherane, you can come down."

A light-skinned girl who looked younger than Latoya, but had a body just as voluptuous, came down similarly dressed in jeans and a T-shirt.

"This what I got. Along with this," Latoya said, handing Ben printed-out internet photos of her naked body published on Greg's website, which was dubbed KittyKats.com. Next, she handed him naked photographs of Sherane from the same site. Ben shuffled in his seat to hide his erection.

"We both took those pictures at his apartment on 13th Street," Latoya said. "That's where me and Sherane met."

Ben wanted to have both of their asses right then and there. They were thick in all the right places and for them to be low-budget Internet porn models, they did a hell of a job posing in all the right positions.

"And so, both of you agreed to do a certain amount of pictures for a certain amount of money and he burned y'all."

"He ain't burn Sherane, but he owes me money."

"So why are you coming forward, Sherane?"

"'Cause she live here with me, she ain't got nowhere to go and that motherfucker owe me money. She is only 17 years old. He ain't have no business taking her picture, putting her online. He ain't make us sign no paperwork or nothing. I met him at D.C. Live and told him

*100*

I used to strip until I had my baby, and Sherane said she met him at the Ritz on 18 and under night and she told him how old she was."

Ben wanted to ask why Sherane wasn't living with her parents or someone else in her family, but he got the gist: If she was living with Latoya, a woman whom she had met a couple of months earlier at a bootleg porno photo shoot, home probably didn't exist.

"I get your complaint, but if you didn't sign any paperwork, that can't help you," Ben said.

"Well, Sherane was there when he told us how much he would pay us. He paid her what he should have paid me, and I got some other girls who will tell you what the agreement was. At this point, I know his bitch ass ain't gon' pay me my money. I just wanna see him get caught up. He must got me fucked up if he think I'ma just take losing money on the chin. He can go to jail for what he did to Sherane. She got a driver's license that shows her age. Show him Sherane," Latoya asked.

Latoya was right. Sherane was 17 and had seven months to go until she was 18. The address listed on it was from Northeast, which must have been where her parents, or foster home was, but Ben didn't press the issue.

"So, what do you think? You got enough for a story?" Latoya asked.

"I think I do. I still have some more reporting to do, and I need to hold these pictures to scan them in, and the pictures where you have clothes on, like a bikini or something. Just give me some quotes and we're good to go. The story could be in Friday's paper."

Revenge was a dish best served cold, and Latoya was going to get Greg back. She enjoyed the thrill of it. She could smell the blood, and after all, everyone loved the get-back.

"I knew I called the right number."

Ben spent an hour at the house, caught a contact high from his two sources smoking a blunt, and clenched his fist when Rashaun came inside to use the bathroom. After they finished the interview, he asked Latoya to walk him back to the bus stop. She knew why he asked and obliged.

As soon as he got back to the West Towers, Ben Bishop rushed to his room and wrote the first 400 words of his enterprise story on Greg's illegal porn endeavor. It delighted him to know that he was finally going to get Greg back for what happened sophomore year. They busted his lip and nose, and left knots on his head. If Ben could help it, Greg was going to be arrested.

The only thing that stopped him from writing another 200 words was the fact that he had more reporting to do. Charlene Jones, the former HUSA vice president who blew the whistle on Falu Davis and others for assorted malfeasance, forwarded him two emails. One that Falu had sent to her, along with her reply to Falu. If Falu took the fall for this story, it was going to be equally as powerful as the Greg exposé. Confirming the story about HUSA was going to be the hard part.

Although homecoming started with the fireworks on Sunday, Wednesday was the night it kicked into full gear, because Wednesday was the night of the step show. Everyone who was anyone was going to be at the step show to watch all nine black Greek organizations vie for the right to call themselves champions for the next year. Some years they had to hold the step show on Saturday nights at The D.C. Armory or Constitution Hall, just to accommodate the crowds.

This year was a special year because Vicky and Ben were making their last attempt at rekindling their relationship, and Ben told Vicky he would be in the front row to cheer her on. He also promised her that he would celebrate—win lose or draw—with her and her line sisters at The Saint on 14th Street, afterwards.

Ben made it back to campus by 7 p.m. for the start of the general assembly meeting that he knew—because it was homecoming week—student leaders would not reach a quorum for to complete the governing body's business. Perched comfortably in the aisle seat of the last row of chairs, in room 142 of the Blackburn Center, Ben waited patiently for a little more than an hour. Meanwhile, every 20 minutes, Falu Davis urged attendees to wait a little longer for people who were not coming.

Only 7 of the 12 people needed to reach quorum showed. Doug Mitchell and Cameron Horn from Social Work. Peter Paul from Engineering. Kelly Simpson and Theresa Black from Fine Arts, and Patrice Garrett and Stephen Hill from the School of Business actually bothered to appear. All of them were waiting for the step show to begin.

Falu sat behind the white, hard-plastic, elongated table and shuffled papers multiple times, whispering to her vice president, Maurice. Occasionally, she smiled or stared at members in attendance. Ben, still somewhat excited from seeing the naked pictures of the two bootleg porn models earlier, also got excited just looking at Falu, who was fully dressed.

Falu was one of the most beautiful girls Ben had ever seen. There were thousands of attractive girls at Howard, but she was in the top 10, top 5, maybe. It frustrated Ben earlier on that he could never have her. Oh, she would dance with him at parties freshman year; she would even turn around and rub her ass up against him and grind. She had to give him a lap dance and kiss him once, during a game of Truth or Dare in Drew Hall years ago, but that was it.

Falu would smile in his face, making him think she liked him, but she always respectfully declined when he offered to take her out. He stepped to Falu before he stepped to Vicky freshman year. The only thought that comforted Ben was the fact that no other guy who was his classification at school had laid a hand on Falu. If he couldn't have her, he was in good company. He knew a couple of upperclassmen had gotten a piece of her along the way, but current rumor had it she was in a long-distance relationship now, with a big shot lawyer. A lawyer had a valid reason for beating out others who wanted Falu: He was a lawyer.

Older guys always won when it came to chasing women, because that was just who women went for at their age. Older guys were more experienced and established—a constant complaint made by women about guys Ben's age. And it made perfect sense for Falu to be dating a lawyer: Her parents were both lawyers and she, being the overachiever that she was, was probably going to be a successful one, too. If only Ben could taste her one time, he would be happy, he thought watching her cross her legs behind the table.

How was it possible for her to make a pair of jeans, black stilettos and a fitted black sweater look so good? She wore her hair out, too, and her curly Angela Davis afro secretly drove Ben wild. If given the chance, he would have paid to have sex with her.

He smiled to himself and broke out of fantasyland. In reality, Falu was a bitch, they hadn't been close since freshmen year, and if the emails he received about her were true, he was going to bury her, plain and simple.

Falu sat up in her chair, flicked on her microphone and said, "Okay you guys, I'm embarrassed for having called you here tonight, but we've been here for a long time and it does not look like we are going to reach a quorum. It's too bad that this meeting came during Homecoming Week, but I tried to schedule it earlier in the day, so everyone could be out in time for the step show.

"What we'll have to do is add more items on the agenda for the next meeting, to make up for what we missed this session. So you guys can hold on to those agendas if you want, but that stuff will be on the ones we send out in two weeks. I know everyone is planning on going to the step show, and so am I.

"Thanks again for coming, and once again, I apologize for the absence of some of our other members. Maybe if this problem persists, we can band together and kick those members out of the Undergraduate Student Assembly for not fulfilling their obligations," she finished.

The seven people present bolted from their seats after she spoke. They knew it would be hell waiting in line in the cold to get into Burr. Going through metal detectors would take another 10 minutes after they finally made it to the front of the building.

Ben waited in the back while Falu gathered her things in a

manila folder and put it inside her briefcase. She said something to Maurice before she made her way up the stairs and gave Ben a fake smile when she reached his aisle.

"Mr. Bishop, how are you? Is homecoming keeping you and your staff busy this week?" she asked.

How did she ever become so fake? Ben wondered.

"It is, Falu, but that's what we do: We work hard so we can be the eyes, ears, and voice of this campus."

"So let me guess, one of this week's headlines, or even an editorial will read *General Assembly members are a no-show for Wednesday meeting*," she said, making air quotes with her fingers.

"That's a good headline, Falu. I think I might have to steal it," Ben said, following her. They were walking toward Power Hall as they spoke.

"You should write something about how students are neglecting the positions they were picked to serve. They never show up for meetings. Never, and students just sit and take it. I will be the first person to go on record and say how trifling it is, just let me know when you want to talk," she said, jiggling the keys for the HUSA office.

"I have to remember that. Look, I know you are busy because like everyone else—including me—you are going to the step show. I just wanted to ask you about something that I heard," Ben said.

"Sure, go ahead," she said, unlocking the door. They were still standing in the empty hallway, listening to distant voices.

"I heard something about a crazy phone bill accrued by HUSA from making multiple national and international calls. And according to my info, someone or some people in the office might have stolen phone cards from other campus organizations to make the calls."

Falu, the preeminent political player amongst students, was shocked. Her face went blank after he spoke.

"How did you hear, I mean *where* did you hear that, Ben?" she said, looking him coldly in the eye.

"Sources. You know how stuff gets around. Any truth to that?

Can I quote you?" he asked whipping out his pad and pen.

"Ben, I don't see how you could even come across something like that, and if I had more time to sit and talk with you, I would explain to you how that is not true. We need to squash all of these rumors as soon as they begin. I can tell you that HUSA might have slightly gone over the limit of money allotted for phone calls, but no more than *The Hilltop* or the Bison Yearbook. I hope you are not planning on printing an article about a rumor," she said.

"Don't bite my head off, Falu. I'm just asking a question. I know you guys don't get the phone bills, so you probably wouldn't know if there was an abuse of phone privileges by someone in your office, but—"

"I know everything about everything that goes on in my administration!" she nastily interrupted him. "As HUSA president, it is my job to stay up on these matters. I cannot stress to you that this is just a rumor!"

Ben and Falu both turned toward the end of Power Hall when they heard Dean Thomas's voice. and they simultaneously got the same idea. But Falu, ever so clever, guessed what Ben was thinking, and moved quickly to head him off. She didn't want him asking the dean questions before she, herself grabbed the opportunity.

"Dean Thomas, are you heading over to the step show? I have something I need to talk to you about."

"Come to my office Falu. I have a few minutes. Hello Ben," Dean Thomas said.

"Hi Dean," Ben replied, wanting to grab Falu by the hair and bang her head against the wall. She was so slick. Luckily for Ben, a source he had to talk to for an unrelated story had just wrapped up a conversation with the dean and was walking out of the building.

"Chief Hicks," Ben yelled down the hall. "You got a minute?"

Ben took off and Falu's heart dropped to her shoe. She thought Ben was about to ask the chief about the stolen codes, but there was no way he could know about them yet. She hated Ben Bishop.

"Mr. Newspaper Editor. What can I do for you," Chief William

Hicks said, extending his hand for Ben to shake.

Chief Hicks was the longtime chief of campus police at Howard. He had a penchant for flashy jewelry, and rarely did you see him without a smile on his face. He pumped around campus in expensive suits and nice ties, waving to administrators and faculty. Female coeds thought he was cute for an older man. He was tall and fair skinned with wavy salt and pepper hair and a trimmed goatee. The guys paid him no mind, just as long as his officers didn't harass them.

"I hate to bug you, Chief," Ben said. "I know this is the busiest week of the school year for you."

"It sure is, Mr. Bishop. As you know, we are expecting a crowd of nearly fifty-thousand this week."

"That big, huh?"

"Of course. You have alumni coming, the students and all the people homecoming attracts locally, we might get more than that."

Ben scribbled down the numbers.

"So, what's the plan?" he asked.

"As usual, late Friday night and all day Saturday, we'll be shutting Georgia Avenue down. We wanted to shut Sixth Street down, but President Humphries doesn't want it that way. Of course, I'm just telling you that. Don't you put that in the paper and say it came from me. Our officers are going to be working 12-hour shifts this weekend. Some are working their first overtime shift tonight for the step show," he said.

"Can you give out any deployment numbers?" Ben asked.

Chief Hicks smiled. "Nice try, Mr. Bishop. You know my policy is to never give out numbers."

"It was worth a try," Ben smiled. Chief Hicks patted him on the back.

"So, what was it you wanted to talk to me about?"

Ben shifted gears quickly. "Ok, so hypothetically, what if I had information about a student using university housing as part of an illegal pornographic operation, what would the punishment for that be?"

The smile left the chief's face.

"Well, Mr. Bishop, if that were true, if you could prove that, then it would be a criminal infraction. As you know, no soliciting or illegal activity is permitted on university property. A student doing such a thing would open him- or herself up to punishment from the academic disciplinary board, which could result in expulsion. And that is *before* any charges are filed by the local authorities."

"I see, and what if this student also involved minors in this enterprise?"

"Minors involved in something like that in a campus dormitory?"

"Oh, my fault. Well, this student didn't involve the minor in anything on campus property, but nonetheless, they did involve a minor in a pornographic enterprise."

"Mr. Bishop, don't scare me like that," Chief Hicks laughed. "That would be something the local authorities would have to deal with. As I said, the thing most concerning to the university is any illegal activity taking place on school premises. Now, a student being involved in any criminal activity with a minor would be admissible in any actions taken by the disciplinary board. I know you guys are afraid to give names, but Mr. Bishop, if you know that this happened for sure, you might want to give me that information before things get ugly."

"Actually, I'm still confirming everything. That's why it's hypothetical for now. But you'll hear back from me."

Ben was lying. He was going to run with the quotes he got from Chief Hicks. It wasn't unethical, but he wasn't going to snitch on Greg by naming him directly. He was going to embarrass him and then have the police track him down. If he would have told the chief then and there, they would have snatched Greg the same night or the next morning, and Greg would have taken the site down.

"If you say so. Be careful, son. Don't take work so serious with this being homecoming week and all. All these young ladies here, all the fun that students have during this time of the year, take advantage of it. Please don't create a mess for me now," Chief Hicks said,

Ben smiled and shook his hand. They were walking toward Cramton, and the step show line extended down Girard Street, where students were lined against the Greene Stadium. Ben thought of one more favor to ask the chief.

"Chief, this line is crazy. Is there any way I can slide past security with you?"

# *Seven*

Although the shoes she wore hurt her feet like hell—as new shoes often did—Vicky and her sorority sisters stood patiently in Burr Gymnasium's frigid hallway, behind the basketball court entrance. All of the step show participants did. Vicky and her sorors assembled like a pristine group of angels, dressed in white pants suits, matching high heels, and white satin neckties loosely tied in Windsor knots.

As with every homecoming show, this one wasn't going to start on time. The D.J., whoever he was, spent 30 minutes hyping the crowd up, playing Outkast's *Rosa Parks*, Jay-Z's *Hard Knock Life*, Biggie's *One More Chance*, and Pastor Troy's *No More Playin' in GA*. After that came a five-minute demonstration by the audience on whose geographical origins reign supreme. Howard being Howard, and located in D.C., meant the East coast contingent won by default; but the Dirty South was a close second.

Next came the West, and last, as always at Howard, was the Midwest. You would find plenty of people from Illinois, Michigan and Ohio, but other than that, you would be pretty hard pressed to find a strong Midwest constituency amongst students. They scattered like leaves in the wind, and affiliated themselves with whatever big city was closest to their town. So, if someone claimed to be from

Chicago, it might have meant that they were from Country Club Hills or Kankakee.

Being in the moment at the step show moved Vicky through a range of emotions, summing up her years at Howard. This was her first step show competition, and as a graduating senior, it would be her last. She didn't participate the year before, her junior year, because she felt fat and self-conscious. The thought of climbing the stage only to wiggle in ways that she didn't think were flattering to her body, and the possibility of falling and embarrassing herself in front of thousands did a sufficient job of beating her confidence down. It was a good thing that the baggage and fear were gone this year, she thought, waiting to see the order in which they would perform.

The brothers of Kappa Alpha Psi went first. She thanked God as they marched by wearing white slacks and red shirts, carrying their red and white canes. Who could stop the surge of erratic nerves that tormented her body? She and her girls picked sixth place.

"I can't hear myself think, it's so loud in there," Vicky said to Jasmine, who stood against a wall rubbing her white-gloved hands over her elbows.

"Me either. And it's too cold out here. I wish there was somewhere else for us to wait," Jasmine said.

"The cold keeps you alert, and that's a good thing. I'm so nervous with all those people out there," Vicky said.

"Girl, please. We got this. You of all people, 'Ms. Keep us practicing until five in the morning and then make us do it again in the afternoon,' should have calm nerves. Remember, if you fall, improvise, if you forget your lines, give me the signal and I'll save you. We can't let none of these bitches beat us this year!"

Vicky smiled. Jasmine's thirst for competition was nourishment for her.

From the early crowd reaction, the Kappas were doing well.

"Listen to them. They're on fire. They must be unbuckling their pants or taking their shirts off," Vicky suggested. "Listen to all those girls screaming."

"I'm not going to the club tonight if we lose. I don't have any time to be partying with people all up in my face asking me what happened," Stephanie snapped.

"Don't be like that, girl. You sound like a sore loser," Jasmine said.

"Call me whatever you want, I can't believe y'all would go if we lost," she said.

"Well, I'm going to see all my prophytes that I haven't seen in years, which is the same reason why you should come, win lose or draw. This is our last homecoming as students. We might all be living in different cities next year around this time, and we might not be able to come back to homecoming and watch our girls step. You gotta live it up no matter what."

Stephanie didn't speak. Jasmine had a good point, but Stephanie was stubborn, and as Jasmine and Vicky suspected, she was a sore loser.

"Vicky, what about you? You partying if we lose?" Stephanie asked.

"Of course. Like Jasmine said, this is my last homecoming at Howard. It has to be memorable."

"Bitch don't sit there and front. You are going no matter what happens because you told your boy, Ben, that he could come with you and y'all were supposed to kick it."

"Ugh! Ben. Are you serious?" Stephanie interrupted. "I thought he was old news. Eww, girl, this is homecoming. All these fine-ass guys down here for this one week, and you want to spend it with Benjamin Bishop?"

"Why do you hate Ben so much, Stephanie, if I don't? I know you are being a good friend, but damn. Like I said, I'm just trying to have some fun. What do you expect me to do? He was my boyfriend. You think I'm just gonna stop caring about him?"

"He was your boyfriend two years ago. Last year does not count because y'all only lasted a few months before he did that foul shit.

But you know what, you're right. Why am I worried? I might not be coming anyway, so at least I won't have to put up with his corny ass," Stephanie said.

Vicky thought the best thing to do was to let the subject of Ben die down. Stephanie was being a good friend, vowing her loyalty to her girl. But Vicky could not make up her mind about Ben, and they had been spending so much time together since the school year started. They talked on the phone most nights and ate out often. It was almost three months into the school year and he had not tried to have sex with her. Maybe Ben was changing, she thought. Maybe he was becoming the person she wanted him to be. Of course she would entertain him, no matter if Stephanie liked it or not.

It took an hour of people sweating and stomping for their dear lives before the number-six seed was called to the stage. Vicky took a series of deep breaths and rubbed her chest to calm down before they ascended the stage. She was the first in line, and she was the first person whose photo *The Hilltop* snapped as they emerged from the darkness.

The crowd sounded more like RFK Stadium than Burr. So many faces she knew watched her. So many prophytes and line sisters gave her hand gestures and yelled their sorority call in their loudest voice. One unpleasant face grabbed her attention quickly and that was Falu Davis'. As one of the judges, she sat at a table in front of the stage. The only pleasure in seeing Falu's face for Vicky was the fact that Falu so wanted to be on that stage stepping with her. Falu and Vicky went out for the sorority together sophomore year. They were dressed somewhat alike in conservative blue skirt suits at rush. Many weeks later, it was Vicky who got the early morning knock on her door to join the line and Falu didn't. That was the one thing that Vicky felt she had over Falu—the beautiful girl who had it all—from the men, to looks and parents with money. Falu had gone out for the sorority their junior year, too, after she and Vicky had fallen out, and it gave Vicky great pleasure to vote "no" on her acceptance to the line.

Behind Falu, sitting in the middle of the first row of patron seats, was Vicky's on-again, off-again college sweetheart, Ben, clapping and smiling. He stood up and yelled something that she could not decipher, but after he sat back down, the show began.

"Ladies and gentleman. This is not a test! You are now rocking with the best! Let us show you how we do it. Alpha Chapter. LADIES!"

STOMP!

They were off. Vicky clapped and stomped and yelled and twirled her upper body in a circular motion before they all stopped abruptly. The crowd loved it. She turned around and went in the other direction and they all tossed their hats into the crowd. There was more clapping, more feet tapping, more stomping. The sweat quickly surfaced on her forehead. Her heart beat faster than a flying bullet. The yells wouldn't stop. More stomping. More stepping. More feet tapping.

The group broke off into two lines on opposite sides of the stage and simultaneously caught 16 white canes that someone from the audience tossed into the air. Now they imitated the Kappas and with one hand each, twirled the wooden sticks with lightning speed, all while singing. Vicky came front and center and did a solo twirl; winding the cane above her head and behind her back before flipping it 20 feet in the air and catching with one hand again. Still lined up on opposite sides of the stage, they marched like military soldiers and lobbed the canes from side to side, while each member traded sides. The audience loved it.

Next, Vicky came out and did a solo singing performance while her sorors stomped their feet and hands. Vicky couldn't stop and she wouldn't stop twirling her cane. She had the hang of it now. As she emptied every drop of air her lungs had stored, they formed a Soul Train line and took turns stepping down it. They gyrated, stepped, clapped, stepped in slow motion, and then sped it up. After Vicky finished her solo performance, she started stepping backwards—all while saluting fellow sorority members in the audience with their signature hand gesture and call.

Variations of this went on for more than 20 minutes without any of the 16 steppers making any mistakes. When they lined up at the end of their routine to catch their breath and strike a serious pose, Vicky reluctantly broke a smile and winked an eye at Ben, one of many standing for an overwhelming ovation. *This* was what she had practiced for, endless hours every day since the beginning of the semester. The other girls called her a stickler, which she was, but Vicky felt that since she was chapter president, she should have a greater sense of urgency than everyone else. Ben blew her a kiss as the stage director dimmed the lights for the next act.

Exactly one hour and fifteen minutes later, Vicky and her sorors were named first place winners in the 1998 homecoming step show, and marched on stage crying when the trophies were presented. Omega Psi Phi took the first place prize for the men, and during each acceptance, throngs of fraternity and sorority members from the audience flooded the stage, sang and stepped.

Vicky would definitely be partying at The Saint tonight, with Ben, Jasmine, a now-certain Stephanie and hundreds of other black Greeks.

Drenched from the sweat that soaked their bodies, Vicky and her sorors emerged into the hallway of Burr Gymnasium to the sound of people congratulating them and whistling. They were surrounded by sorority hopefuls, alumni and administrators. She walked toward the glass doors in front of Burr and saw Ben standing with a *Hilltop* photographer and a reporter. The same freshman reporter Vicky remembered Ben talking about taking under his wing. She remembered that Brandon was his name and that she had seen his name in the paper many times. She also remembered he would often call Ben asking questions while she and Ben were out together or watching television.

He held a notepad in one hand and wedged a pen above his ear as she approached them. Both Ben and the reporter clapped for her. She hugged Ben and called the rest of her sorors over so they could share the spotlight of having their picture taken and being quoted in the school paper.

"Congratulations. I knew you had it in you, but damn, you kicked it, Vic," Ben said hugging her.

"I'm warning you I'm sweaty," she laughed.

"I don't care. Give me everything you got," he said, pulling her closer into a bear hug.

She squeezed him back and poked him in the side. They stood back from each other and the smiles on their faces took them back to when everything between them was fresh and new. When their love first took root roots. Anyone watching could see that they still felt something for each other. Brandon suspended the moment with his first question.

"Hi Vicky, I'm Brandon from *The Hilltop*, Ben's protégé," he joked. "How does it feel now that you've won it all?"

Burgundy and gray Polo rugby? Check. Black Polo jeans? Check. Black, low-cut leather Timberlands? Check. Brandon unbuttoned two of three buttons on his shirt, which exposed the silver Cuban-link chain he bought from a street vendor at Eastern Market in Southeast a few weeks prior. It glistened, contrasted against a black T-shirt. He touched his head with a drop of pink moisturizer lotion and brushed his waves down. Two splashes of Eternity cologne and he was done.

A handsome, boyish reflection stared back at him in the mirror, making him smile. His looks were only responsible for fifty percent of the grin. The other half was silliness—the natural effect a blunt and a tall cup of rum and Coke could do for you. He and Frank shopped at Pentagon City Mall earlier in the day for homecoming outfits. Oh, how quickly they learned that it cost big money in college dollars to keep up with the Joneses for homecoming.

Freshmen usually went all out because they were new and they had to impress people. New clothes had to be bought for campus events and the club, money had to be pocketed for club entry and accessories like marijuana and liquor. Brandon was thankful that he knew Greg and Ben, because Greg gave him free weed and a fake ID. Ben gave him free tickets to various events since he was covering them.

After Brandon and Frank dressed, they switched on the ceiling fan in their room to kill the weed smell. They could get kicked out of school if caught blazing up in the dorm. They removed the bath towel from the bottom of the door (another trick people used in dorms to keep the skunk odor from seeping into the hallway).

"These IDs Greg gave us better work tonight, Brandon, or I want my thirty-five dollars back," Frank said.

"You can kiss that money goodbye. You know damn well Greg ain't coming up off no dollars."

"That's easy for you to say. You didn't have to pay for yours."

"Quit complaining. You didn't have to pay for that weed we just smoked, did you? It's homecoming, nobody is trying to hear all that complaining. Let's get out of here so we can get on some of these girls. I can see the line at Burr from here," Brandon said, looking out of the courtyard window of Drew Hall, which gave a great view of the gym.

Ten minutes later, they were standing in line like hundreds of others waiting to get in Burr. Their eyes were bloodshot red, and they both smelled like contraband mixed with cologne, but it was home-coming—they weren't the only people in line who smelled that way.

While Frank spoke to people he knew and made sure that no-body cut them in line, Brandon was on celebrity watch. He wanted to see who would show up to the step show. No one, so far, but he did see a few familiar faces.

Falu Davis, the beautiful HUSA president, passed him and Frank, walking quickly up to security and bypassing the line. Brandon wanted that kind of power. Brandon wanted her, but he knew he could never have her. The one time he interviewed her for a story about a donation Microsoft made to the school in the form of new computers, Brandon was afraid to look her in the eye until she noticed and told him to. She was polite, he thought. She was driven. He asked her what she was going to do after she graduated and she said with such conviction that she was going to law school at either Harvard or Yale, but most likely, Harvard, if she could have her way. Brandon fed off of it.

After Falu Davis bust the line, Brandon saw his boss, Ben, slipping a notepad into his coat pocket, and sliding with the chief of campus police past a security blockade. There wasn't a person on campus that had any sort of importance that Ben didn't know. Girls waved to him from the line and guys threw him the peace sign.

"Yo, don't you work for homeboy right there? Stop him before he goes inside, so we won't have to wait in this line, dawg," Frank pleaded.

"Nah, let him do his own thing," Brandon said. "I ain't begging nobody to get me in."

"But you write for the paper," Frank insisted. "You're covering the step show, and it's cold as shit out here. We got at least another twenty minutes in this line, B."

"Yeah, and if I tell them I write for the paper, they might let me in, but what about you? You don't do shit, but smoke up all of my free weed. Just shut up and stay in line. This is where all the girls are anyway," Brandon said.

He was right. There were too many pretty girls in line for him to choose whom he would approach before they went inside. If he talked to one girl and got turned down, others would see it and that might mess his game up. What if he stepped to one girl and her friend was more attractive? That sucked. Instead of approaching anyone, he and Frank stood in the chilly November air until they passed the metal detectors, and followed the music up the steps into the rafters.

The rafters were packed. People had to squeeze past seated

spectators and search for empty seats. Old faces, young faces, male and female, caught his attention as he searched.

Brandon had never been to a step show before. The closest he had come to seeing people step was back in high school in Philly, when a group of Alphas from one of the local schools came and spoke to his gym class about fraternities and sororities. The Alphas urged their young audience to look into Greek life, particularly Alpha Phi Alpha for the boys, when they got to college. He also once saw a group of Deltas stepping in the street at the Penn Relays at The University of Pennsylvania.

"We made it just in time," Frank said, following Brandon to the top of the bleachers. "They just cut the lights off."

When they sat, the music started and everybody jumped out of their seats and started dancing.

"Damn, look how much love the Greeks get. That might have to be the move for us," Brandon said.

The step show was memorable to say the least. That night, Brandon and Frank made up their minds that they would pledge before they graduated. The spotlight and attention for girls sucked them in. To them, fraternities were synonymous with multiple sex partners and parties that lasted forever. Afterward, Frank followed friends he knew outside while Brandon had to wait around and interview the winners.

"Stay right here. They'll be coming out from behind the court," Ben said, and tapped Brandon on the shoulder. "I'm keeping you busy this week, huh?" Ben asked.

Brandon tried not to make too much eye contact with Ben because he was high, and he knew that Ben would know that he got the weed from Greg if he saw him high. He wouldn't have gotten in trouble, but Ben was one of the people Brandon wanted to impress. So was Greg, who stood at the front doors of Burr watching him and Ben waiting on the side.

Brandon was playing both sides of the field, he thought, while waiting there. He was caught up in a deep-seated hatred the two upperclassmen held for each other, when all he was trying to do was have fun.

The winning sorority came out first, and Brandon watched with admiration how Ben scooped up one of the prettiest members and laughed with her in his arms. It was the same girl Brandon had seen with Ben many times before, including the very first day he met Ben on the Yard. She would call *The Hilltop* office for Ben periodically when Brandon was there. When he asked Ben if she was his girlfriend, he was shocked when Ben said no, but that he wanted her to be. Victoria Mourning was her name. Brandon had heard freshman sorority hopefuls reduce themselves to whispers when she walked by their crowds.

Her beauty made him admire Ben even more for seemingly having her. Brandon wanted a girlfriend just as attractive, if not more so, one day. While they hugged and joked, Brandon looked over at Greg, who was still watching them. He regretted telling Greg some of the things Ben had said, because he knew Greg would start trouble.

Brandon turned back around and Vicky was poking Ben in the side, looking in his face. Frank was waiting for him outside and he still had to interview the Omegas. He would have to butt into their celebration. Her quick glance was his opening.

"Hi Vicky, I'm Brandon from *The Hilltop*, Ben's protégé," he joked. "How does it feel now that you've won it all?"

She beamed at Ben and said, "You train 'em young, huh? Your protégé, huh? Well, Brandon, this feels great. Our sorority is built on the principle of sisterhood and that is what this win was tonight. We practiced hard for this night. We stayed up late, all while maintaining our grades because we wanted to give the people a show. We wanted to show them what real sisters can accomplish when we come together," she smiled.

Brandon's work was practically done. One question was actually all he had to ask her. The story he was writing was only 400 words, and had multiple photos to go along with it. Besides, the standard "sisterhood" and "brotherhood" responses and praises for each of the winning organizations would be the only quotes they gave out all night. As soon as the Omegas emerged, he would ask their chapter president the same question, and he and Frank would be off to the club.

Brandon listened to Ben and Vicky talk about partying at The Saint later that night, and waited with them while they waited for more of her sorors. When he looked across the lobby to see if Greg was still watching them, he was startled to see that Greg was less than 10 feet away.

"Hey yo, Ben, somebody told me you got a problem with me," Greg said, walking up to Ben's face.

The smile on Ben's face disappeared. Vicky grabbed his arm and told him to follow her outside. Brandon stood still. They stood face-to-face now. Greg was a few inches taller and more muscular than Ben. His nostrils flared in Ben's face and his jaw muscles clenched. Neeko and Poncho were nowhere to be found.

"If I had a problem with you, you would know it," Ben said.

"Nigga, whatever. I know about the fucking story that you tryna do. You got something to ask me, then ask it and stop acting like a bitch! Otherwise, my name better not be in that paper on Friday or I'ma fuck your shit up!"

"We can handle this right—"

"Do we have a problem here?" a campus police officer said, walking over to the crowd. "Let's break this up, fellas. Everybody out!" he yelled to the crowd surrounding them.

"This is why they're gonna stop letting these kids have stuff on campus, for all this fighting and stuff," the officer said to another officer. "Come on, son. Let's go," he said, grabbing Greg's arms.

"I'm going, I'm going, Greg said. I'll see his bitch ass later."

Ben and Greg studied each other's faces with nasty sneers until Greg was out of the doors, out of sight. The crowd followed Greg out the door. Brandon thought that Ben looked afraid. He waited with Ben while Vicky went to get her car, so she could drive him home, since campus police wouldn't let him go.

"Nothing good can come from you two young boys fighting," the campus cop said to Ben as he was leaving. "Let that die down, son, before something happens to one of you."

Ben, whose eyes were full of fire at that point, ignored the old man and left the building.

# *Eight*

It was 4 a.m. by the time Ben and Vicky got back to her room. The Saint had been packed with black Greeks who celebrated the step show together. Ben and Vicky spent the whole night dancing and drinking with each other; he even fell inside the club and was the butt of many jokes.

He stumbled down the second-floor hallway in the East Towers, knocking on random doors and making music with his knuckles.

"Wake up, bitches. It's homecoming, goddammit. Let's have some fun," his voice slurred. Vicky laughed at him, which only encouraged him more.

"I said wake up, goddammit!" He knocked on a door in the hallway, snapped his fingers and spun around in unison. Predictably, he lost his balance and crashed to the cheap, teal hallway rug. "Ouch!"

"Ben, get up," Vicky giggled. She was tipsy, too, but not like him. Ironically, she was the one who should have been celebrating wildly, not him. "Ben, stop banging on people's doors. It's late and you might wake someone up."

"They need to get up. It's homecoming. Nobody should be sleeping during homecoming!"

"Shhh. Ben, yes they should. What do you think is gonna happen when you get to my room?"

"I don't know," he looked at her and smiled after she helped him to his feet, "you tell me."

Vicky knew what he was talking about. She frowned at him and let his arm go.

"Everybody, get up!" he said.

"Ben, I said stop. I'm gonna leave you out here and I bet someone will call the RA. Then what? *The Hilltop* editor gets kicked out of the East Towers for being drunk, making loud noise in the halls late at night. You better be quiet and come on."

Vicky had a room that faced the West Towers, which meant to get there she had to go through a series of turns and passages. It was funny how the East Towers looked the same as the West outside, but was designed slightly different inside. She kicked her shoes off when she opened the door, and held it open for Ben. He stumbled through and used the weight of her bedroom door to prop himself up. Vicky nudged him to the side and felt the weight of his body against her back. It felt good. Ben ran to her twin bed once inside and collapsed.

"Take your shoes off, Ben. You can't sleep on my bed like that."

He did her one better. He took his shoes, shirt, and pants off and tapped on the bed for her to join him.

Vicky went to the bathroom to change into her night pajamas. When she came back, she was wearing a long white T-shirt. She turned around to click the light and Ben caught a glimpse of her ass. Immediately, he got excited.

As soon as she lay down, he wrapped his arms around her and turned her in his direction. They kissed a sloppy, drunken kiss and breathed heavily on each other. He fondled her soft breast and rubbed his hands down her thighs. She was warm. She felt good. He was solid as a rock. She kissed him back and moaned when he kissed and lapped at her neck. This continued for 20 minutes, until Ben messed up the foreplay by trying to get on top of her and take it further. She wouldn't let him, so as a result he spent most of the night unable to sleep, with his horniness quite tangible.

Hours later, his hangover was coming down and he was traversing campus to meet with his managing editor, Forrest, on the Yard by the flagpole. Forrest was dressed in navy green cargo pants, brown wool jacket and Timberland boots. His back was turned toward Ben.

"Give me all your money," Ben said, covering Forrest's eyes.

"Ben you can't disguise your voice. I wish you would stop running up on me like that," he said, turning to shake Ben's hand.

"Whatever. What's going on?"

"How come you didn't call me back last night? I called you a million times. Word is you and Greg almost got into at the step show."

Ben sucked his teeth, remembering the night before. He wanted to punch Greg in the face until the blood from cuts he caused squirted back into his own .

"Damn, Howard people don't waste time spreading the news. I was at the club with Vicky last night, and yeah, we had words, but that was it. He called himself trying to punk me in front of Vicky and them, so I couldn't just stand there."

"What's the deal? I heard he was saying something about, 'if you got some shit to say to him, say it to his face,' or something like that. What kind of beef you got with Greg-, well I mean what kind of *recent* beef you got with him? Everybody knows what happened sophomore year," Forrest said.

Ben made a sweeping view around the flagpole to make sure not too many eyes were watching. "I'm about to embarrass his ass on Friday, *that's* what, and he knows it, so he's getting scared," Ben said.

"Embarrass him? What? How? Tell me—don't leave me out. You got some dirt?" Forrest's eyes lit up at the possibility of a good story. Ben told him everything that he had on Greg and stood back watching his reaction, smiling. Forrest returned the smile.

"Oh damn, that is a big story. That crazy dude might hunt you down for that one, Ben. Is that the story you were holding from me?"

"Yeah, I had to. You got a big mouth."

"A big mouth? Your mouth is way bigger than mine, but I won't get into that now. This is the biggest story this campus has seen in years, well that and this HUSA story if it's true. So, Greg heard about the story and he was trying to scare you into not writing it? Nah, fuck that, we gotta write it. You can put my name on it too if you want to. How did he hear that you were writing about him?" Forrest asked.

"Brandon."

"Brandon? Our Brandon?"

"Yeah. He and Brandon are close, too. His punk-ass got Brandon to a write a couple of papers for him. I'm telling you Greg is like a disease, but everybody around here is too afraid to stand up to him. Fuck Greg. What do I have to lose?" Ben said.

Ben swore Forrest to secrecy, even from the staff writers, and specifically from Brandon. They were finishing the last touches on the paper tonight, but he wanted even the other writers to be surprised. Everyone on campus loved Greg, and Ben was going to blow him out of the water. It gave him a sick and twisted pleasure.

"I can promise that I won't say anything, but neither should you. Man, Greg does not live by the same rules we live by, Ben. If this website is making him money and you come along and fuck that up—which is what you are doing—he is going to come after you *hard*. Harder than last time, and what happens if no one is there to back you up?"

"Oh well, I'll cross that bridge when I get to it. People deserve to know what this dude is up to."

"Are you sure this is all about pointing out that broke the law? You sure this isn't a personal vendetta?"

"It doesn't matter if it is, Forrest. I'm doing the story!"

"Well go ahead, do your story, but what if I told you that Greg carries a pistol in his glove compartment and sometimes on him?"

Ben didn't respond. He was running late for a political science class, his last of the day. He had no time to listen to Forrest try and talk him out of engaging with Greg. Forrest gave good advice: Ben could get killed or badly bruised and he did not have money to pay for a lawyer. Poncho and Neeko were business partners with Greg. Ben covering the story might mess up their money and he might become their target now. Now, Ben had to think more seriously about whether he was going to take the stand he originally wanted or live with punking out,—if only for self-preservation.

An hour later, Ben sat in the back of his Third World Politics class, ruminating on whether to put Greg on blast in the newspaper. Which was more important, his manhood or immediate safety?

"So, as you see class, although it did not turn out to be a successful revolution, you see how their actions were the catalyst for generations after them. Sometimes that is all it takes, for one person to stand up—no matter if they die or not—to set it off. Not to sound corny, quoting the popular movie, but you guys get my drift," Dr. Banks said, standing in front of the class. He was normally one of Ben's favorite professors, but today Ben was out of it. Dr. Banks noticed.

"Mr. Bishop. Mr. *Hilltop* Editor, what other famous revolutionary attempts had a lasting impact on the generations to come after them?"

"Huh?" Ben asked, snapping out of a trance.

"Not with us today, Mr. Bishop, I see. It's homecoming. I understand," Dr. Banks laughed. "But let me help you out. I bet you didn't know that one of your cultural icons was named after an unsuccessful revolutionary."

"Who?" Ben asked.

"Well, I'm sure you're a fan of Tupac Shakur, and before I go any further, I am not going to debate whether he is still alive or not. Like I was saying, Tupac was a cultural icon for most of you right? It's quite an interesting coincidence that his songs were militant and dealt with violence and poverty. Did you guys know that he was named after a Peruvian rebel who led a charge against the Spaniards in 1780? He was originally named Jose Gabriel Condorcanqui, but he later changed his name to Tupac Amaru II, after his great-grand-father, the last Incan ruler. He led a charge against the Spaniards that ended with his men capturing and executing a governor. Now, he was eventually captured, tortured and killed, but look at what he meant to revolutionary tales. Tupac Shakur's mother knew just what she was doing when she named him," Dr. Banks concluded.

"That's the end of class for the day. Enjoy homecoming and please, young people, have fun responsibly. I'll be at the game on Saturday, so I'm sure I'll see some of you there."

Ben waited in the back of the class until it was empty. He caught Dr. Banks just as he grabbed his briefcase and started for the door.

"Dr. Banks."

"Yes, Mr. Bishop. Do you have a question?"

"That was an interesting lecture. Tupac is one of my favorite rappers, and I never knew the origin of his name."

"See, Tupac's mother was a Black Panther, you know? She knew what she was doing. It's too bad he had to die the way he did. But anyway, what was your question?"

"Well, I don't know exactly. I'm going through something personally and I'm caught in-between standing up for what I believe in and backing down, but then I have to live with the feeling of being a coward. It's kind of a tough decision, you know?"

"Hmm. I'm guessing this has something to do with the paper you run, Mr. Bishop."

"Of course. There's a controversial story that I got my hands on, but the person that it implicates might want to take matters further than an article."

"I see. Well, I think if you have fears of being a coward and having to live with those feelings, it means that you have had to swallow your courage before. Think about how that made you feel. Think about a pattern that is developing inside of you at a young age. Now, sometimes you have to be smart and win the war by fighting each battle one at a time, but forgive me if I am a little cynical. This is college, Mr. Bishop. Hopefully all of you students here—and I'm assuming this issue is with a student—but hopefully you are all here past that schoolyard mentality. I say go with your gut feeling."

Ben thought over what Dr. Banks said. His gut feeling was to write the article about Greg.

"You're right, Dr. Banks," he said patting his stomach. "It's already in here. I'll go with my gut."


She knew the numbers would be the same. She had made the calls to Africa and stole phone codes from several other student organizations, but somehow, she wished that AT&T made a mistake. She hadn't planned on telling Eric and she decided to wait to tell her parents until they got to D.C. on Friday. They were coming for homecoming weekend and the annual Board of Trustees dinner where student leaders were invited to socialize with the board.

Falu was alone in her office playing solitaire when the phone interrupted her. She wasn't focused on winning; she just needed to keep a distraction from thoughts of the inevitable. Then the phone rang.

"Howard University Student Association. How can I help you?"

"Falu this is Mrs. Pearl. Dean Thomas will see you in her office now."

"I'll be right there."

Falu said a prayer before she opened her office door and went out into the hallway. So many people were in good moods this time of the year, as they should have been, and Falu was faking smiles left and right. It felt like the corridor grew narrower with each step, and she felt the lights dim. She thought of categorically denying every charge, but no one would buy her lies.

"Hi Mrs. Pearl," Falu said, walking into the Dean's waiting area.

"Hey, girl. She's expecting you. Just go right in."

Mrs. Pearl avoided eye contact with Falu. That was another bad sign. Falu tapped on the door three times before she entered, and found the dean flipping through white invoices.

"Sit down, Falu," the dean said without looking at her.

Falu sat for what seemed like an eternity before the dean cleared her throat and placed the packet in the middle of her desk. She looked at Falu with a serious face, as if she was her mother, and was about to scold her for bringing home a bad report card.

"We got the numbers back from AT&T today and they're sticking."

Silence.

"Did you hear what I said?"

"Yes, Dean. The numbers came back the same."

The dean's cell phone rang, but she quickly silenced it after she acknowledged that it was someone she didn't want to speak to.

"So, if the phone company double-checked the numbers and they came back the same, I would say that HUSA has a really serious problem. I'm not going to ask them to check the numbers again, Falu, because we have dealt with them for years. They handle all university phone services and the reason we have dealt with them for years is because they provide service that we like. What are we going to do about this?"

Falu fought back tears.

"I told you I would personally pay for the cell phone charges and I am prepared to lose my university stipend. I was going to suggest that HUSA borrow money from the university, and as you know, student leaders have been discussing whether they would recommend an increase in the student activity fee for next year, which means that HUSA would have a bigger budget and maybe that could help pay down the debt."

The dean burst out laughing. "Falu Davis, why should next year's administration suffer because of this? You will be gone, out of here, and these students will have to deal with not having programming funds. I don't think so. And as far as an increase in the student activity fee goes, the increase your office will get, which has not been determined, won't cover the damages. I think we are going to handle this issue sooner rather than later."

"What are you suggesting?" Falu asked.

"The best thing I can suggest. HUSA's executive account will be frozen as soon as I finish talking with you, so I advise you to let your staff know that they have lost their stipends for the rest of the school year. We are going to have to confiscate your university-issued cell phone. And what I like the least is, we are going to have to recoup some of that money from your programming budget."

Damn, Falu thought. That was the deathblow. After the administration took money from both of those accounts, HUSA would be close to bankrupt for the year.

"So what are the other student groups supposed to do for programs that they have already planned? We have already appropriated money for that."

"I know you have, but it won't be allocated. As I said before, drastic situations call for drastic measures. I will not let this administration pass this debt on. It's simply too big and it would compromise the future administration's budget next year."

"I can't believe this," Falu mumbled to herself.

"Well, believe, Falu. My office is too busy this week with homecoming activities, but there will be an emergency general assembly and HUSA policy board meeting tomorrow. Your secretary will get a copy of the memo from me later today. What I think you should be more concerned about, Falu, is the phone codes that were used by someone in your office to call several numbers that we traced back to Africa," the dean said, shooting her a sinister glare.

"Is that everything?" Falu asked.

"For now. Please close the door when you leave."

Falu stood up and released the clip from her cell phone, turned it off and placed it on the dean's desk. She opened the door and rushed out of the office without saying goodbye to Mrs. Pearl. She walked quickly around the corner to the women's restroom, where once inside she scrambled to get into the first empty stall. In there, she burst into tears.

She rested her head against the metal door and massaged her temples for the next 20 minutes. All the brain power she possessed could do nothing for her now, because she could not think of a way to get out of the mess she had gotten herself into. The pending embarrassment to her and her family, her academic standing if found guilty by the disciplinary board, and her plans for law school were shot to hell. She quieted her sobs when she heard someone enter the bathroom. Whoever it was looked at herself in the mirror, fixed her shirt and left. Falu emerged from the stall with a ball of toilet tissue to wipe her soaked face. Her eyeliner ran down her cheeks, tragically framing her bloodshot eyes. She wasn't going to make her afternoon class.

"Hey Falu, what's wrong?" Melissa Powell, a campus pal, asked coming through the bathroom door.

"Oh nothing," Falu said fixing her face. I'm just really emotional. I'm okay. How are you?"

"I'm doing good; glad homecoming is here and I'm done my last..."

Falu stopped paying attention to Melissa and focused on the ringing sound in her head. She saw Melissa's mouth moving, but didn't hear a word coming out of it.

"Well, have fun this week, Melissa. I'm sure I'll see you out at a party or something," Falu said, tossing tissue into the trash near the door. She walked back to her office to collect her briefcase. Although she had made up her mind that she was not going to class for the rest of the day, she still felt hungry. Normally, she would have eaten in the cafeteria or at the Punchout, so she could monitor the pulse of what went on with other students. But today she was liable to break down and cry again, so she decided to walk to Labomba's at the corner of Georgia Avenue and Euclid Street, across from Howard's School of Business.

The quicker she slipped out of the back door of Blackburn Center, the less likely people were to stop her, especially someone from her staff. At first, she walked quickly across to the Yard with long, striding steps, but she slowed when she saw *Hilltop* editor Ben Bishop talking to his managing editor, Forrest Hunter. Ben, that pain in the ass, had asked her about the phone bill and she told him to check back. Now what would she tell him? She had instructed her office that if he called while she was in, to say that she was not there. She didn't want to be embarrassed on the front page.

When she thought they made eye contact, she bent down and opened her briefcase. She faked a search through its contents, smacked herself on the side of the forehead and shook her head.

"I knew I forgot something," she said to herself, loud enough so that anyone around her could hear and know that she wasn't crazy. She turned around and walked toward the front of Blackburn. When she got toward the garden where people sat on the wall, she looked back and saw that Ben and Forrest were still talking. She walked briskly behind the Fine Arts building to avoid seeing or being seen by Ben. There was nothing back there but the old women's gym, parking spaces for faculty and administrators and the back of Greene Stadium, when she made it to the other side.

She walked the sidewalk next to Cramton and glanced to her left to see if Ben was coming her way. He hadn't made it that far. She continued her walk down Sixth Street and crossed at the light.

Labomba was easy to overlook if you were not looking for it. It was a nondescript corner store with tiny windows that didn't let in much light from the outside. Falu snuck into the empty establishment unnoticed. She sat at a two-seat table near a video arcade game next to the wall. She ordered a grilled chicken sandwich with lettuce and tomato and a medium iced tea. While she waited for her meal to cook, she deliberated her fate. Usually when she sat alone with her thoughts, it was about what she was going to achieve next, but paranoia was the best she could do today.

Falu's position as HUSA president gave her an unduly inflated impression of her own stature. She likened herself to Andrew Lip, a former Howard University president who ran the school in the '70s and '80s. He was a pillar in Howard's history, increasing alumni

*133*

contributions and enrollment, and adding several schools to the university during his tenure. He had won countless national educational awards and had served as an ambassador to Ghana. President Lip won that country over with praise as an academic and businessman.

After serving for more than 20 years as president, he resigned and several years later declared bankruptcy. The government had gone after him relentlessly after a D.C. cable outfit that he started with a Maryland state senator and a local D.C. congressman went belly-up. Lip was a member of the board of the Urban Cable Network, which started out offering cable to all of the Howard dorms and the university hotel before expanding into the city. He faced a slew of charges, some of which the government found him guilty of, including gross negligence. They won an almost $3 million lawsuit against him and recovered Rolex watches, a 45-foot boat, his Maryland home and pieces of artwork and other valuables. The embarrassing chapter stained President Lip's legacy forever. To Falu, she had everything to lose, and her pending presidential collapse—though on a much less grandiose scale than Lip's—would feel to her just as devastating.

# *Nine*

Ben was a tall drink of water, which was how she liked her men. He was dark—her mother always advised her on the sweetness of chocolate men. His smile was beautifully pearly white, and he had ambition. All his personality signs pointed to him probably being a good father someday—seeing as how he tutored, mentored and ran a journalism program for local kids in the Washington area.

If they had children, he could pass his height on to them. They would probably be a perfect peanut butter brown, mixing his dark complexion and her caramel skin. Would her fat gene persist though? Who would they favor? Would they be silly like him or more serious like her? She and he both liked music, books and movies, although they differed most in the latter category.

The standing debate between them was which *Godfather* movie was better, One or Two. Three, they both agreed, was good, but not as well-written as the first two, and too many years passed in between the trilogy's completion. Vicky favored number one because of Brando. He made it. He had the best character, the audience got a chance to see how Michael's character developed from a military schoolboy to Mafioso supreme, ordering more hits than Barry Bonds on a great day. Overall, to her, number One just had more memorable characters like Sunny, Luca Brasi and Johnny Fontane—whom many people suspected was based on Frank Sinatra's real life story.

To Ben, writing was king. The screenplay had to make sense, and above all, the dialogue had to be great. For him, Number Two passed the test. Flashbacks of Vito's early life in Italy and New York, played by a young Robert DeNiro, were brilliantly done. What he liked most about the second movie was the genius of Michael Corleone's character, how he intercepted the greedy Hyman Roth's plot to assassinate him and discovered that Fredo was part of the plot. Such drama. And the ending was perfect, in addition to a good Hollywood story. Fredo had to die, and he had to die by Michael's will, otherwise the whole script would have been compromised for one small mistake. Ben and Vicky could debate movies forever.

As for books, they read the classics: Baldwin, Malcolm, Dr. King, Shakespeare, Truman Capote. Ben was everything she wanted in a man. She could forgive him for trying to make her choose between him and pledging, and for being superficial when she gained weight. Those memories stung like hell, but she could make an effort to forget the past. She had already forgiven him.

All these thoughts ran through Vicky's mind as she shuffled in between her room and the tiny little kitchen area in her second-floor room in the East Towers. She tuned out the weed smoke billowing from under her roommate's door. The towel didn't always do the trick of keeping the smell contained. Roberta Flack was singing. Vicky's kitchen smelled like a restaurant.

She skipped the fashion show afterparty at D.C. Live with Jasmine, Stephanie and their other sorors, because she had promised Ben that she would cook for him on Thursday. It was her way of helping him out, since he would be busy finishing the week's paper. Besides, all her girls wanted to do was continue basking in the glow of winning the step show, rubbing it in the face of whatever Greek organization that was not theirs.

They would undoubtedly step at the club, and Vicky had had enough the night before, partying with them and Ben at The Saint. Ah, Ben. Thoughts of him and what they could be refreshed her.

There was a possibility that they would make it this time; that they would be everything she knew they could be. Stephanie told her that she was crazy to skip a party to cook for a man who had at one point treated her so terribly. She was crazy to disrupt the unadulterated fun of her last homecoming as a student at Howard, Stephanie admonished, but Vicky ignored her. She had spent every homecoming with her girls, and although they were graduating, they would get to spend more time together. She and Ben had wasted time that she couldn't get back, but wished she could. And counting time was not as important as making whatever time you had count.

Thursday nights were when Ben earned his money. He stayed up through the night editing copy, fixing stories and designing pages for Friday's paper. Over time, Vicky had heard him complain about sections that blew deadline, computers that broke down, photographs that had not been taken, and stories that still needed more work at the eleventh hour.

Her baked salmon would make the night less stressful—temporarily. She baked four pieces, three for him, one for her, and seasoned them with dill weed, butter and a little lemon sauce, the way her mother did. Brown rice and fresh spinach came on the side. The old Vicky would have baked a potato and stuffed it with every bit of cream she could find, but her new objective was to keep the weight down. He would have to settle for store-bought pink lemonade. Just the thought of him enjoying her cooking gave her pleasure. The ultimate pleasure was giving pleasure.

Staring at the electric, black and white stove in her kitchen, she took the food from the oven, placed it on a plate and covered it with aluminum foil. Wednesday hadn't been the night for sex, but if he hadn't been so busy with work Thursday and had tried again, she might have given in. After they got back from the club on Wednesday, Ben was drunk, her feet ached and she was tired from dancing all night. She was apprehensive when he made a move, so they groped and kissed briefly and settled for a few hours of cuddling before they had to wake for class. The weight of his body on her back felt so good; how he wrapped his arms firmly around her waist, his hard chest protecting the back of her head.

During intervals she felt his stiff penis on her back. Fear overtook the hormones, but oh was she horny. Vicky hadn't had sex in almost a year, when Tyrone Blue, then a graduate student, gave her a wham, bam, no thank you, ma'am one Saturday night after a fraternity party. He had climbed on top of her, pumped faster than a jackrabbit and was done within minutes. The only temporary pleasure he gave her was a magical lapping from his tongue.

She was uncomfortable with Tyrone, too, because by then people had started making comments about her weight. She was so uncomfortable that she insisted having sex with her T-shirt still on. At least if she decided to have sex with Ben, she would be comfortable. She had many offers since Tyrone, but she declined, going months without being touched, even refusing to do so herself. It took everything she had not to devour Ben's solid body as they lay in her bed the night before.

She carried the food across the courtyard that separated the two tower buildings, snuck past the one-eyed security guard so she wouldn't have to show ID or be signed in, and traversed two long corridors until she got to *The Hilltop* office. A sign on the door asked for anyone entering to knock, because they were on deadline. Her first knock went unanswered. She knocked a second time and Forrest answered.

"Something smells good. Did you bring some for me?" he joked.

"I'm a poor college student. I don't have it like that but if I could I would, Forrest," she said.

"It's too late," Ben said, walking over and grabbing the plate, "I'm hungry and this food was promised to me. Your word is everything," he said hugging her.

Vicky followed him into the newsroom where he sat in a beat-up wooden chair and began circling errors on print outs in red ink. She admired his work ethic. Every day he did this. He wrote editorials, sometimes took pictures and set up drop-off times for the paper to be delivered to the printing plant. Sometimes he skipped class to take it there himself.

A flurry of reporters and editors, some whose faces she had seen earlier at the fashion show, were present, laughing and writing. Vicky had no desire to be a journalist. She didn't like the idea of always having to talk to people or be in their business, but she respected what they did. She took inventory of the storyboard on the wall outside of Ben's office, where editors kept up to date with what reporter was writing which story. Under "front page," next to "website," was Ben's name.

"So, you're going ahead with the story?" she asked.

He looked back at her with a mouthful of food and nodded his head yes. "Why not?" he asked, accidentally spitting out rice. "I'm not afraid."

"Well, have you interviewed Greg? Did he deny it?"

"That's my last call. I'm waiting for Brandon to get back to me with his cell phone number so I can call and ask him," he said.

"But what about what happened before?" she asked, referring to the ass whipping Greg and his crew gave him.

"Follow me," he said, standing up and escorting her into his office. He stood while she sat in his chair.

"You know they're violent, Ben. They might come after you."

"Let them come. Greg is involved in some serious shit. Two girls contacted me about this story. I didn't go looking for this, but now that I got it, I'm running with it," he said, opening the drawer, tossing photos at her.

Vicky studied the naked shots—one of a 17-year-old—without comment. All of a sudden, a big bang came from the newsroom.

"Excuse me, you have to knock before you come in here. We're working," Vicky heard Forrest say.

"Shut the fuck up! I need to see Ben!"

She recognized the voice. Her fears were coming to fruition. She followed Ben into the newsroom and locked his office door behind her. Greg, Neeko and Poncho flanked each other and faced Ben. All three dressed in Dickies work suits.

"Instead of using Brandon as a middle man, say whatever you got to say to me like a man, you pussy!"

"Ain't nobody using a middle man. I needed your cell number, so I could ask you a question," Ben responded, visibly nervous.

"I'm listening."

Vicky's hands shook standing next to Ben. Neeko and Poncho stood next to Greg with clenched fists and evil looks on their faces.

"Why did you have a minor pose naked for a pornographic website?" Ben asked.

The room fell silent and all eyes watched. Ben pulled a note-pad out of his pocket like he was about to take a quote. Greg gritted his teeth and flared his nostrils. One second later he threw the first punch. Vicky ran for security.


Sex was the best way for Greg to relieve stress. Homecoming could be stressful. It was only Thursday and he had been to at least seven parties, and had hosted three. And there were three more big ones to go. His take so far in the week was almost 10-stacks ($10,000) and the weekend hadn't even come. It might not seem like a stressful situation on the surface, but the casual observer couldn't see how promoting parties, being the number-one supplier on Howard's campus of whatever drug students desired, and making a feeble attempt to do class work could fray the nerves. Adding to his agitation was the huge chunk of time he spent thinking about the confrontation he had with *The Hilltop* editor, Ben, after the step show. Given the massive trouble Ben's snooping could cause Greg's business, one could appreciate why when Greg got a chance to relieve stress, he took it.

Shelly was his fourth body of the week, and second of the day on Thursday. She was a freshman, which meant that she was a more-than-easy catch for him. Greg didn't even know her last name, just that she was from a small town in Alabama and had literally thrown herself at him the night before, when he made his first stop of the night at the popular freshman club, The Ritz. The only reason he hadn't taken her home that night was because he had more partying to do, and there was a possibility he could come up on something better.

He took her number and promised to call later. By 5 a.m. when Poncho and Neeko dropped him off home, he was too drunk for pussy. But later, after a day of actually going to class and completing two midterms, calling Shelly wasn't a bad idea.

Oh, how easy it was. He called. She giggled and teased about how horny she was. She didn't even make an effort for him to chase her, like other girls did. Shelly was a month away from her 18th birthday and away from home for the first time. At first when she told Greg her age, he thought about turning her down. But Greg had been moved past the guilt of having sex with under-aged girls. Although he was 24, he was a college student, and to him, any girl in college like him could get served. Besides, if he didn't do it, someone else would have. There was a time when he might have warned one of his boys about messing with young girls; they got clingy, rushed to get the girlfriend title and ran their mouths like faucets.

Shelly was red, very fair and tall, and thick. She had ass for days and chest to match, with a stomach as flat as an ironing board. On the way to his apartment, she bragged how she was a big girl and how she could take whatever he dished. Her parents would cringe if they heard the way she talked, how she confessed that she wasn't a virgin, and had been with men older than him. They would fall out if they heard her promise how she could take it like a big girl.

Greg made her show him how much she could take and gave her vicious back shots that triggered loud moans—almost screams— from her, as he smacked her ass hard and roughly grabbed fistfuls of her cascading brown and black streaked hair. With every dirty word he whispered, she moaned more. He turned her over, pushed her arms toward her head and she grabbed the back of his head and asked for more. All of this was being filmed on his camcorder, which she gladly smiled for after he was finished, and before she took him inside of her mouth to prepare for a second go-around.

Afterward, he lay calm in his bed, sweating. They shared a joint and listened to Tupac. Shelly wanted to go again, but Greg couldn't muster it, and committed to his memory just how much of a freak his new young find was. She would definitely be getting more calls in the future.

He didn't want to answer the university number when it showed up on his phone, because he thought it was probably someone on campus trying to track him down for an insignificant amount of weed or ecstasy.

"Yo, who this?" he asked answering his phone.

"Greg, are you busy?"

"Brandon?"

"Yeah, it's me. Are you busy?"

"Why? Tell your boys I'm not coming over there unless they're buying weight. I'm talking at least an ounce. I can't be running back and forth for all this nickel and dime shit!" he lashed out.

"Huh? I'm not calling about none of that."

Brandon's voice sounded serious, like he was in some trouble. Greg sat up in bed.

"What's up, B? Somebody fuckin' with you?"

"Nah, not at all. I'm good. It's just…It's just—"

"Spit it out."

"Ben asked me to call you and see about either you calling him or me giving him your number so he could call you."

Greg knew what this meant, but he still had to ask further questions. Ben Bishop wanting his number wasn't a good thing. It was a sign that his scare tactic the night before had not worked. Therefore, his stress level began climbing.

"Ben? What that fuck he wanna talk to me about?"

"You know," Brandon said with fear in his voice. "I think he's going through with that story. I just wanted to give you a heads up on it. I think he wants to see if you're going to comment or not."

Silence. Greg was brewing in bed. *The Hilltop* came out on Friday, which was the next day and just so happened to be Yardfest, one of the premier events of homecoming. Thousands of people would be on campus, playing games, eating fish from tents and listening to whoever performed at the concert on the Yard. They would all be reading copies of *The Hilltop* with his name plastered across the front page, under a byline that read Benjamin Bishop.

"You tell Ben that if he writes anything about me that I will… never mind, B, thanks for letting me know. I'ma go talk to Ben myself. You don't have to be the go-between anymore. Good looking out."

He hung up after and looked at Shelly.

"Get dressed. You gotta go."

"But I thought we were going to chill for a little bit."

"I said get your shit and get dressed! You gotta get the fuck out my house! Damn!"

She rolled her eyes at him and yanked the covers off of her. Greg was already standing in front of a dresser putting on boxers.

"Go in the bathroom and get dressed. I gotta make a phone call," he ordered. She did as she was told.

He dialed seven digits with the quickness and only said two things.

"Meet me over at the dorm where the newspaper is. We gotta handle some business."

Twenty minutes later, Greg, Neeko and Poncho were standing in the courtyard of the West Towers speaking to familiar faces. The guards at the Towers knew Greg's face, because he was a student, had stayed at the Towers years ago, and still came through to see girls. He had a contact in the office of Residence Life who programmed his ID card to unlock the garage door in the Tower's basement, but he needed his car to be parked on the street and in position to pull off, in case he came out running. All three of them parked on 9th Street, besides Banneker. They waited outside until a cluster of students went through the doors, creating a large enough distraction to sneak by without getting carded.

They breathed hard walking through the halls. Greg hadn't been this upset in a long time, not since he had to beat up a junior who got loud with him in the cafeteria one day. It turned out that the guy was a transfer student from New York who didn't know Greg. Greg accidentally bumped him in line one day and he confronted Greg, talking loud and threatening to whip his ass. Security defused the argument, and the kid swaggered around the cafeteria with his chest puffed out, talking loudly about Howard was full of punk bitches that couldn't fight.

Through all the New Yorker's macho talk and braggadocio, Greg sat and ate, and waited. He skipped his next class after lunch and waited for the guy for an hour. When the guy came out of Douglas Hall, he shook hands with his friends and walked across the Yard toward the Human Ecology building. He walked out the university gates and crossed the street. Greg made sure to stay a good distance behind his quarry. The kid turned left into the Annex courtyard and was met by Neeko, who purposely bumped him and knocked his book bag off his shoulder. When he picked it up, Neeko was standing in front of him and Greg was running up behind him. He turned just in time to catch the first punch to his nose. Five minutes later he lay on the ground, almost stomped to death. He bled profusely from the head. It concluded with him suffering a broken nose and jaw. That was first semester, 1997. He didn't come back to school after that.

That fight was the last time Greg had been this upset, and that was just because he had been publicly disrespected. What a fool, Greg thought—every student at Howard knew better than to do that, unless it was a football player with size, someone who could handle Greg by himself.

Greg had tried to scare Ben Bishop, another fool who needed some *act-right*, but the warning didn't work. So Greg was through talking.

Neeko snatched the sign off of *The Hilltop* door that asked for anyone entering to knock because they were on deadline. Poncho kicked in the door.

"Excuse me, you have to knock before you come in here. We're working," Forrest Hunter, a guy with whom Greg had a math class one semester, blurted out.

"Shut the fuck up! I need to see Ben!" Greg ordered.

Seconds later, Ben emerged from his office with his sorority girlfriend behind him. Greg wanted to rush him.

"Instead of using Brandon as a middle man, say whatever you got to say to me like a man, you pussy!"

"Ain't nobody using a middle man. I needed your cell number, so I could ask you a question," Ben responded, visibly nervous.

"I'm listening."

The sight of Ben's petrified face comforted Greg. Neeko and Poncho were standing by his side waiting for him to make the first move and for them to jump on anyone who tried to break up the fight. Greg already knew what his response would be to whatever question Ben asked. Ben still had the nerve to pull out a notepad, as if this were going to be an official interview.

"Why did you have a minor pose naked for a pornographic website?" Ben asked.

Greg swallowed hard and flared his nostrils. Ben's look of fear had turned into a smirk.

Out of nowhere, Greg jumped across the distance separating them and connected his fist with Ben's left jaw. Loud, protesting voices sounded in the background, but were met and silenced by Neeko's and Poncho's fists. Ben and Greg rolled around on the floor exchanging blows. Although Greg was winning, Ben had punched him in his face twice and had landed significant body shots. Greg drove his hands into Ben's jaw and tried to get him in a headlock, but Ben rolled over on top of Greg and fed him another fist to the face. Now Greg rolled and kneed Ben in the groin, which gave Greg the advantage. Ben lay curled up on the floor in pain while Greg stood and issued directives to his crew.

"Cut those computer cords y'all."

He stood over Ben to make sure he wouldn't make a dash to stop Neeko and Poncho while they ripped cords from the sockets. Forrest tried to stop Neeko from grabbing the server computer, but Greg ran over behind him and leveled him with a right hook. Forrest fell, and Greg snatched the cord from the wall. Neeko picked up the server computer—the computer that linked all of the work reporters and writers did together and served as the paper's recovery hard drive when they lost stories. He slammed it viciously to the ground and watched as it cracked open and began smoking.

"Write a story now, punk bitch," Greg said, looking back at Ben. They heard voices from the hallway and rushed toward the doors. A security guard extended his hands to block them, but there was only one of him and three of them. Neeko and Poncho threw him to the floor. Greg jumped over him and pushed Vicky out of the way, leading the blaze of sprinting feet out of the building.

By the time Brandon could say anything that he thought might have calmed Greg down, his volatile benefactor had already hung up. Brandon witnessed Greg's violent temper before. Once at a gas station on New York Avenue, when Brandon was riding with Greg to make a "pick up," something he knew he should not have done, Greg was accosted by a homeless man asking for money. Greg told him no and the man grabbed Greg's arm. Wrong move. Greg punched him in the face twice and he fell to the floor. A security guard from inside the store came out and scared Greg off as he stood over top of the man and was about to stomp him.

Brandon knew this violent tempter could turn toward Ben easily, seeing as how he suspected that Ben and Greg had a history of not liking each other, and because Brandon knew Greg was involved in a slew of illegal enterprises that Ben could expose.

He dialed *The Hilltop* office from inside the computer room in

Drew Hall, where he was typing the results of the fashion show for Friday's paper. He wrote his story in the Drew Hall computer lab because he didn't feel like walking to the Towers to type his story. No one answered the phone.

"Damn," he said, looking around the empty room. He could see a group of freshman guys leaving out a side door, laughing and dressed for the club—where he wanted to be. His *Hilltop* responsibilities came first, and if anything happened to Ben, he would have felt responsible since he was the one playing message boy between Ben and Greg.

He emailed the half-finished story to himself and logged off the computer. As much as he wanted to avoid working from the office, he would not be able to.

Brandon stuffed his notepad in his back pocket and burst through the front door of his dorm. He started a steady jog that proceeded through Burr Gymnasium parking lot, down Girard Place, down to Sixth, where he turned right after the School of Social Work and went down the hill to get to Georgia Avenue. Being out of breath after running less than a mile was a sign that he had been smoking too much weed and needed to get in shape.

He hustled past students on Georgia before crossing over to Barry Place. The sidewalk to the Towers was packed with people hanging outside or standing in front of cars with music playing. He ran in the street past the people and cars. Brandon stepped into the Towers courtyard and stopped as Greg, Neeko and Poncho ran toward him. None of them stopped or acknowledged him, not even Greg. Seconds later, a security guard labored up the courtyard, huffing through a walkie-talkie. Brandon, like other bystanders, watched and wondered what the hell had happened. But more than idly watch, he feared that Ben had been hurt.

He ran into the building and sprinted the long hallways until he got to *The Hilltop* door, which was half open. Inside, a crowd consoled Forrest, who wiped blood from his leaky mouth, and Ben, whose mouth and nose bled. Vicky Mourning, the girl Brandon had interviewed the night before for winning the step show contest, was crying, standing next to Ben.

Two hours later and the staff was finished giving a report to campus police about three attackers—one student and two D.C. locals—who broke into the office and ransacked it. They had completely destroyed one computer and had successfully ripped the cords to seven more, rendering them out of commission. Even Brandon had to file a report, saying that he enabled the fight by passing on a message that Ben wanted to speak to Greg about a story.

When campus police asked Brandon for Greg's contact information, he declined to give it. His reluctance stemmed at least partially from fear of the same thing happening to him that had just happened in the newspaper office; but also kept his mouth shut out of loyalty. Ben would hate him for it, he thought, but if the situation had involved Ben getting in trouble, he would protect Ben just the same.

Burdened with guilt, Brandon volunteered along with several other staff members to take turns completing the paper through the night. They used the Tower's computer room to write stories and emailed them to Ben's account. Ben was smart enough to have a backup server on the computer in his office. It would take all night to lay out the paper from his one computer, but he was determined to do it, and promised extra cash to any staff member who stayed late to help him. They were disgustingly efficient during the night, writing and editing the stories from the computer lab, which they got special permission to keep open all night, and only needed to use Ben's computer for design work. By 5 a.m., the printer's courier had picked up the paper.

# *Ten*

Ben slept hard through the early part of Friday. As was the case whenever he spent overnight hours putting the paper out, he skipped statistics and art history, his early morning Friday classes. He skipped them so much that by November it was impossible for him to get an A in either course, because of the attendance requirements. The best he could hope for was a B, and he was close to being dropped to C status.

Ben made a mental note of every staff member who stayed overnight to help him put the paper out, and promised to pad his or her check when payroll came around. Multiple worries faced him, like making sure he called the IT guy to replace the cords and computers that Greg and his crew damaged. The staff rallied behind him to put the paper together at the 23rd hour, but they couldn't operate that way for the entire year. They had to turn around and publish the special homecoming edition, which ran the Monday after homecoming and served as a wrap-up of the weekend's events. It would also feature the grade they gave the homecoming committee.

Having to get IT to fix the equipment would cost *The Hilltop* a few thousand, which meant that he would have to switch a few things around in his budget to pay for it. He counted it as another lesson learned: He should have budgeted for office emergencies. But who could predict that Greg Harris and his boys would storm into the office and trash it? Who could predict that Greg would be smart enough to know that all of the stories were linked to the server and that if he destroyed it, he destroyed the stories?

Ben's saving grace was the backup server in his office. He and Forrest took turns laying out the paper after the stories were finished. Ben would sit at his computer until his eyes got tired, and then Forrest took over. Payback was on Ben's mind. Greg got the best of them in their fight, although Ben got a few good shots in, but Ben would have the bigger laugh once everyone on the Yard saw a copy of the paper. Chief Williams said there would be at least 50,000 people on campus this weekend. After the game on Saturday, Ben planned on hiring a group of high school kids from the mentoring program he ran to walk around the Yard handing out papers. Knowledge of this made him sleep better—until the phone calls started.

The first one woke him at 9 a.m.; just in time to catch fresh rays of sun fight their way through the dusty beige blinds in his room. He put the ringer on vibrate and went back to sleep without seeing who called.

Thirty minutes later, the phone had vibrated so much that it fell from on top of the dresser to the floor next to Ben's bed. That crash woke him, and he finally reached down and answered it when he saw that it was a university number.

"Yeah, this is Ben."

"Mr. Bishop. Are you asleep? Did I catch you at a bad time?" Chief Williams of campus police asked.

Ben rested the phone on his face, stretched his arms and rubbed cold from his eyes.

"Chief Williams, not at all. I was just waking up. What's going on?"

"You tell me. The other day you warn me about the possibility of one of our students being involved in illegal activity on university property, and I come in this morning and read the overnight log to find that you were in a fight and that the newspaper office was vandalized."

Ben heard the chief shuffle papers in the background.

"My report says here that there were three guys, and that you got into a pretty bad fight with one of them. They assaulted one of my officers and members of the newspaper staff and broke some of your equipment. Do I have that right?" he asked.

"That's about it," Ben said, walking to his window. Below, backpack-wielding students who had partied the night before staggered off to their last classes for the week.

"I see. And was this the student you alluded to the other night?"

"Pretty much, Chief. That's him."

"Greg Harris, the report says. The University doesn't have an updated address on him, because I checked. I was wondering if you had any contact information for him."

"I don't. We're not friends. As you probably read under the story in today's paper, the incident last night resulted from me trying to get in contact with him to get a quote about the porno website."

"Mr. Bishop, I'm sorry, I thought because they damaged the computers you weren't able to publish a paper. There were none in the bin when I came in this morning. No one has one."

"What?"

"There are no *Hilltops* in this building, Mr. Bishop. I also thought that maybe the printer missed us during their distribution route, because I know they have before. But I looked for one this morning after I left a meeting in the administration building with President Humphries, and I didn't see any there either—so I figured that you didn't go to print. But you are telling me that you turned the paper in last night?"

"Yes, Chief Williams. I'm telling you that my staff and I stayed up throughout the night editing and designing the paper. I personally met the delivery guy from the printer out front and handed him the envelope with our pictures and ads that had to be scanned in down at the press. I'm gonna have to call them and look into this. Can I call you back in a few minutes after I straighten this out?" Ben asked.

The chief gave him his private office number, which Ben committed to memory in case he needed direct access to the chief for any stories that might come up later in the school year. As soon as he hung up the phone with Chief Williams, it vibrated again—it was another university number.

"Hello."

"Ben, what's going on, it's Brandon. Did you know that there are no *Hilltops* on campus today? I went around to three or four buildings, and none of them have papers. Did everything go alright with the printer?"

"I don't know. Someone just called me and told me the same thing. I gotta call the printer right now to see what happened. Give me a few minutes and I'll call you back."

"No problem. I'm in my room, just so you know," Brandon said hanging up.

Ben dialed *The Washington Times*, the company that printed *The Hilltop*, and checked with their production manager. *The Hilltop*, Ben was told, was printed and distributed between 6 and 7 a.m. on main campus and the law school campus. They had a distribution checklist to account for all 10,000 copies that had been delivered. Ben's other line clicked while he was on the phone with *The Times*, and it was another university number—probably someone on his staff, he thought.

"I already know. There are no papers on campus. I'm on the phone with *The Times* now and they are saying that they delivered the papers."

"Yes, and I think it's because they were stolen, Ben," Dean Thomas said on the other end of the phone.

"Huh?"

"I came in early this morning to get copies of the papers ready, so the Board of Trustees members could read them at their meeting later today, but there were none here. I know a lot of people read the paper, but I also know that they didn't take *that* many papers *that* early in the morning," she joked. "I called around to some of the other schools, and they didn't have papers either," she said.

"I know. I'm on the phone right now with *The Times*, and they said they printed and distributed them."

"That's what they told me when I called," Dean Thomas said.

"So why do you think they were stolen?" Ben asked. "Who would steal copies of the paper?"

"A custodian from the law school called me back and said that they saw two guys running from the building with bundles of paper, putting them into the back of a truck," Dean Thomas said.

"That fucking pussy!" Ben blurted out accidentally.

"Excuse me, Ben."

"Oh, I'm sorry, Dean. I don't know if you heard, but there was a fight in *The Hilltop* office last night, and they destroyed some of our computer equipment. I'm sure they stole the papers."

"They? Wait a minute. Slow down. Who are 'they,' and why were you fighting?"

"It's a long story Dean, but in short, I had a disagreement with Greg Harris over a story I wrote, and he didn't like it, so he brought his friends with him to the office and we got into an ugly fight."

"Did you report this to campus police?" she asked worriedly.

"Yes. I reported it to them last night. I just got off the phone with Chief Williams a few minutes ago. I don't know what to do about the papers. That's seven thousand in printing fees down the toilet," Ben said.

"Well, call *The Times* back and order another 10,000 copies of the paper. It's homecoming, Ben. We have to have a paper. We'll discuss how you'll get the money back in your budget, but just do that for now. And I need to see you in my office before noon to discuss this fight. I'm calling Chief Williams now."

*The Times* promised to have 10,000 copies of the paper delivered to main campus within two hours. As exhausted as he was, Ben couldn't get back to sleep after that. He called all of his editors and told them the news. He called Brandon next.

"Hello," Brandon said.

"So, whose side are you on, Brandon, mine or his?"

"Huh?"

"Don't play dumb with me. How did Greg know that we still put out a paper after he destroyed the server?"

"I don't know what you're talking about."

"Greg and his boys stole the papers, Brandon! That's why you don't see any on campus. He destroyed the server on purpose because he knew that was where the backup drives were for all the stories. He didn't know about the backup server in my office. Someone must have told him."

"It wasn't me," Brandon said defensively. "How could I? I spent the night in the office with y'all and slept on the sofa until my first class today, remember?"

Brandon had a point. Ben had personally gone over the fashion show article with him and had marked his name down as one of his staff members who stayed late. He apologized for accusing him of telling Greg about the backup server.

"I'd advise you to stay away from Greg Harris, Brandon, because he is in a lot of trouble, as you know," Ben said before hanging up.

He thought about telling Brandon to call Greg and let him know that they were on to his scheme, but he decided not to, just in case Greg and his crew hijacked the second batch of papers. Yet nonetheless, he wanted to—if only for the personal satisfaction of letting Greg know that he was still one step ahead of him.


Greg, Neeko and Poncho split up after they ran from the Towers. They bolted past students in the Towers courtyard, jumped into their respective cars and fled, all to a different girl's house that they thought they could trust to keep them safe. They agreed to meet at The Diner in Adam's Morgan around 4 a.m., after all the bars and clubs had closed.

Greg showed up first, and immediately regretted suggesting the diner as their rendezvous. He recognized every Howard student that walked through the doors. He moved his seat to the back and positioned his back to the wall, so he could see whoever walked through the door. He was lucky to get a table at that time, with all the hungry bar and club hoppers who stopped there before they went home. Adam's Morgan was the meeting ground where all races coincided. White twenty-somethings shuttled there in droves and engorged themselves on beer by the pitcher. They smoked and fought outside and threw up on the street when they were done. Asians came, too. So did the Latinos. In 1998, the District might have still been the Chocolate City in terms of population, but the other flavors were gaining, and they all flocked to the same trendy areas. Greg was too hungry to wait for his cohorts, so he ordered a chicken parmesan sandwich with fries and washed it down—first with a glass of D.C. tap water with lime, then followed by a cool sip of Hennessy and Coke.

His nerves bothered him as he sat. Ben had found out about the site, and Greg knew that Latoya was the person who tipped him off. It was so stupid of Greg to think that with her earlier threat against him, she meant that she would try to get someone to fight him. He should have been thinking ahead, he told himself as he sat alone. When he called Latoya back to threaten her about running her mouth, he could hear the joy in her voice from knowing that she had exacted such painful retribution. What was $150 anyway? If he would have simply paid her, none of this would have happened.

To end the call, *she* hung up on *him*, which stung Greg even more. That was twice just now that she'd played him like a punk bitch—the first time being how she snitched on him to Ben. That was it. He made up his mind that she would get dealt with, too, and that like Ben, her punishment would be physical.

He finished the first glass of liquor before he finished the sandwich, and ordered another drink. It would help ease the headache. There were only two other times in Greg's life where had been so anxious. The summer after his freshman year at Howard, he went back home to Los Angeles where he rekindled things with his on-again, off-again girlfriend, Crystal. They communicated via phone and snail mail during the school year and hooked up when Greg came home for the holidays. Unlike Greg, Crystal opted not to go to a university and headed for cosmetology school.

Before he went to Howard, Greg considered Crystal his crowning achievement, because she was prettier than the other girls at Crenshaw High School. But the girls at Howard and in D.C. were from another world, a world that embraced him and turned him out. Greg had gotten involved heavily with the party scene. He went to clubs literally every night and had finished his first semester with a 2.3 GPA. In order to keep his tuition scholarship, he had to maintain a 3.0 for the entire year and he was going to have to be damn-near perfect second semester to redeem it. Instead, he did only slightly better and had come back to California dejected, depressed and embarrassed.

The uncertainty of whether he would return to school ruffled his feathers, because he had fit in with a new crowd of older, money-making, do-whatever-it-took-to-get-ahead D.C. hardheads and a few Howard cats. They promoted parties, supplied students at local colleges with bootleg CDs and tapes, weed, coke—whatever they needed. Greg felt more a part of a family running with them than he did back home with his mother and grandmother, who never gave him much support and had barely congratulated him after he had won the scholarship.

Being back in California, he had to answer to the same teachers who helped him get the scholarship, the same teachers who would admonish him for losing it. What was he going to do, tell them that instead of taking class seriously he smoked and drank, spent time in the streets trying to make money, and had sex with as many girls as he could instead of going to class? So, he avoided them. He fell back into the hands of Crystal, and by the end of the summer he had gotten her pregnant. It put the fear of God in him when she warned him that she was going to keep it and that there was nothing he could do about it. She warned him that if he didn't want to take care of it, she would take him to court and make him pay child support. Greg attempted every trick in the book to get her to abort, but she was dead set on keeping it. Before the summer was over, he sent a wire back East to one of his drug-dealing mentors, and he responded by giving Greg enough money to get back to D.C., where he would hustle and work off his debt.

Crystal eventually had the child, a boy, whom she named after Greg. In five years, Greg had seen his son a handful of times, only when he was back in California and his mother or grandmother watched the baby. Eventually Greg stopped going home. He switched apartments in D.C. frequently and didn't give his mother or grandmother his address after they forwarded a picture of Greg Jr. to him. He trashed it and kept it moving, denying that responsibility.

The second time he had gotten so anxious was a couple of years prior, when he had sold a freshmen girl some liquid E at a house party in Ledroit Park. The girl started throwing up and hallucinating, and collapsed in the backyard of the house. She scared the crowd away and had ended the party early. Greg originally wanted to dump her body by the reservoir, because he thought she was dead, but heard her breathing and choking in the back of his car. So he and Neeko dropped her off at the Washington Medical Center and left. The girl eventually recovered, but word of what happened at the party spread amongst students and had somehow gotten back to a nosy-ass *Hilltop* reporter, Benjamin Bishop. Of course, word got back to Greg that the paper was going to print a story about it.

Greg warned Ben not to pursue the story when he came around asking questions on campus, but Ben was relentless. One night, Greg, Neeko and Poncho followed Ben around campus and caught him coming home from the undergraduate library after midnight. Ben was oblivious to his surroundings, and had cut through the Engineering parking lot. Greg sped up behind him, and before he could put the car in park, Neeko and Poncho had jumped out of the car and attacked Ben. Greg rushed over and had gotten in a few shots— enough to let Ben know that it was he who did it—and fled the scene.

Ben never reported the girl's overdose story, but after that, whenever he saw Greg on campus, he had always given him the most hateful stares.

Greg knew Ben hated him, and probably wanted revenge for what happened. He thought about that when he heard that Ben had found out about his website and had started to snoop. What he didn't think was that Ben would not back down this time. Beating Ben up might not have been enough to stop him from running a story that could possibly land him in jail, Greg thought to himself as he sat in the diner. This time he would have to take extra steps. Where the fuck were Neeko and Poncho?

Just as Greg flipped open his cell phone to call them, he saw them enter the dining room. He stood up and waved them back toward his table.

"It took y'all long enough. I couldn't wait. I had to get something to eat," he said, sitting, stuffing the last of his sandwich into his mouth.

"I dropped my car off at Poncho's so we could come together," Neeko said.

Greg called the waitress over to his table and ordered Hennessy and Coke for his friends.

"Damn, we could have used three cars, but it's cool. Don't worry about it," Greg said.

"Use three cars for what?" Poncho asked.

"I can't take any chances with this shit getting out. Tomorrow is Yardfest, and everyone will be on campus. I need y'all to help me with one more thing."

"We cyant get to dat boy now," Neeko said, slipping back into patois. "He got the whole police force at Howard looking for us," he said, referring to Ben. Neeko would have been more than happy to give Ben more punishment.

"I'm not talking about him, at least not for now. I'm not finished with him, but I'll catch him later. We broke their server, I got a gut feeling that that might not have been enough."

"You think they can still put out a paper? I thought you said if we destroy the main computer, it would erase all of the stories," Poncho said.

"It will, and I know we broke it, but just in case we need to make sure they don't publish that story. We could face prison if they print it, or if they find Sherane. I think that bitch is staying with Latoya, but we can't get over there yet either."

"Why not?" Neeko asked.

"Because keeping this story from running is more important, and that bitch's brother just got out of the pen; nigga supposed to be some Southeast gangsta. I'll get her in time. We gotta deal with this *Hilltop* shit first."

"What's the plan?"

"We gotta scour the whole campus and collect the bundles after the paper boys drop them off."

Neeko and Poncho smiled at Greg's plan. They acknowledged that they would not have thought to do such a thing after they destroyed the computer, but they privately knew that Greg was smarter than them anyway, and that he and his ideas were their meal ticket. They were just muscle.

"I've been at this school for six years. I know every drop point for *The Hilltop*. We'll start on main campus, then hit the law school. I'll take the top of the hill, and y'all take everything below, like architecture, engineering, communications and the health clinic. If I finish on top of the hill before y'all I'll come help. They should start delivering the papers in an hour or so. We can leave from here," Greg said.

Two hours later, the sun pathetically pierced the sky, leaving just enough darkness for Greg to make an attempt to dump the papers he stole into the Potomac River from the 14th Street Bridge. Each bundle was tied together, making them heavy enough that they should've sunk into the river, but they didn't. After he saw that the first bundle he dropped simply fell apart in the river, he instructed Neeko and Poncho to meet him at his apartment.

There, they used a 55-gallon drum in the alley behind the building to burn the papers, which turned out to be the best decision. It caused a smell, but Greg's neighbors would assume that it was the regular group of bums who congregated in the alleys and street corners around burning flames to keep their hands warm. Overall, the disposal plan was messy and tedious, and Greg smacked himself for being so dumb as to think that the first bundle would sink into the river. Yet, almost two hours after they started their mission, they were finished and smelled like smoke.

Neeko and Poncho went home. Going against the recommendation of his friends, Greg parked his car two blocks away on Lamont Street and went back to his apartment. He slept peacefully with his pistol under a pillow next to him.

# *Eleven*

Music blasted through refrigerator-sized speakers in the background, and students laughed together in circles—all dressed in new outfits—but Brandon sat on the steps of Locke Hall dazed, not participating in any Yardfest activities. At the beginning of the week, all he could think about was how much fun it would be to see the concert on the Yard, the freestyle battle—which some of his dorm mates had signed up for—and to see a bunch of pretty girls dressed in provocative skirts and shirts. This was homecoming. This was what he had heard about for years, what Biggie rapped about. All his upperclassman friends who worked for the newspaper had bragged to him about homecoming, and Brandon was alone sulking, worrying and ruminating over how his life was about to come crashing down.

He was dressed for the occasion: New sneakers, fitted cap, jeans and Nautica jacket. But his mind was on Greg and what had happened the night before, what had happened that morning, and what he read in his hands.

Brandon woke early on Friday to read the story that Greg had tried so hard to keep from getting into the paper, but when he went to the first floor of Drew Hall, there were no papers. He checked in Douglass, Locke and The Blackburn Center, but there were no papers, anywhere. Ben later told him that Greg, Neeko and Poncho had driven around to all the distribution sites and stolen the papers; worse yet, Ben had suspected him of tipping off Greg's crew that the staff had produced a paper, in spite of their destructive efforts.

Hours later, after the printer ran off the 10,000 additional copies, Brandon sat, reading Ben's expose with racy pictures of an underage girl posing on the very website Brandon had been writing material for. His stomach sank as the story revealed to him, for the first time, the extent of Greg's criminal activity. Ben's story showed PG-13 pictures of young women, some Howard students, posing in kitchenettes in the West and East Towers. Two girls, one whose face Brandon recognized, were photographed wresting with each other in lingerie. The story was all anyone on campus could talk about all day. Greg Harris, the story had said, would have to face a university trial, where he would have to go in front of the disciplinary board and plead his case as to why he should not be expelled. There was a possibility that the Howard students he photographed on campus property might have to do the same thing, the story said.

Ben went a step further and placed pull quotes from the campus chief of police and a D.C. police sergeant from the third district, whose jurisdiction Howard fell under.

In the story it said that Greg was 24, had knowingly coaxed a 17-year-old girl into posing naked on his website and had possibly supplied the girl with narcotics such as marijuana or ecstasy. Even though Brandon was just now learning these sordid details, he worried that he might face any disciplinary action for writing biographies of certain women on the site. At the start, Brandon just thought he was doing an innocuous gig for a modeling site that hadn't been launched. And, he reasoned, he was never present while the models were photographed.

It all made sense to Brandon why Greg didn't want Ben to run the story. It also now made sense that Greg had hung up on him the night before and rushed over to *The Hilltop* office to trash it, destroying the server in the process. The guilt Brandon felt had shifted gears from Ben's side back to Greg's. He worried that he had contributed to the possible demise of one of the few people who had taken him under his wing.

Ben had taken him under his wing, too, and he looked up to him just the same, but Ben wasn't facing expulsion and possible jail time. It all made sense why Ben had been so hush-hush about the story, and had been so adamant about staying up through the night producing the paper. Even with a busted lip and nose, he worked through the early morning hours with a sick glaze in his eyes. At the time, Brandon couldn't fully grasp what the look was about, but he knew for sure, now.

Making matters worse, Ben had added a small blurb of text at the bottom of the front page of the paper, reading: "Mr. Harris and two associates stormed *The Hilltop* office late in the evening, destroying university property and assaulting a campus police officer."

Brandon felt used, as though he had been the middleman for two people who clearly hated each other. He had called Ben early in the morning after he couldn't find any papers to let him know that they hadn't been delivered. Ben later told him that it was Greg who had stolen them. Brandon called Greg to see if the rumor was true, but Greg didn't answer. He called later, after the papers had been reprinted and started circulating on campus, but still there was no answer. He thought about walking to Columbia Heights to Greg's apartment, but decided against it, seeing as how there were police officers looking for him.

"All the girls are out on the Yard. Why the fuck are you sittin' over here reading the newspaper?" Frank asked, walking over to Brandon.

Brandon didn't answer; he just shook his head and buried his face back in the paper.

"You're worried about that?" Frank said, pointing to the story about Greg. "Why do you care if the cops catch him? I mean, it would be messed up to have our weed connect locked up, but it's more places we can buy weed. If anything, you need to be asking him why he ain't tell you about the models, so you could've been over there watching 'em strip and shit," Frank joked. "That's what I would be mad about."

"You are too fucking stupid to see that I could be caught up in this shit, Frank," Brandon said raising his voice. "If they get Greg, do you really think they'll stop with him? My whole shit is fucked up over some dumb shit."

"Brandon, they can't expel you for not knowing about something. That's what you tell the cops if they come asking you questions. I don't even see why you're so worried. Greg is the one who should be worried, not you."

"I feel like I set him up," Brandon said, looking up at Frank.

"Who Greg? How? You told him what you knew about Ben."

"Yeah, but Ben scared me and he really had me thinking I could catch some heat, so I told him about all the stuff I wrote and I look stupid as hell, talking about 'I'm writing for a website that Greg is about to start', not even knowing that it was up and running."

"Well, be mad at Ben. Be mad at Greg. I don't care who you get mad at, just get up off these steps. Look out there," Frank said, pointing to the Yard. "I see nothing but scattered ass out there, and a whole bunch of ugly-ass niggas getting all those numbers when that should be us." He patted Brandon on the back and smiled. It was enough to make Brandon stand and glance at the paper one last time. It was the first time he had noticed that two stories he had written, one about the step show, and the other about the fashion show, had appeared on the front page. He balled up the paper and simulated a series of dribbles before he jumped up and shot it into a trashcan below.

"Eww. I'm like Mike. I need to say fuck this school shit and get a contract," Brandon joked.

"Nigga please. It's easy to make a shot with balled up newspaper. Do it on the court and talk that shit, you bum."

Brandon laughed. It was a temporary reprieve from the doldrums he felt most of the afternoon. But before he could kick into homecoming mood and enjoy the Yard festivities, he suffered one more setback. Ben Bishop was walking across campus talking with

President Humphries. Brandon froze in his footsteps and waited to see where they were going. Ben was all smiles on the Yard, and Brandon hadn't disliked him more than at that moment. It was a dislike more intense than any of the many times Ben had gotten on him about blowing deadline or not seizing opportunities when they arose. His paranoia gave him the urge to confront Ben and ask why he was trying to get him into trouble, by snitching to President Humphries. What if Greg found out that he told Ben about his involvement?

Finally, President Humphries and his entourage of administrative flunkies left Ben behind and headed toward Blackburn. Ben had stopped on the Yard near a bench across from Blackburn. He started dialing numbers on his cell phone when Brandon emerged.

"Ben."

"Brandon," Ben smiled. "We got him. I want to see his punk ass show up on campus today. Thanks for all your help last night. I know I overreacted earlier on the phone. My fault. I didn't know how he could have known about the backup server, but it doesn't matter now. Everything turned out okay, and I liked your stories, too. What did you think about them?" Ben asked.

"I don't know," Brandon shrugged. "I don't give a shit about those stories."

Ben frowned and cocked his head back. "What?"

"Ben, you realize that the same thing that happened to you might happen to me now, because of this shit?"

"Is that what the problem is? No fingers point back to you, Brandon, so catch your breath. I would have done this story without you."

"Yeah, but you wanted me to hook you up with his number and now all this stuff happens. I ain't want nothing to do with this story from the get-go."

"Calm down, Brandon. You don't want to have anything to do with the story? Fine. I was gonna ask you to do a follow- up on it for Monday, but forget about it."

"A follow-up? Are you crazy? Why don't you do it? You don't

mind fighting a fight you can't win."

When Ben stared back into Brandon's eyes, he saw worry and anger, which explained Brandon's last comment. He decided to let it slide.

"Look, I know Greg was your boy, but I told you that he was into serious stuff. I told you that you were in over your head. I'm not gonna stand here and argue with you. I don't have a problem writing the story, but I got something even bigger running on Monday, that's bigger than your boy, believe it or not."

Brandon didn't respond, but he wanted to. What story was so big that Ben Bishop was willing to pass along a promising follow-up story on Greg?

"Guess you can't tell anybody what that story is either, huh? Anybody going to jail for that one?"

Ben smiled. "I can't tell you just yet, and to answer your second question, no, jail might be a stretch for this one, but it's big. Wait and see."

The funny thing about fear is that it can be a great motivator, but of what? Usually when people refer to it as a motivational tool, they mean that fear—defined by Webster's as *a feeling of anxiety and agitation caused by the presence or nearness of danger, evil or pain*—could compel one to overcome an otherwise insurmountable obstacle. And to overcome that obstacle is a good thing. It is a progression of sorts, serving as a mental victory over a stifling, reoccurring theme.

But what about when fear was just fear and it left you terrorized? When it boxed you into a corner and presented two options, both of which you dreaded?

It would have been a great boost to Falu Davis's self-esteem and psyche if someone could have answered that question with a response that she wanted to hear. The news about the fiscal fleece, and the information pilfering she had done to carry it out, wouldn't stay trapped in the closet forever. She had not yet told her mother, whom she had seen earlier at a Board of Trustees breakfast.

Falu, flanked by other student leaders, gave a state of the university speech to the Board in the President's conference room that morning, and her mother beamed with joy as Falu captivated her audience with powerful, witty, articulate speech. How could Falu ruin her mother's trip to D.C. (her father was flying in on a later flight for the board of trustees dinner at night) with this awful news? How to explain that she had stolen from the university and sabotaged student programming for a whole school year, as a result? Everyone expected more from her. She was a third-generation Howardite representing the Davis family; a future attorney, part of that Talented Tenth that Dubois spoke of and her parents referenced often.

As she sat in her office with the blinds closed off to the festivities outside on the Yard, she did everything but cry. Her stomach felt icy and empty, and her heart stung almost as virulently as the first time it got broken by a boy. Eric, the man she hoped would be her future husband, couldn't help her. Although he had potential written all over him, he did not yet have the money to give her or the political clout to pull her out of this one. He was thousands of miles away in Africa teaching, working for people who earned less than $1 a day. What could he do? He asked her as she sobbed to him via a telephone conversation she purchased a calling card to make. She had never told him about the codes she stole to call in the past. When he told her in the past to wait for his calls, she defied him, arguing that he would not call as frequently as she wanted him to. That was a part of the reason she stole the codes.

Rocks had started to fall from the fortress that was Falu Davis, the seemingly invincible student who was dangerously beautifully, disgustingly intelligent, and driven. Falu knew it was unlikely that rumors would spread along Power Hall of the trouble she faced, because she knew that Dean Thomas had something to hide as well. The Dean, Falu knew, would have to answer to President Humphries or one of the vice presidents about why student phone accounts had not been monitored more closely, and why year-old phone bills had just surfaced.

The dean was distracted with homecoming this week, but Falu knew that the wily administrator was preparing to throw her under the bus. The emergency general assembly meeting and university trial board were both the dean's ideas. At this point there were only two ways rumors could start spreading: Charlene Jones, the evil bitch of an ex-best friend that had snitched on her; and Ben Bishop, the nosy newspaper editor who Charlene had already tipped off. He had already started asking questions, possibly setting the rumor mill in motion.

Charlene was far away, but Ben could be a problem, Falu thought. If she had never paid him attention before, she certainly did now. Looking at the front page of *The Hilltop*, she took note of how he had pretty much set campus and metropolitan police on Greg Harris.

Everyone knew that Greg Harris sold drugs to students, they just never snitched on him. Everyone knew Greg had beaten up a student or two, or three, in his day at Howard, and Falu knew that Greg and his boys had beaten up Ben sophomore year.

If Ben could uncover a pornography website Greg ran that used local, underaged girls as models and university apartments as backdrops, Ben Bishop could bury her. Everyone read *The Hilltop*. Although there was a student-run radio show, no one listened to it. Board of Trustees members all had subscriptions mailed out to them once a week, and so did more than 500 prominent alumni.

Ben posted PG-13 rated pictures of the site on the front page. He quoted two girls who admitted to being given partial payments by Greg—one of the models was 17. Chief Williams was quoted. Howard students' pictures were shown. Another, smaller piece mentioned that Greg had stormed into *The Hilltop* office the night before with friends and attacked staff, broke equipment and assaulted a campus police officer. Ben Bishop's byline was on both stories, and he had the nerve to be calling her, trying to get information about phone usage irregularities involving HUSA staff members. Like she would really agree to be interviewed for *that* story.

Falu's directive to her staff was simple: If Ben Bishop called, she was not available. She kept her office door closed just in case he came by her office, in which case she would be "in a meeting" or "unavailable." She had already turned in her university-issued cell phone to Dean Thomas, so he wouldn't be able to reach her there. "Why," they asked? She wouldn't tell.

If only the story Ben was trying to write about her was a positive story, like the special section *The Washington Post* ran in the Style section about Howard homecoming: Its history, the money it generated for the city from clubs, restaurants and hotels, and how the event was so popular that it ballooned to something bigger than the game on Saturday.

"Falu, aren't you going to come on the Yard and celebrate with everyone today?" Maurice asked, bursting through the office doors. Falu was startled when he walked in carrying a plate of funnel cake and a can soda. He flopped down at his desk, which was across from hers.

"You scared me," Falu said.

"Can you believe it?" he asked, nodding toward the newspaper she held in her hands.

"Everybody knew Greg Harris was into illegal stuff, but it finally caught up to him," she said.

"Aren't you on the disciplinary board? Do you think that that's something that could get Greg kicked out of school?"

"I'm sad to say, but I think it is," she said. She couldn't help but think about herself and what she would soon face. Falu wanted to tell Maurice about the ax that was about to fall and separate their heads from their bodies, but she couldn't risk it. Maurice was her vice president, and although she was supposed to trust him, Charlene was once her vice president and that bitch completely turned on her.

"I gotta hurry up and eat this funnel cake, so I can get back on the Yard; everybody's out there. Why don't you have the blinds open? What's wrong with you? You're normally the one out in everyone's face."

"Nothing," she said, looking out of the blinds. "I just wanted some time alone. This week was crazy with midterms. My parents are in town. I'm still studying for the LSAT; it's a lot. I think I might go back to my room and skip the Yard this year."

"Skip the Yard on your last homecoming as a student?" Maurice stood, stuffing a piece of cake in his mouth. He held his index finger out indicating that he wanted her to wait until he could speak. The cake flushed down in one big knot down his throat and he chased it with a healthy swallow of Sunkist.

"Falu, if I have to drag you out on the Yard, I will. You are student government president. You can't miss homecoming."

She stared at Maurice with an exhausted look and said, "Sometimes you take this student government stuff too serious, Maurice. That's why they call it student government. It's not that serious. It's doesn't go beyond Howard, and once we get on the other side of these walls, we'll have real-life issues to deal with, not catering to a bunch of students who don't know what we do and who don't care about what we do in the first place. People won't be so apathetic once we graduate. All the politics here and the cliques people fit into mean nothing in the real world, and nobody will care that you were in student government," she said. She needed to relieve stress, and since Maurice was there, he took it. He didn't know how to take it, but he took it.

"Where did all of that come from? You love being HUSA President. If you couldn't be HUSA President, your life at Howard would be so boring, Falu. And now you're telling me that the job is not that serious. I don't get it," he said. He had finished his snack.

"Of course you don't get it. I'm HUSA President today, but what about tomorrow? What will I be? Anything could happen. Just ask Greg Harris," she said, lifting the paper and smacking it back down on the desk. "He is one of the most popular students on this campus and now there's a city-wide search for him, all because of one news story. Just like that, his life is forever changed."

Maurice still couldn't understand the parallel between her pessimistic diatribe disguised as candid talk about the "real world," and Greg Harris's current legal trouble, so he didn't respond to it. He shrugged his shoulders and said, "Maybe I don't get it, but I know I'm not staying in this office all day, and neither are you." He grabbed her hand, and she pulled back.

"Maurice, let go of me. I don't feel like going out on the Yard."

"Every other student leader is outside except for you. You gotta come," he yanked.

Every student leader? That meant Ben Bishop. Falu was definitely not going outside and when she did, it would only be to escape him on her way back to her dorm. She looked through the blinds again and could not see him. She didn't want to ask Maurice if he had seen him, because he would get suspicious.

"I saw all of them already at the breakfast this morning and I'll see them again tonight at the dinner with the Board of Trustees. I'll pass on the Yard." She was still looking out of the window.

"I tried. I know *The Hilltop* will have something to say about this in Monday's paper; the fact that you were nowhere to be found during Yardfest, but at least I tried. I hope you feel better at dinner tonight," he said, tossing a paper plate into the trash and heading for the door. Considering what she faced, she hoped the only thing *The Hilltop* wrote about her in Monday's paper was that she wasn't present on the Yard.

"With both of my parents there, I'll have no choice but to be."

# *Twelve*

Argh! Which way was it? Was it big fork then little fork, or little fork then big fork? Both forks actually looked the same size. She went through all of this over some salad. At least it looked tasty. The server, a short Latino man with a stocky build, clean-shaven face and low-cut haircut, smiled at her and her tablemates without showing any teeth. He placed a serving plate, replete with a predetermined amount of crisp, mint-green, arugula leaves stacked on top of each other, in front of each of them.

He made sure not to lose that smile. The dressing he poured over their salad looked Italian and smelled vinegary. Vicky was the first person he served.

"Salad?" he asked, staring down at her.

"Yes, please."

"How about dressing?"

"Just a little. Thanks."

"Not a problem."

How long before he lost that smile? Vicky wondered while sitting there. She noticed him wearing it earlier in the night during the one-hour meet-and-greet session. He and a cluster of other well-dressed servers—attired immaculately in creased black slacks with starched white tuxedo shirts tucked tightly inside of them, silver cufflinks and bowties—followed her and at least one hundred or so guests around the ball room, offering clams casino, shrimp cocktail and Cantonese shrimp spring rolls.

The university knew how to spend money when trustees hosted a function. For this night, they rented out a ballroom at the Ritz-Carlton hotel in Georgetown for the formal affair. They ate the aforementioned appetizers and listened to a jazz quintet play center stage. All the while, they took turns positioning their champagne flutes under the free-flowing fountain where two statues of white men playing a harp, poured a vintage brand into attendees' empty vessels. At the open bar, stocked with XO and VSOP cognac brands, bartenders delicately dispensed about an ounce, or a third of a cup full, into brandy snifters and waited while Board members sniffed, swirled the liquor and tasted it, giving smiles for approval.

The server at Vicky's table had personally filled her wine glass twice with a sweet chardonnay. The second glass made her lighten up some, and she started smiling more, speaking to more of the students, faculty and Board members present.

Now she was sitting at a dinner table with other attendees, some of their faces familiar, , but others not so much. She felt palpably self-conscious about not knowing which fork was the proper fork for her to grab first. She waited until everyone else was served and watched as a woman she did not know—but had overheard earlier in passing conversation say that she was a tenured professor in the law school who taught contract law— grab the first fork on the left.

Thank God.

Now Vicky could eat. She smiled at the woman— Constance Mobley was her name—as she picked up her salad fork and started to chow. Vicky went to plenty of scholarship dinners over the years and sorority banquets, but she sometimes forgot the proper etiquette when dining. Pass the tongs when dropping sugar blocks into the tea, because everyone had to use the one set. Why? Never stick your pinky finger out when sipping a glass of tea. Why? She knew that it was imperative for her to know these things as chapter president, but to

*173*

her it wasn't that deep. And tonight was a night that she couldn't remember all the rules, so she decided she would do as Constance did.

Constance, Vicky thought, was her in 20 years anyway: A nice looking, professional black woman, probably busting her ass as a full-time career woman, mother and wife (she sported a huge rock on her wedding finger) in a male-dominated world. She was forced to be a bitch at times to get the guys' respect, but be quietly polite and put-together at others. The thought of being successful with a career, husband and kids excited her, but everything else, Vicky was unsure about.

Devon Knox sat next to Constance Mobley. He was one of her pupils. He was a bald-head, clean-shaven, double-dimpled-face, caramel skin brotha who was a second-year law student, and he had been sharing his experience of working in the public defender's office in D.C. over the summer. He bragged that next year he would work as a summer associate at a prestigious firm in New York City, and hopefully that would turn into a job.

Professor Mobley, proud of her student, assured him that she was confident it would. Next to him was Lisa Cooper, an undergraduate—a junior who Vicky knew on a name basis because Lisa was a member of the Fine Arts Student Council. Lisa was a dancer from Massachusetts. Next to Lisa was Dr. Philip Johnson, an alumni board member and leading surgeon at a hospital in Richmond, Virginia. Dr. Eunice Baker, a longtime faculty member in the school of social work, sat next to him, and then the rest were students: Ashley Heard, Sean Fleming and Kevin White.

Missing from her table was the one person she wanted to be there, Benjamin Bishop. Seating arraignments were made by President Humphries's secretary in an effort to mix up the crowd and let board members interact with the everyday faces of the university, and Ben was at the most coveted table. President Humphries, his wife and Michael Jared, president of the board and CEO of a Fortune 500 company—one of the few black CEO's of the country's biggest companies—was sitting there, too. Michael Jared and Dr. Humphries were both Howard graduates and undergraduate classmates.

It was amazing to Vicky how those two powerful, important men were once where she was sitting, and were now rich, successful and living their dreams. There was hope for her.

She caught glimpses of Ben throughout the night laughing and talking with the people at his table. Ben was a hit at the dinner. Even people at Vicky's table were talking about the week's issue of *The Hilltop* and how no one thought Greg Harris had a chance in hell of being excused by the university disciplinary board. The overwhelming consensus was that he should get to packing his bags now and not step foot back on university grounds.

Vicky stood and talked with Ben before the dinner started and watched as students, faculty and board members congratulated him on a solid issue of the paper. He smiled back and shook hands, but only Vicky knew the fear he was now living with, wondering what corner Greg and his squadron of thugs would appear from to beat him unconscious. Vicky tried her best to assure him that they wouldn't. She would fight alongside him if they did.

Her defense system was breaking down, and Ben Bishop was winning her heart back by being patient and sensitive and thoughtful. She smiled, sitting at her table thinking about the compliments he showered her with when he met her out in front of the East Towers, before they went to the dinner together. She *fit perfectly into the black fitted dress. She smelled sweet, and would be the most beautiful girl there.* That was his compliment, if she remembered correctly. He smiled his brilliant smile at her, held onto her and embraced her with a tight hug. She could have melted in his arms. She wanted to.

Ben didn't look bad either in a black, single-breasted suit with a red power tie, a fresh haircut and new, square-toe leather shoes. He smelled just as good to her as she did to him, so when he embraced her, she took in his scent and smiled. She was beginning to think that giving Ben another chance wouldn't be so bad after all; forget about what Jasmine and Stephanie said.

"And here is our main course for the night," the server said, interrupting Vicky's thoughts as her eyes scoured the room.

"Oh," she jumped. "I'm sorry. I was in a daze," she smiled.

He smiled back and said, "No problem. I could tell. I'll take that salad plate and leave this right here for you. You really liked the salad, huh?"

"I did. I could've eaten just salad to be honest, because I know I won't eat all of this," she said pointing to her new plate.

"Just try it. We got a new executive chef a few months ago, and the people can't stop talking about him."

This server was nice. He was polite and friendly and provided good service. Vicky noticed him checking her out earlier, but even still, he did his job well. She would take his advice and try the food—well, some of it.

She had given up red meat, so the filet mignon would sit on her plate unless she could substitute it with a grilled or baked piece of chicken, but the lobster she would definitely try. She grew self-conscious at the table, thinking that people were watching her eat. And to make matters worse, the server had commented on how she cleaned her salad plate completely. She was trying to get full off of the arugula, so she wouldn't have to eat the dinner. All it would do, she feared, was add pounds. Pounds were bad. Pounds were her enemy. She would have to run an extra mile tomorrow, after she ate the potatoes and asparagus, and an assortment of appetizers.

There was still dessert to come after the entrée. And what about the liquor? People always told her that alcohol added weight.

Dessert came by way of two options: Either German chocolate cake or a slice of warm apple pie with a scoop of vanilla ice cream. Vicky started not to eat anything at all, but once again, the nice waiter suggested the apple pie and ice cream. It was his favorite, he told her.

As people scooped the last morsels of dessert, President Humphries rose and went to the podium to address the room.

"Welcome," he said to applause. "One-hundred and thirty-one times, this university has been able to say that at the annual meet-and-greet between the Board of Trustees, faculty, and our most prized asset, our students."

The audience clapped.

"I hope you all have enjoyed the fine food prepared for us tonight and I hope you all have gotten a chance to mingle and get to know one another. Often times, we find ourselves so busy with the day-to-day work that we forget that there is one thing that we all share in common. We all want Howard University to be the best university in the world. We serve as ambassadors to this great institution, both home and abroad.

"I was in Africa this past summer visiting Ghana, and during a guest lecture I was introduced to a 24-year-old man who said that he had just graduated from high school and that he had been accepted as a freshman to Howard. I welcomed the young man to our family and assured him that with hard work, he would see his dreams come to fruition from his time at Howard. Now, 24 is old for someone to just be graduating from high school, so I asked this young man why it took him so long. And as I suspected, the school system over there is not what we wish it was, and he had to stay home and help his family raise money to feed his 10 brothers and sisters after his father died from AIDS. He was finally able to go back to school for a short time, and then his mother died from AIDS," President Humphries said, looking out into the see of faces who were now staring back seriously.

"That's nothing to laugh about, am I right? So, I asked him how he did it. I asked him how he managed to hold his siblings together, work, go to school and get accepted to Howard. The young man told me that he had always dreamed of learning in our fine community, since a guest lecturer came to his school and talked about his experiences here. This man, whose name escapes me, went to Howard from Ghana, came back to his community after spending several years working in the States, and built a school in his village. From that point on, this young man said that getting to Howard was a life goal, because to him, Howard represented the impossible and he wanted to do the impossible and come go back to Ghana and make a change. That story made me feel proud, and at this time, I would like you all to give Mr. Djimon Okaba a round of applause," President Humphries said, pointing to an African man who was also sitting at his table.

Djimon received a standing ovation from the crowd and looked quite embarrassed as he thanked everyone. President Humphries went on.

"Every day, Howard University students, both here and out in the world, are doing the impossible. And whatever they give to the world, they got it here. I look at people like Falu Davis, who knows? She might be a future Supreme Court Justice, someday. I also look at students like Benjamin Bishop. If I live long enough, I'm sure I'll see his name on the masthead of *The New York Times*. So, in closing, I just want to say that for those of you on the faculty and the Board, I'm glad you could come this evening and share time with our future."

Everyone stood again after President Humphries left the podium and for the first time at dinner, Vicky noticed Falu Davis. They made eye contact, and Falu issued a quick fake smile before her father held his arms around her—no doubt congratulating her on being given a shout out by the president. It all helped with her mother's Board of Trustees campaign, Vicky thought as she stood there watching. Girls like Falu had it all. Vicky sulked quietly, fuming at how Falu could be so ridiculously beautiful, smart, ambitious and connected. Vicky knew she would be hearing big things about Falu one day. It was just written in the stars for her.

Instead of letting her jealousy get the best of her, she focused her attention on the other student the president had called out, Ben. He was smiling and shaking hands with people, looking handsome. Vicky couldn't wait until the ride home from the banquet, so they could talk. She would invite him up for tea.

People lingered and talked for a short time after the event was over, and Vicky got caught up in conversation with a student, some girl named Rochelle, who was trying to be a member of the sorority.

She considered Vicky sitting alone at her table as the perfect opportunity to take a shot at getting on good terms with her.

"Hi Vicky, how are you? Where did you get that dress? It looks beautiful," Rochelle asked.

"Oh this? Thanks. Actually, I got this from a boutique in Georgetown, but I can't remember the name. It cost an arm and a leg," Vicky joked.

Rochelle chuckled. While Rochelle spoke, Vicky was only able to take in part of the conversation after she looked across the room and saw Ben and Falu talking in a corner.

Why the fuck was Falu Davis talking to Ben, her Ben? Falu could have any of the guys there. They looked like they were talking about something serious, which puzzled Vicky, because it didn't look like Ben was trying to lay any game down. She was still curious. After a few minutes of watching them go back and forth, Ben came over to her table and asked if she was ready to leave. She was, she just had to say bye to a few people. Ben told her that he would be waiting out front in the car.

Vicky stayed a few more minutes while Ben retrieved the car from the garage, and she made one last trip to the bathroom before leaving. As she walked out of the bathroom, she stepped into the spacious, dark, empty corridor and heard a stern voice.

"Are you kidding me, young lady? How do you expect me to explain this? I can't get you out of this. How could you do this to me?"

The voice belonged to a tall chocolate woman with a beautiful face and a patch of gray hair. She was dressed in a black power suit with killer heels and a rock the size of a dime on her ring finger. The woman looked familiar, Vicky thought, as she walked closer. The distinguished woman was too busy scolding someone in a corner—someone whom Vicky could not see—to notice her.

It wasn't until Vicky walked by her, when the woman temporarily lowered her voice, that Vicky realized from where she recognized the face. That visage belonged to Falu Davis in a good 30 years, because the woman was her mother—the Chicago lawyer extraordinaire and front-runner for a seat on the Board of Trustees. The funny thing about the encounter was the person she was scolding in the corner was a frightened, embarrassed, shaken, Falu Davis. Vicky had never seen Falu look so shaken before. She was always calm and collected, and the envy of every female and serious undergraduate so-called "intellectual" on campus.

"Is this the same guy whose name Milton mentioned after he mentioned your name?" her mother asked.

"Yes," Vicky heard Falu answer. "Mom, I'm sorry."

"Did he write that front page story in today's paper?"

"Yes."

Vicky was out of earshot to hear anything after that, so she grabbed the tail of her gown and ascended the steps. What the hell had Ben Bishop said to Falu Davis to make her break down like that, and to make her mother rip her to shreds?

"I just saw Falu and her mother talking in the hallway and her mother was asking about you," Vicky said, rushing to the car.

Ben looked at her with big brown eyes and said, "Are you serious? What did she say?"

"She asked who you were and if you wrote the story in today's paper, and she also said she wouldn't be able to explain it, but I don't know what *it* is, so what *is* it?" Vicky asked.

Ben smiled at her. "You sound like a nosy little reporter, you know that?" he asked, pulling out onto the street. "A damn good-looking reporter, might I add."

Vicky smiled at the compliment, but didn't give up on finding out what had happened.

"Thanks for the compliment, but don't try to change the subject. What's going on?"

"Vicky this can't go outside of this car. You already know the shit I'm going through with crazy-ass Greg, and this might be the second big story I break in less than a week."

"What is it?" Vicky asked excitedly.

"That bitch ran up almost sixty-thousand in phone bills, making calls to Africa and whatever-the-fuck-else place in the world where she knows people. And she stole phone codes from other student organizations to pull it off, if the information I have is correct."

"What? Oh my goodness. How could she be so stupid? What are you talking about 'If the information I have is correct?' Didn't you hear me say that her mother said she couldn't explain this?"

"Yeah, but Falu said she has backup documents or something like that, and she can show that the debt isn't what I think it is, and that someone else is responsible for stealing the codes."

"I can't believe this. This is huge."

"It is, Vicky, but like I said, you can't mention this to anyone. Promise you won't."

"I swear. I'll just wait 'til Monday to read it."

"Good. I hope after I drop you off tonight, I won't have to wait until Monday to see you again. I can't get over how good you look in that dress."

Ben was putting her on the defense a little, but this time she didn't mind.

"Of course you will. As a matter of fact, I'm not partying tonight, because I'll be hanging out with my sorors tomorrow night for the homecoming game afterparty. So you can come up tonight and have some tea with me, if you don't have any plans," she offered.

To that he smiled, which in turn made her smile.

"I like the sound of that. I'm laying low for safety purposes anyway. Tea sounds just about right."

Hours later, in the middle of the night, Vicky and Ben Bishop lay sweaty in her twin bed, naked after having sex three times. It got better every time for Vicky, and with every soft kiss and caress on her body from him, she fell back in love. He was forgiven for the past. Their new relationship had been consummated, and she had decided to follow her heart and not worry about getting hurt again.

She melted with every touch of his hands, and felt angelic lying with his arms wrapped around her stomach, as he nibbled on her ears and played in her hair. Ben admitted to her that he never stopped caring about her, and that she could blame the way he acted on immaturity, which is what she suspected in the first place. He thought they had a future together, and so did she. They didn't get much sleep that night, but they did get in lots of kissing and laughing and hugging and play fighting. It felt good to be back in love.

# *Thirteen*

Not even a throbbing headache that made one's head feel as heavy as a bowling ball could stop someone—a Howard student—a freshman on top of that—from missing the Saturday homecoming game. It was like a rite of passage. It wouldn't satisfy the curious freshman to watch on the local Howard TV channel, or from a room in Cooke Hall, which was right across from Greene Stadium; or from the hall window of Drew Hall, which was right behind the stadium. You had to be there, to be in and of it.

So far, the events leading up to Saturday had been memorable for Brandon. He had never gotten so high or drunk in his life. He had never been around so many beautiful black girls at one time, and been lucky with them. Twenty-four hours before this moment, he was sulking on the Yard during Yardfest, worrying if he was going to be suspended from school for his obscure involvement in an illegal porn/modeling website run by one of his mentors, Greg Harris.

That feeling of fear lasted all but a short part of the afternoon, but he overcame it by partying. After the Yard cleared out and the pep rally was over, Brandon, Frank and the rest of their crew headed to Georgia Avenue to become a part of the crowd: thousands of undergraduates and locals walking up and down the strip, sipping milkshakes from McDonalds, stopping street traffic and listening to music blare from open SUV trunks.

People showed off, riding motorcycles up and down Georgia and popping wheelies, while hustle men hustled books, boots, Outkast concert tickets, and fake Howard paraphernalia including sweatshirts, hats and jackets. Lots of flirting went down. Numbers were exchanged, along with hugs, screams and expletives for some rowdy members in a given group. The writhing mass of humanity was the equivalent to a club letting out times 10, except there was no club around. And it would be hours before people would actually start partying.

Hours later, Brandon and his crew found themselves high on marijuana and drunk from rum and Coke when they stumbled into the Blackburn Center for a homecoming party thrown by the Louisiana and Texas clubs (LATEX). The Southerners turned the second-floor ballroom of the university center into a club and had several of the hottest DJs in D.C. take turns spinning southern classics from Outkast, 8-Ball and M.J.G., Scarface, Master P, and the Hot Boys.

They mixed in East Coast artists like Nas, Jay-Z, Biggie and Puffy, but it was the late 90s, and the beginning of a new trend of popular southern music had begun eating up the charts. Brandon had never appreciated southern music until he got to Howard, because he never saw anyone dance to it back home. But once he got to school, he quickly learned that southern music was the music of choice in the club. It didn't matter if whoever was rapping wasn't saying anything of substance on the mic; the girls bounced and shook, and popped nastily to it, and he sweated hard trying to keep up with them.

Fast-forward 10 hours to Saturday, game day, and Brandon found himself and only half his crew up and ready to go to the game. He wasn't fully rested, his eyes were bloodshot and he hadn't eaten, but the crowd seduced him. On the walk from Drew, he could see the sea of brown faces crowd the stadium. Horns were playing, courtesy of the Howard University Showtime Marching Band, which got the audience crunk, and the chants—the chants were loud and energetic.

*I'm so glad I go to Howard U*
*And not a white school*
*I'm so glad I go to Howard U*
*And not a white school,*
*I'm so glad I go to Howard U*
*Glory hallelujah, I'm so glad*

Two hours later, after the band obliterated the Morehouse band with an array of classic cuts from Earth Wind and Fire, Rakim and new stuff from Lauren Hill's *The Miseducation of Lauren Hill* album, the actual game teetered on a knife edge. Morehouse had taken a three-point lead off of a field goal with less than two minutes left, and the Howard Bison, led by NFL prospect quarterback Jason Brown and junior wide receiver Earl Knight, found themselves on the 50-yard line with no time outs left.

They ran a no-huddle offense and hiked the ball out of the shotgun to keep Morehouse confused. Brown dropped back several yards and looked left, but his receivers were covered. Knight cut across the middle of the field at the 35-yard line, and the safety sticking him tripped on the grass. Brown fired a rifle-like shot across the middle that hit Knight in the chest, right before he was hit by a Morehouse linebacker. But it was enough for a first down, and if need be, a field goal to send the game into overtime.

Brandon, and everyone else in the crowd went crazy.

*First and ten! Bison!*

That first down ignited the otherwise stunned crowd, and on the very next play, with less than 30 seconds left, Jason Brown and Earl Knight made magic once more. Knight ran straight down the right sideline, matched up with Morehouse's star cornerback, Trevor Hayes, who stuck to him like white on rice. Trevor Hayes's mistake was made when he played Earl on the outside, allowing Brown to drop a ball into his hands perfectly. Trevor Hayes had fallen after he flew in the air and attempted the interception, which gave Earl Knight enough room to ease into the end zone.

The bleachers where Brandon sat behind the goal felt like they were going to collapse. Everyone jumped into the air and started hugging each other, glad that Howard would not be getting upset and embarrassed at Homecoming. A loss on a random Saturday afternoon was fine, but not on Homecoming, when people from around the country came to watch them play ball. Brandon and Frank knew what chant was coming next, so they jumped up from their seats, prepared to go first.

*Do it, do it, do it!*
*Do it, do it, do it!*
*Do it, do it, do it!*
*Now stop, and let the freshmen do it!*

All the freshmen got up from their seats and pumped their fist in the air. Some danced and screamed at the top of their lungs. It was when Brandon jumped up and pumped his fist in the air that he saw what he thought were two ghosts. Neeko and Poncho were sitting at the top of the opposing team's bleachers, both dressed in dark clothing with hoodies on. He had hung around them long enough when they were with Greg to notice them, and they both stood ice grilling the crowd, numb to the celebration.

Brandon couldn't see them after he sat down, because after the freshmen went, it was the sophomores' turn to do it, and then the juniors and then the seniors.

Brandon jumped up when it was the seniors' turn, but he couldn't see the ominous duo, because Frank grabbed his arm.

"Brandon what are you doing? You're not a senior. Everybody knows you're not a senior. You're embarrassing me, sit down man," Frank said, and tugged at his arm.

"Man, fuck them. I saw somebody I knew and now I missed them because of you," Brandon said.

Brandon would get one more chance to see if it really was Neeko and Poncho in the crowd. No doubt they were there looking for

Ben, who was not there. If he was, then as a student leader he would have been sitting in the president's section, along with Falu Davis, her staff, and others.

*Now stop,* the chant went on
*And everybody do it!*
*Do it, do it, do it!*
*Do it, do it, do it!*
*Do it, do it, do it!*

Brandon looked for them as he pumped his fist, but they were gone. He was sure he saw them there. How long had they been there? Were they looking for him as well as Ben? They couldn't have been looking for him, because he called Greg's cell number multiple times and Greg never answered. If Greg was trying to have him set up, he could have easily answered the phone and told Brandon to meet him in a dark alley or somewhere else, and the three of them could have dealt with him that way for being affiliated with Ben Bishop.

After the game was over, as is standard, the cheering crowd gathered on the Yard, so alumni who hadn't seen each other in years could hug and get caught up on each others' lives. This also gave people a chance to flirt with each other. The president went around shaking hands with major contributors to the capital campaign and so did Board of Trustees members.

Brandon bought a fish platter from an African stand in front of Douglas Hall, but he barely touched it—he was too occupied walking back and forth across the Yard, looking for Neeko and Poncho. They didn't go to Howard, so it was easy for them to stay under the radar of the police while interloping on campus. But Greg, because of his fugitive status, wouldn't be caught dead on campus for the homecoming game. And as Brandon learned from looking into the tens of thousands of faces, Ben wouldn't be caught on the Yard on that day either, considering the heat that followed him.

"Yo, B, you acting real funny today. What's up with that?" Frank asked, following Brandon across the Yard.

Frank couldn't understand Brandon's paranoia. All he thought about, like Brandon thought about on a normal day, was girls.

"Hey, B, I gotta sit down somewhere and eat my fish before it gets cold. Who you looking for, a girl?"

"Nah man, I think I saw two of Greg's boys at the game," Brandon finally answered, after leading Frank on a scavenger hunt across the Yard.

"We've been all over the Yard, man. Whoever you saw ain't here no more, and who cares if they came on the Yard. Everybody is on the Yard."

"Yeah, but they don't go to school here, and they wouldn't just be hanging on the Yard, especially without Greg, and I know he isn't crazy enough to come up here today."

"So why you think they came up here?" Frank asked, seeming more interested in the thought of a conspiracy unraveling.

Brandon was walking across a path on the east side of the Yard, across from Locke Hall, when he heard a loud shrieking sound and saw at least a hundred women gesture their hands in the air. Some were student faces he recognized, others were young, but not students, and others were old with strands of gray hair stylishly done. He directed his attention toward the circle.

"Now you wanna watch them step, huh? That's more like it," Frank said.

Brandon ignored him and walked to the back of a crowd that pressed around the sorority members as they stepped. His eyes scoured the circle until he saw a familiar face. Vicky Mourning was her name, and as far as he knew, she was Ben Bishop's girlfriend. She was with him and Ben the other night when they stayed at the office all night putting out the paper. She had brought Ben dinner that night. Brandon admired Ben for having a girlfriend so attractive and put together. She was president of her sorority at Howard, and he knew she would be on the Yard stepping for homecoming.

Maybe Ben would be in the background watching. Maybe she would know where Ben was, since it seemed that he was reluctant to come on campus for the game. Brandon thought about sticking around until after she and her sorors finished stepping to ask her. Vicky and Brandon were on a first-name basis because of Ben.

They stepped for what seemed like forever and at the end they reconvened in a huge circle and held hands. It took them another 20 minutes after they did their last step just to stop crying and hugging each other. Brandon looked around and saw that other fraternities and sororities were doing the same thing. Seeing that only reinforced Brandon's resolve to pledge as soon as he earned the 30 credits required to do so. He loved seeing the camaraderie they shared. Plus, in his young mind, all he could think about was the girls he would get because of his affiliation and all the social connections being Greek would create for him once he graduated.

He blended into the crowd after the stepping was over and noticed Vicky talking to two girls he had seen her with on several occasions in the Punchout and on campus.

"Yo, I'll catch up with you in a second, Frank. I need to talk to somebody real quick."

"Fool, stop playing. You don't know her," Frank said, seeing which way Brandon was walking.

Brandon turned around and looked at him like he was crazy.

"Why can't I know her? She's not famous."

Brandon stepped up behind Vicky and her friends and said, "Excuse me, Vicky."

She turned around. "Hi Brandon," she said, giving him a hug.

"Hey, I was wondering if you saw Ben up here? I called him and he didn't answer his phone," Brandon lied.

Vicky smiled and said, "He's not coming on the Yard today. He wanted to sleep in," she said, remembering their night. Ben was asleep in her room, in her bed. And if she wasn't president of Alpha chapter, and it wasn't Homecoming, she would have been lying right beside him. But, she had to show face for alumni big sisters from her sorority.

She noticed the worried look on Brandon's face, however.

"What's wrong, Brandon?" she asked.

"I was at the game, and I could have sworn I saw Neeko and Poncho there. I wanted to give Ben a heads up, but he's straight if he's not here," he said.

"I wish I would've seen 'em. I would've called campus police. I'll let him know when I see him. You be careful out here, Brandon," she said.

They said goodbye and she was back to talking with her two friends, one of whom Brandon heard ask who he was. Ben, he thought, was definitely laying low.


"Do you think they were there looking for you?" Forrest asked Ben, sitting across from him at a heavy wooden table in the middle of the newsroom floor early Saturday evening. Ben momentarily stopped scribbling in red ink on a printed sheet of paper that contained the 400-word follow up story on Greg Harris for Monday's paper. This story really had nothing new, except that police had been looking for him and had not found him. That was subject to change, however, seeing as how it was only Saturday. Ben just completed the story early because he had nothing better to do, and he and Forrest wanted to have most of the stories edited by Saturday night. The exception was the last-minute story Ben was working on about HUSA.

"Why else would they be there? They probably saw Brandon at the game, and if they didn't, they know how to get in contact with him," Ben said to Forrest, worriedly.

"So, what are you going to do?"

Ben started to answer him, but gestured his right index finger to his mouth for silence, as he tried to hear the commotion outside of the newsroom doors. He thought it might have been someone trying to break in, but on further inspection, it was just a group of rowdy students laughing and playing in the hall. That happened on a regular basis. Ben and Forrest were the only two people in the office and they had the door bolted from the inside—a new deterrent to stop thugs like Greg and his crew from coming into the office and destroying property. They had to use emergency funds out of their budget to get the IT guy to come in on a Saturday and fix the server.

"I don't know what I'm going to do. I was up on the Yard yesterday for Yardfest, and if I wasn't so tired this morning, and if I didn't have to let the IT guy in here to fix the computers, I might have gone on the Yard today and then I would have confronted them. They wouldn't have tried anything stupid in front of a crowd like the one there today."

"Maybe they just came to see the game and they weren't looking for you. I was at the game and I didn't see them. I would have recognized them and I damn sure know they can recognize me."

"Come on, Forrest. They aren't students here. I never see them at any regular games, and this just so happens to be the day after I put Greg on blast? I gotta try to think like Greg on this one, and that motherfucker is sneaky. For all Brandon knows, Greg might have been hiding in a car on campus, watching everything that went down. The cops haven't caught up to him, but I bet he hasn't left town. The university doesn't even have an up-to-date address on him," Ben said.

Forrest looked at him as if to say, "How the hell did you know that?"

"I know someone in enrollment management who checked for me. I'm not a stalker," Ben said.

"Okay, so what, are you gonna stay in the Towers from here until graduation? You gonna keep running from this dude? Not me."

"I'm not running," Ben said, flashing back in his mind to the night when they jumped him in the Engineering building parking lot, and to Thursday night, when he and Greg fought heads-up. The beatdown sophomore year was bad, because he just flatout got jumped and pummeled, but Thursday he'd fought back and didn't come up as short as he'd feared.

"Well, if it means anything, I got your back."

"Thanks Forrest," Ben said, balling his right hand into a fist to give Forrest a pound. "I appreciate it."

Ben acted tough or nonchalant in front of Forrest, because he felt as if he had to act that way in front of his staff. He had to lead by example, so they would know that when it came to exposing ugly stories that some people might not want to get told, that he would support them. He had to let them know that they were doing the right thing. But he was afraid. Greg was someone Ben thought had a little sense. A fistfight might be all that there was with Greg, seeing as how he was actually a smart guy.

Ben could handle another fistfight, but what about Neeko and Poncho? Unaffiliated with the university, these two cats took pride in being thugs. They could try to escalate the situation into something out of control, and because of that threat, Ben worried. This was college. No one was supposed to be fighting and trying to be a thug. They were supposed to be learning, preparing for the future and dreaming big, but people like the ones looking for him were not envisioning the same future he saw for himself. They needed immediate satisfaction and they handled beef with physical confrontation.

An awkward silence in the room followed. Ben went back to marking up copy, and Forrest put red check marks on the back of photographs that they were going to use for Monday's paper, including pictures from the Outkast concert, Yardfest and the game. He checked off on his clipboard all completed tasks, then got up from his seat and went to the chalkboard outside of Ben's office. for the board listed all front-page stories.

Four of the five stories had brief headlines on them, except for the one Ben was doing, which just read his name. He and Forrest decided not to put the subject on the board, because no one knew about the story except for those two, and they wanted to keep it that way. If anyone from UGSA or one of the student council boards found out, they would have been bugging Ben and Forrest to leak the story to them first. Ben and Forrest wanted to break the news.

"You haven't said much about this," Forrest said, tapping at the board where Ben's name was with a piece of chalk. "I hope we still have this story coming in."

Ben looked up from the table and smiled.

"I have most of it written and saved on my desktop in my office, and the rest I'll finish tonight."

"I can't believe Falu Davis could be so stupid," Forrest said.

"Me neither. But it gets better. I saw her at the Board of Trustees dinner the other night and she tells me that she has a different set of invoices that has the bill much lower, and that she knows who the thief was in her office who took the codes."

"But I thought for sure that the thief was her, and that Dean Thomas had the phone company double-check the numbers," Forrest said.

"She did! Falu is scrambling at the last minute. I'm just curious to see what she can come up with and who she is going to try to pin this on … although I think I already know that."

"Who?"

"Charlene Jones, the one who leaked this to me in the first place. Charlene is in Japan, so she is the easiest target, but Charlene already accounted for the phone calls she made to Asia. Falu can't explain thousands of dollars' worth of calls to Africa to some guy."

"It's a wrap for Falu. Oh, how the mighty have fallen. Isn't her mother running as an alumni member of the board?"

"Yep. Vicky heard her mother talking about me the other night at the trustees' dinner. I feel kind of bad for Falu, seeing as how she probably was a shoo-in for Harvard Law if she got a decent score on the LSAT. But with this on her record, it's a wrap. We might win a Hearst award for the news we're breaking," Ben rejoiced. Hearst awards were to college students what Pulitzers were to working journalists.

Ambition is a wonderful thing. The thought of humbling another student walking around with an inflated ego gave Ben a rush. He had changed gears from being afraid that Neeko, Greg and Poncho were going to beat him worse than they did before, to ruminations over his staff winning the collegiate equivalent to a Pulitzer.

"Let's do a checklist of everything we have for this story, Ben, just to make sure you're not getting all excited," Forrest said. "Do we even have all of this confirmed?"

Forrest would be a great successor to Ben as editor of the paper the following school year, Ben thought as he stood up, walked to his office and went inside. When Ben lost focus, Forrest was there to catch him, which was what he was doing now, but Ben had covered his behind.

"Here is an actual invoice," Ben said, throwing a thick stack of papers into Forrest's hands.

"But how did—"

"Dean Thomas and Falu weren't as tight as you might have thought. I ran into the Dean at Yardfest yesterday and I told her about the story. She pulled me to the side and told me to follow her to her office. I told her I knew how much money the university owed and who was behind it, and she didn't refute it. The only thing she did was cover her ass, attributing the late invoice to AT&T. I asked about the stolen IDs and all she said was for me to keep following the route that I've been on. And I quote, 'This is a classic example of a student getting a little drunk off of the power of being a student leader. I have seen this happen a million times in my day, but never to this magnitude.'"

"Dayum! She said that?"

"Yep. That's why I think it's hilarious that Falu told me that she has a separate invoice. I almost told her what the Dean said until she lied to me about that. I just want to see what she comes up with so I can put it in the story."

"I can't believe the Dean threw her under the bus like that."

"Why not? I can. She had to cover her ass. And the last thing I found out was that Dean Thomas went to school with Falu's mother."

"Really?"

"Yep. And just like all the girls here hate Falu's conceited ass, they all hated her mother when she was here. This story is deep. I have a new respect for how crafty and sneaky Dean Thomas is after this. This was a slap in the face to Falu and her mother, and it's going to ruin both of them," Ben said. Then the phone in his office rang.

Ten minutes later he came back out smiling.

"That was her."

"Falu?"

"Yeah. Got a meeting with her at the Annex in a couple of hours."

# *Fourteen*

Anyone who knew Greg Harris knew that he was vindictive, and that there was no way he was going to let what happened to him the day before go unanswered. As observers might say in the local slang, he *got carried*—he was thoroughly embarrassed on campus after a nosy college newspaper editor put his online operation on blast. So yeah, anybody who knew Greg knew beyond a doubt that he would get his payback. Ben should have known it, and in a sense he did—that's why he walked the streets looking behind his back every few feet, and traveled with a switchblade in his pocket. Memories of what happened to him before when he got tangled up in Greg's business replayed in his head.

But this time Greg was more angry, more ruthless and more willing to hurt Ben Bishop to get his point across. It infuriated him that he, Neeko and Poncho scoured the main campus and law school during the early morning hours, patiently waiting for the carriers to deliver the papers that he and his crew later pilfered—only to have *The Hilltop* print another 10,000 copies.

Luckily for Greg, a customer in the West Towers called him early Friday afternoon, just before he was about to dress and head to the Yard for Yardfest. The client said to read the story printed about him in the paper. He stopped short of driving to the Towers, going to Ben Bishop's room, and heaving him out of his bedroom window. Instead, Greg had to quickly pack up his pistol, pills, weed and cash, and flee his Columbia Heights apartment, just in case the cops came knocking. The university didn't have an up-to-date address on him, and he arranged that on purpose. But various people on campus and across the city knew where he lived, including the two women Ben quoted as saying that Greg had short-changed them for a job. He would get them back, too.

Everyone knew Greg drove a black Expedition with D.C. plates, so he had to dump it temporarily. He stashed the car in a supplier's mechanic garage in Suitland, Maryland, and traded it for a beige, 1988 Pontiac 6000 with tinted windows. That provided an effective disguise for him to roam the streets of Northwest. Friday night he didn't make any stops on campus or at the clubs after Yardfest. He took orders, but got Neeko and Poncho to handle them, and Greg spent the night at Neeko's apartment in the Brookland section of Northeast D.C. He chose to chill at Neeko's apartment because Poncho lived too close to his own house.

Before dawn Saturday morning, the day of the homecoming game—which he wouldn't make an appearance at either—he woke, went to his apartment at 13th and Irving to do inventory, grabbed more clothes and left quickly before anyone could notice him. He spent the morning at Neeko's, but it didn't take him long to realize that he wouldn't spend another night there. , He couldn't because Neeko's kids and their mother drove Greg crazy with all the running back and forth across the living room floor while he tried to sleep. And Neeko's babies' mother asked way too many questions.

*Neeko, why is he here? How long is he staying? Is somebody chasing him? Why would you bring him here?*

Out of respect for Neeko and to avoid confrontation, Greg didn't answer her when he heard her ask questions. He had to find another place to stay for the night, and he found that in a 28-year-old woman he was occasionally dating named Tiffany. She conveniently lived in Oxon Hill, a black section of Maryland just outside of Southeast D.C. She worked for the government and wasn't affiliated with Howard in any way. Greg met her at a barbecue over the summer and had maintained a relationship with her. Tiffany's house would be the stop after tonight—after he handled the business ahead of him.

"This motherfucker creeping over to the Annex on the late night, looking over his shoulders every five seconds, just to get some pussy," Neeko said, sitting in the passenger seat of Greg's temporary ride.

"Did you see the look on his face when we passed him the first time? He looked like he wanted to turn around and run all the way back to the Towers, fucking punk bitch," Poncho added. He was sitting in the back seat of the car.

Greg, Poncho and Neeko were parked on Fourth Street, up the street a little from the Bethune Annex dormitory. A succession of other student cars from residents in the Annex, the Quad or anyone foolish enough to be actually studying in one of the campus libraries during homecoming week, were parked in front of them. It was a perfect spot for them to blend in. From where they were parked, they could see anyone who left the Annex Courtyard or the back exit down the steps near the garage and down Bryant Street. That would be the way Ben would have to go if he took the back exit.

They had spotted Ben when he walked up from under the ramp to the underground West Towers garage; he wore a black hoody, black jeans and black sneakers. He had the drawstring pulled down and the hood stuck to his head, looking over his shoulders. From the ramp, he crossed over to the East Towers ramp, out onto 8th Street, and through an empty parking lot.

Greg, Neeko and Poncho would have missed him if Greg had listened to Neeko and parked outside the front entrance to wait on Barry Place. Since Neeko and Poncho said that they hadn't seen Ben at the homecoming game, Greg figured he was hiding, trying to keep a low profile; Greg's hunch paid off.

They kept the Pontiac's lights off when they started the car, and waited to pull off from the circle in the back of the Towers until Ben reached the parking lot about to cross Georgia Avenue. Greg drove slowly across the East Towers ramp, across 8th Street, and into the parking lot. By this time, Ben had passed the Howard University Hotel and started walking down Bryant Street. They stalled and waited until he got further down the street.

When they got to Bryant Street, Ben was walking in front of the C.B. Powell Building, home to the School of Communications. They eased down the street behind him and right by him when Ben turned and looked with suspicion at them and a car behind them passing by. The tinted windows kept him from recognizing his pursuers. They stopped at the light at Bryant and Fourth, by which time, Ben had caught up on them some. Greg fought off an urge to jump out of the car right then and there to attack him, but there was a car with witnesses in it behind them.

When the light changed, they proceeded slowly straight down the block, and by the time they got to a small side street off of Bryant, they could see that Ben was heading into the Annex. They made the block and found parking on Fourth.

They waited with the car in "park" and all the lights off. Greg killed the music inside. No one walking by would be able to see that there were three armed thugs in the car, ready to do damage to a Howard student.

The plan had changed many times. First, they were going to hit Ben over the top or in the back of the head with the butt of a pistol and kidnap him. They would find a place to take him and get rid of him. Greg didn't like it. The second plan was to simply drive by him when they noticed him leaving the building and just let off a succession of shots, but Greg didn't like that either, because it could cause a nasty scene and draw too much attention to them. Gunshots would garner attention and someone would inevitably get up from their desk or bed and look out the window. Now they didn't even have a plan. The goal was just to fuck Ben's troublemaking ass up as bad as they could and leave it up to whoever found him to deal with whatever was left of him.

Greg hadn't felt this way in years, since the first time he shot someone. It was in Oxon Hill, outside of a strip club. Greg and the crew of D.C. cats he had gotten cool with were partying there, celebrating the last night that a girl they were cool with, Mystique, would be dancing there. She was headed off to Los Angeles to begin her porno career, and Greg and his friends, the ones who introduced him to drug dealing, partied with her. Early in the night, someone in Greg's crew got into an argument with someone in a crew from Southeast, and Greg and his boys ended up being the ones kicked out of the club.

Just like the present moment, Greg and his crew had found themselves parked outside of the club waiting for the opposing faction. Greg knew what they were about to do, because unlike him, everyone else was armed. Travis, a person who Greg considered to be a mentor, handed Greg a pistol and a blunt. He took them both and took a puff of what he thought was weed, but ended up being angel dust.

It was the first time and only time he had ever smoked angel dust, and it created a monster that night. Greg's heart beat so fast that he thought it would burst, and he became anxious and disoriented, slobbering down the corners of his mouth to his chin. His speech became slurred and his hearing and visual senses became heightened, almost like he was hallucinating.

After an hour of waiting in the car, the group they had tangled with came outside, and following his mentors, Greg exited the car. In the most psychotic rage of his life, he fired a barrage of shots into the crowd. He saw one man clutch his leg and another his stomach. Who knew if it was one of the shots he fired that did the damage?

Greg and his crew fled the scene and were the quarry of local police authorities who said on the news that they didn't have descriptions of the shooters or their getaway car. Greg never heard anything about the two guys injured in that shooting dying, but it forced him to lay low for a second, because he feared payback. Karma hadn't reached him—at least not yet. But it came to claim Travis two years after that incident, when he was killed outside of a strip club.

"I wish this motherfucker hurry up," Neeko said. "He been in there almost an hour."

"Just chill, Neeko," Greg said, looking over at him and tapping his shoulder. It was one of the few things Greg had said all night while they were in the car, as the marijuana he had smoked to get him ready for the night's task settled in.

This time, instead of being restless he was heavily sedated, and his eyes were half-shut. Thoughts raced in his head of Ben's face when he saw Greg coming for him. Did Ben Bishop really think he would let this slide?

"Yo, yo, there he goes right there. Ain't nobody with 'im. Let's go."

Greg slowly placed the car in reverse to get out of the parking spot, but stopped. For a second, it looked as if Ben was going to walk up Fourth Street from the courtyard and turn left on College Street. That would have been perfect for them, since no one was ever on College Street. They could get him and drive off scot-free. But Ben stopped midway through crossing the street and turned back toward the Annex. Greg waited until he got closer to the intersection before he would turn right on Bryant, headed back to the Towers. Then, someone he couldn't recognize from his parked location called Ben's name to get his attention.

"Aw shit," Greg said, stalling the gear. "We gotta wait 'til he finish talking."

"Yo what the fuck! Whoever this bitch is, she 'bout to catch the same thing he is, if she don't go back inside," Poncho said, angrily.

Just as she expected, Falu's parents didn't take the news too well. They were furious—her mother was so upset that Falu thought she actually might slap her in public at the Board of Trustees dinner the other night in Georgetown. Maybe the fact that they were in public was the only reason her mother hadn't smacked her in the face, Falu concluded. But truthfully, after her mother scorned and emotionally abused her, there was nothing a smack could do to hurt Falu more.

She had failed, posed a humiliating embarrassment for her family and short-circuited herself in the process, her mother told her. This was an offense that, even if she weren't found guilty by the university disciplinary board, would be reported as part of her tenure at Howard.

Once it hit *The Hilltop*, it would be part of Howard history: The HUSA President who fleeced the students. She could forget about a recommendation letter to Harvard from President Humphries after he learned of her transgressions; and could probably wave goodbye to the support of all other members of the powerful board. The most hurtful thing was that her mother, for whom Falu would certainly ruin any chances of becoming the next alumni member to the Board of Trustees, had proclaimed that she was through with her own daughter. Falu's father, the more laid back of the two, tried to calm Falu's tears and assure her that her mother was speaking from emotion and that she didn't really mean what she said. But Falu wasn't buying it. She could read the hatred and disappointment in her mother's eyes. And when her mother slammed the bedroom door of her hotel suite, leaving Falu and her father in the living room area, it was confirmation enough for her.

Her mother, the woman she had looked up to all of her life, the woman to which people often attributed Falu's good looks and her maneater, unrelenting determination, had dropped her like she was hot. Friday night, Falu cried harder than she had ever cried before. It was a good thing that it was Homecoming and her roommates were out, drinking, dancing, and partying like everyone else. Otherwise they would have heard the loud sobs she projected from a darkened bedroom. What would her life become? Maybe she wasn't cut out to be a lawyer. Eric wasn't answering when she called, and she didn't really have any close friends left at Howard. That's because at some point—as was the case with Charlene Jones—she had quarreled with all of them, or they simply grew to hate her for some reason or another, be it jealousy or her seemingly standoffish nature.

Falu felt stupid, unsure, and afraid. Only her mother's disapproval could make her feel this way. It made Falu question all of the dreams she had been chasing of becoming a big-time attorney with aspirations to reach the United States Supreme Court.

It was possible her dreams could have been her mother projecting unfulfilled dreams onto her. Her father pushed her for greatness, too, but it was unlike her mother's unrelenting expectations. This pressure had infiltrated her being. She could only wear her makeup a certain kind of way, because it was what her mother taught her. She could only mess with a certain kind of guy, because she had an image to uphold and people were always watching her, waiting for her to fail. Never show emotion, and keep it moving like a rolling stone that gathers no moss. Because friends would come and go over the years, and the jealousy would cause them to turn on her and attempt to slander her, her mother warned her. This was the way her mother carried herself.

Falu aspired to be her mother, but often, secretly questioned if it was the life she wanted for herself. Falu, an only child, had spent many nights at home with a nanny or away at camp or boarding school, because her parents were too busy working to spend much time with her. She had the newest and the latest material items, but she didn't have her parents' time. Instead of her mother preparing home-cooked meals, Falu grew up eating pre-cooked meals that her mother purchased from the grocery store on her way home from a late day at work. Did Falu really want that life? Was it worth it? Her parents had thought about divorce before, but fought through it. They traveled the world, drove nice cars, and frequented a plethora of exclusive Chicago social gatherings, but were they happy?

All of these thoughts surfaced again Friday night as she lay in bed, but by Saturday she had gathered herself. She had smiles to share with alumni, faculty, staff, and students at the game. Hundreds of hands had to be shaken of all the people who would be introduced to her as HUSA President.

Pictures had to be taken for local media and the Bison Year-book. Only a select group of people knew what she had done, and surprisingly, when she ventured onto campus Saturday afternoon, she didn't see them. Dean Thomas was nowhere to be found. Falu was glad, because she had grown to hate the Dean in recent days, and had learned that the Dean was to her mother, what girls at Howard were to her: Jealous.

The most important person who knew what Falu had done, and who could cause her the most harm, was also not there. Where was Benjamin Bishop, she wondered? She saw his latest girlfriend, Vicky Jones, sitting by the goal line with the rest of her little sorority friends. Ben had buried Greg Harris in Friday's edition of the paper, and she knew that everyone would be reading the special post-home-coming Monday edition to see the grade the paper gave this year's events. If Ben had his way, they would also read about her.

Her last option after her parents told her that there was nothing they could do for her, was to doctor an invoice from AT&T with a lower amount. She could then provide Ben a proposal she had draft-ed on how student organizations could recover some of their pro-gramming money from an emergency fund from the office of Student Affairs. She also prepared a note that she was going to present to the university disciplinary board, accusing Charlene Jones of stealing phone codes. It was a stretch, but it was her last shot at saving herself from embarrassment, at saving her law school recommendations. She was going to tell Ben about all of this on the Yard if she saw him, but he didn't show. So, she called him at work later that night.

"*Hilltop*, this is Ben speaking."

"Ben?"

"Yes, who's calling?"

"This is Falu Davis."

How many Falus did he know? She just always had to be pro-fessional.

"Hey, what's going on?"

"Did I catch you at a bad time?"

"Not at all. I'm in the office putting the paper together for Monday, and I need to speak with you anyway, remember," he said. She could hear him shuffle papers in the background.

"Right. Here's the thing. I can talk to you, but not over the phone. Can we meet? I have those papers I told you about to show you."

"We can meet. Give me a time and a place and I'll meet you there."

"Good. I'm really not in the mood to go anywhere. Meet me at my dorm. My suitemates should be leaving for the club, or wherever they are going tonight, in about an hour or so."

"Uh, okay. I can do that. You live in the Annex right?"

"Right."

"I'll see you in an hour or so."

It was 11:30 p.m. when Ben finally showed up at her dorm. She signed him in and took him to her room.

"Interesting art work," Ben said, admiring a Chicago black art gallery piece that her parents had bought her for her room.

"Thanks. It was a gift from my parents. They know the artist."

"And what about this?" Ben asked, pointing to an African mask close to the window.

"I got that when I went to South Africa for the summer," she said.

"Africa, huh?" Ben asked, with a funny look on his face.

She knew what the look meant. She went to Africa and a lot of the calls made on those stolen phone codes were made to Africa. Some people on campus knew about Eric as well.

"Can I take your jacket?" she asked.

Ben looked perplexed by the offer, but obliged and when she took it, a switchblade fell from its pocket. She shot the same funny look right back at him. She knew what Greg Harris had done to him sophomore year, and she read the story he wrote about Greg and his friends assaulting *Hilltop* staff members in the office Thursday night. Anyone who knew Greg Harris suspected that Ben Bishop had another ass whipping coming.

"Oh my God, Falu. I'm sorry. Sometimes I just carry this at night, because you know it's crazy out here. I walked from the West Towers over here. I just needed protection in case anything happened," Ben said, scooping the blade off the floor and placing it back into his pocket.

Falu shrugged her shoulders nonchalantly. "You don't have to explain anything to me. You're not the most popular guy with some people right now," she said, pointing to Friday's edition of *The Hilltop*, which was lying on her desk. Ben laughed.

Falu and Ben spent the first 30 minutes drinking tea that she had made and sharing their plans for life after graduation. This was how they used to talk freshman year when they were still cool, when Ben thought he still had a chance of having sex with her.

"So how come you aren't out tonight partying? This is your last homecoming at Howard as a student," Ben said.

"I could ask you the same question."

"Fair enough. Besides, I have a paper to run and before I take up too much of your time, do you have the papers you told me about?"

Falu opened her bottom desk drawer and pulled a manila folder from it. "Here you go," she said.

Ben, who was sitting in a chair across from her desk chair, sat his mug on the floor, which internally infuriated Falu. What the hell had she bought coasters for if people weren't going to use them? She retrieved his cup and placed it on the desktop. She stood and walked over to her window. No one was outside. The occasional car passed down the street, but that was it. After studying the documents for 10 minutes, Ben finally spoke.

"Falu, how come the records you have are different from a copy of the invoice that I have?"

"You have a copy? Where did you get a copy of the invoice?"

"Dean Thomas," he said, staring into her face.

That bitch!

"Well, Dean Thomas had several copies of the invoices, because she asked AT&T to recalculate everything," Falu said, fumbling for an explanation

"I know that, and I got an updated copy from her yesterday with the latest bill, and it's higher than what you're showing me."

Falu was running out of lies.

"Well, I don't know what she's trying to do. I don't know why she would give you a copy in the first place, unless she was trying to ruin me. Her and that bitch, Charlene!"

Ben jerked his head back in surprise. Falu had never acted this way before, and she knew that was what he was thinking. It was too late to try to take it back.

"I'm sorry Ben. I've ruined everything," she began to cry. "I won't be going to Harvard when people find out about this, and if I get kicked out of school, I won't be going to law school at all. They're all jealous of me and they always have been," she cried, "and you are trying to embarrass me like you did Greg Harris. I don't understand this."

"Falu, I'm not trying to embarrass you." Ben stood up. "Someone told me about this story and I followed it. Hey, you're a smart girl, your parents know people, you'll be alright."

"My parents? My parents are embarrassed, Ben, and if you write this story, my mom definitely won't be elected to the board." She sat down on her bed and wiped her eyes.

"Falu, I, I'm almost speechless. I have never seen you like this before. I don't know what to say to you."

"Please don't print this story, Ben," she stood. "I'll do anything for you."

Her facial expression went from sheepish fear to whatever, whenever, whenever. She had seen the way Ben often lustfully looked at her, and although she thought it was demeaning for women to use their sexuality to get ahead, the most important thing to Falu was getting ahead. As Ben stood three feet away from her, sizing up her body, thinking about her offer, she went in for the kill, and stepped to him, kissing him. He didn't fight her off. They fell back on her bed and she rolled on top of him, kissing him on his lips and neck.

He moaned slightly. She stood up and removed her gray and blue Howard sweatshirt. She wasn't wearing a bra. Ben caressed her breasts, sat up, and started kissing them. Next, his shirt was off. Then they were both naked, kissing all over each other.

"Let me get a condom," Falu said, stopping him from kissing her. She stood up and got a condom from the top drawer of her dresser. She turned around and Ben was smiling at her, stroking himself up and down. She smiled back and then walked over to the light switch and killed it.

# *Fifteen*

Benjamin Michael Bishop is dead. His lifeless body was found in a bush in front of the C.B. Powell building by a group of freshmen from the Quad, on their way back from partying early Sunday morning. Multiple stab wounds killed him. Two to the back and even more in the front; none of them were defensive wounds, initial police reports said. No weapon was recovered at the scene.

The Howard University Hospital Emergency room at one point was filled with two-dozen students—most of them *Hilltop* employees—who came with tear-filled eyes to see if what they had heard was true. It got so thick inside that doctors had to complain to campus police, because they grew tired of coming out into the lobby area to break the news. Ben's body lie in a morgue there, but it would be transferred.

Chief Williams, who got the early morning call at his Bowie, Maryland, home, led campus police in rushing to the scene and directing traffic away from the hospital. President Humphries arrived and was genuinely teary-eyed as a result of the news.

"One of our brightest stars has been taken from us," he told the news cameras as they fired questions at him from in front of the emergency room.

"At this moment, we don't know what precipitated this tragic occurrence, but campus police are working with the metropolitan police department to solve this one. This one hurts. We see murders every day in this city, young people just being swept up in these streets, but this young man I knew personally. This young man served his peers and classmates as the student editor of the campus newspaper, and I cannot imagine that he would be involved in anything that warranted his life being taken away from him," President Humphries said, surrounded by all of his aides and university officers.

Howard's campus was put on lockdown. All dormitory visitations were temporarily suspended, streets were closed for the day, and campus police officers were stationed in front of Blackburn and the gates to the main yard, checking the identification of anyone who tried to get through. If they were not affiliated with Howard, they had a better chance of walking on water than getting past those guards.

At the spot where Ben Bishop fell, a candlelight vigil started by *Hilltoppers* decorated the sidewalk and the front of the Communications building. There was barely enough room on the front steps of C.B. Powell for people to enter or exit the building. Colorful flowers decorated every inch of grass in front of the building. Even some professors who knew Ben Bishop showed up on a Sunday—their day off—to pay their respects. The news media got footage of this, too.

This was a black eye for Howard: A murder right on campus, under everyone's nose. The worst part of it all was that it happened during homecoming weekend. Howard had long been under much scrutiny by media pundits. One black columnist at *The Washington Post*, Curtis Mallory, a tall yellow man whom the Howard community had dubbed an Uncle Tom, stood out in particular. Through years of sharp criticism, he always referred to Howard as a party school, where they cared more about dressing up for class and frittering time at extracurricular activities than achieving. This tragedy would only fuel his campaign to suggest that Howard students were living off of a legacy built by the Stokely Carmichaels of the world. Somehow, he would conveniently forget that Howard students were Rhodes, Truman, Fulbright and Marshall Scholars.

President Humphries knew this placed the university squarely into critics' crosshairs, and so his public relations team worked all day that Sunday. This killing was not one related to homecoming; he wanted everyone working to assure the media. It wasn't because the weekend attracted large, out-of-town crowds who liked to party, listen to hip-hop, or drink liquor. It was isolated, and in the end, it would be proven that a monster, not the masses, was behind this savage murder.

*The Hilltop* office was inundated with calls and visits. Would there be an issue on Monday, seeing as how the editor was dead? Who killed him? Was it true that Ben Bishop was a drug dealer and that all his dirty D.C. deeds had caught up to him? Did a crew from Hobart Street, whom he had been down with since his freshman year, catch up to him and stab him? How many people were the police looking for? When was the funeral?

Every phone rang. Every board was filled with messages from concerned students promising that they would help out if they could. The English department chair called and said that if they needed help copy editing the paper, she would come in and provide it. National news affiliates such as Fox, CNN and MSNBC wanted to do satellite interviews with the newspaper staff to gauge what the mood was like in the newsroom, now that Ben was dead. They wanted to know if the paper had any photographs of him at work, which it did, providing several copies to national media. They wanted videographers to get footage of Ben's private office. Everyone dug in their archives to see when was the last time a student editor had been killed.

Several unfamiliar cases surfaced, but none related to Howard. When was the last time a Howard student was killed? Howard students and alumni died, unfortunately, all the time, just like students and alumni from any other school. There was a case that *Hilltoppers* had heard about where a guy was killed in front of the Towers, but that was years before any of them stepped foot on Howard's campus.

It was difficult for Forrest to deal with all of this at once, especially given how he had seen Ben in the office, just hours before his body was found. One moment they were discussing Monday's paper. The next, his friend's life was snuffed out. Forrest replayed everything for the police when they came to the office. He printed out a copy of both stories Ben was working on: The follow-up story to Greg Harris's illegal pornography website and the HUSA phone bill scandal. Staff members gawked as police left the office with papers in their hands, and a copy of Friday's issue with the story about Greg Harris. That evidence-gathering created suspicion in the minds of most about whom police would consider their first suspect in Ben Bishop's murder. They just couldn't believe that a story in the newspaper would lead to this.

Jasmine and Stephanie couldn't come see Vicky because visitation was suspended, so she went to them and spent the whole day at their apartment, shocked, broken and bewildered as to how something could happened to Ben—two days after they had finally gotten back together.

"Girl, if you really think it was Greg Harris you need to tell the police about it," Stephanie said, holding Vicky tightly. They were sitting on a living room sofa drinking tea—well Stephanie was drinking—Vicky hadn't touched hers. Vicky hadn't stopped crying, shaking and asking out loud, "Why," after Stephanie picked her up from in front of the Towers.

Vicky had gone to the press conference and heard President Humphries' remarks. She saw dozens of familiar faces as people walked up to the hospital. Before she went outside to be picked up, she had gone to *The Hilltop* office. Since reporters who lived in satellite dorms wrote for *The Hilltop*, they were allowed into the West Towers with proof of ID or if Forrest, who had been designated overseer of the paper now, had come to the front of the building to sign them in. He signed Vicky in and brought her up to speed on his last moments with Ben. She sat and watched as police grabbed a few things from his office and watched as one of them doubled back to get a copy of Friday's issue of *The Hilltop*, with the story about Greg Harris circled in red. That crystallized her suspicion that Greg Harris and his friends—the same ones who vandalized the office the other night when she had cooked for Ben—were behind his murder.

"They already know. I told you that one of them went back into his office and came out with a copy of Friday's paper. He had the story about Greg circled in red. That could only mean one thing. I called Brandon, and he said that he had been trying to get in touch with Greg, but Greg wasn't answering his phone. I made him give the police Greg's number and tell them where he lived," Vicky sniffled.

"You should have, Vicky. I hope they find him and lock his ass up for the rest of his life," Stephanie said. Even she was crying. She didn't like Ben, but this was murder, and as much as she didn't like him, she wouldn't wish this on him. Plus, she had heard about Friday night. She and Stephanie got an earful on the Yard Saturday after Brandon, Ben's newspaper protégé, came up to Vicky on the Yard. They remembered him from the night at Burr when they won the step show, and Ben and Greg were about to get into a fight.

"Greg is so stupid," she continued. "I can't believe he thought he was going to get away with this, especially after everything at Burr the other night, and then at *The Hilltop*. He should've known he would be the first one the police came looking for."

Vicky didn't speak. She just rocked back and forth in Stephanie's arms. How could Greg Harris be so evil, she wondered. One had to be evil to take the life of someone else. She had seen the look in his eye the other night at the office, when he attacked Ben. He wanted to do serious harm to Ben. She reminded Forrest of this and was glad that he had been seeing things the same way she had. She also took comfort in the fact that he'd already told the police about it, as well as the sophomore year incident when Greg and his friends jumped Ben over something similar.

"All he was doing was writing about something that was true. I could see if it were false, but it was true," Vicky rocked. "If Greg couldn't handle all this, he shouldn't have been doing it."

Vicky and her friends watched as the evening news led with a breaking news story out of Washington D.C.

*When is rambunctious hip-hop partying, wild drinking, throngs of people in the streets, and a city turned inside out too much? And tonight, folks, we have news of a murder on the campus of How-ard University during the busiest time of the school year. Its annu-al homecoming celebration, which brings in thousands from out of town into the city each year to party—many of them not affiliated with the university—has left the editor-in-chief of the student news-paper dead, stabbed to death. Was this a random murder? Or was it a predictable culmination of the week's events, the annual football game, and a slew of afterparties? Tonight, we hear from local police, university officials, and students at the school.*

"It was Greg Harris, you stupid bitch!" Vicky yelled, and hurled the spoon she stirred her tea with at the screen.

"I can't believe they're gonna try to blame this on homecom-ing. They look for a reason every year to take it away from us," Stephanie added.

"Argh! Can we call them and get a retraction? I can't believe this," Jasmine finally chimed in.

They flipped through several channels and most newscasts led with the same erroneous stories. How irresponsible. Jasmine and Stephanie's landline phone started ringing off the hook after this, with other incredulous coeds asking the same questions, threatening to write letters to whomever directed the news coverage.

"What if they never find him?" Vicky worried. "What if Greg gets away with this? They gotta catch him. They can't stop looking until they catch him," she cried. Vicky was a mess, and her friends knew it. They killed the television, picked up the spoon she threw at it, and escorted her to Jasmine's bedroom, where Vicky laid down for some rest. She hadn't gotten any all night. Hopefully, they tried to assure her, the police would catch up with Greg that night.

When you came down from an angel dust high, you really came down. Greg could barely sit still in the cold orange metal chair from inside the recording cell at the Metropolitan Police Department's third district. His hands lay cuffed on his lap, his eyes half-closed to the world. The guard, a short, stocky, middle-aged black cop with a salt-and-pepper beard, shook the chair violently every time Greg's head fell to his chest. With every shake, he would jump up, shivering with bloodshot eyes, wishing he could rub his arms to create a warming sensation. A urine smell permeated the small cell, and Greg sat plastered in front of a gray cinderblock wall, staring into a black video camera, as a judge spoke to him remotely.

"Did you hear what I said, Mr. Harris? Mr. Harris!"

The guard came from in front of the cell again and shook Greg's chair.

"Wha-," he said jumping in his chair. Greg hadn't gotten a good night's sleep, and it was late Sunday afternoon.

"I said, did you hear me?" the judge asked again.

"Well, answer the man," the cop ordered.

Greg raised his two shackled hands and dug his two thumbs into his eyes.

"Can you repeat the question?"

"That's can you repeat the question, *Your Honor*," the officer corrected him.

Greg stared at him, hating him for being a cop, but hating him for being a black cop even more. Greg was from Los Angeles, the place that birthed the original members of the rap group N.W.A. When they screamed, "Fuck the police," so did he, and like Ice Cube, the group's most talented lyricist said, black cops will show out for white cops at the drop of a dime. Greg thought about this when he looked at the cop, who was looking back at him, pointing for Greg to look into the camera and answer the judge.

"I said, can you repeat the question please, Your Honor."

"I said, do you know what you have been charged with?"

"No sir."

"Reckless endangerment of a juvenile, illegally participating in child pornography, aggravated assault, and fraud. I know you've been in lockup, Mr. Harris, but this is an arraignment proceeding from here. You are being formally charged, and you will have a preliminary hearing in three weeks. An attorney will be provided for you if you cannot afford one. I am releasing you under your own recognizance, young man. Do you hear me?"

"Yes, Your Honor," Greg said, looking into the camera. On the side of the tripod was a 20-inch color television, where he could see a live image of the white-haired white man dressed in a black robe talking to him. He was nestled comfortably on a cherry wood bench in a courtroom somewhere, a place where Greg and all the people brought in lockup to the third district didn't even have to go. They told him when they first booked him that his arraignment would be fed via satellite to a judge downtown. Greg knew the police would catch up with him sooner or later for the website stuff. He was just happy that they weren't charging him with what he initially feared they were going to when they first pulled him over.

He had sped off from the scene after Ben Bishop fell to the ground. Anyone around could have heard his tires screech. Now that he thought about it, somebody had probably gotten the license plate number of the car he was driving, because no one knew that he had switched cars except for Neeko and Poncho. Instead of lying low after everything was done, like they had initially planned, Greg went back to Neeko's, where they ate spaghetti and replayed everything that happened. Feeling safe and secure, after he stashed his weapons at Neeko's, he made one trip to his apartment before planning to go to a female acquaintance's house. That was his mistake.

They let him go into his place, but once he stepped outside, thermal shirt in one hand, set of keys to the hooptie that wasn't his in the other, six officers yelled for him to freeze, all with their weapons drawn. He took inventory of the scene in front of him, the flashing lights coming around the corner, and decided not to make a run for it back into the apartment building. He yielded, and felt the hard shoves as they rushed him to the ground and cuffed him. They had accused him of murder and a slew of other offenses, and stuffed him in the back of a squad car. They made him wait in the back of the car and left him subject to inquiries from nosy neighbors who were awakened by the shouts and flashing lights, and wanted to walk up to the car and see who it was. He heard some of them volunteer that they had seen him come in and out of the building and that he didn't speak much.

He regretted all of the stupid moves he had made that night, and how, if he were more disciplined, he would have evaded the cops. Why did he go back to his apartment? He should have gone straight to Maryland after he dropped Neeko and Poncho off. It wasn't supposed to come to this, he thought, sitting in the back of the car. All because he had shorted a couple of girls a few dollars from a photo shoot.

Murder? How could it be murder? He knew that he hadn't committed a murder and neither did the people he was with; and after spending several hours in jail, he was glad that the police finally knew that and had dropped the charge they initially levied against him.


For all the tears Brandon cried, his mother couldn't console him enough. He spent Saturday night drunk; partying with every other freshman that club-hopped, courtesy of two shuttle buses that left from in front of the quad once an hour after 11 p.m. The shuttles provided by the university dropped students off at three different clubs—all freshman-targeted, 18-and-over clubs. If there were any fast freshmen that had access to fake IDs, they skipped catching the Howard shuttle and caught cabs or the Metro, which was D.C.'s public transportation system.

By 3:30 a.m., Brandon was out of it, but was trying to make it into D.C. Live, a 21-and-over club, but fell short of getting inside when he started vomiting on the street in front of the club. All he could remember later on was sitting on the freezing sidewalk, wiping vomit from the corners of his mouth, denying cheerful and drunk passersby offers to help him up or call him a cab.

Embarrassing was an understatement. He knew most upper-classmen would look at him and call him a stupid freshman when they saw him outside, stapled to the ground, across the street from the club with throw up on his face. But he wished he could have avoided it. Like most freshmen, Brandon had tried so hard to be older than he was. It was a natural outgrowth of spending so much time around the likes of Greg Harris and Ben, seeing all the attention they got from girls on campus.

Outside the club, Brandon had run across *Hilltop* staffers who teased him and admonished him for drinking too much, and he eventually got a ride home with one—he couldn't remember who. But he was not prepared for the *Hilltop* news that would wake him up Sunday.

"Hello," Brandon offered, half asleep on Sunday morning.

"Brandon, have you heard?"

"Hello."

"Brandon, wake up," the voice said, tears audible from Brandon's end of the phone.

"Forrest?"

"Ben is dead."

"What?"

"It's Ben. He got stabbed to death. They found him in front of the School of C this morning."

Ben immediately broke down crying on the other end of the phone and snatched the covers completely off of himself.

"What? What time was this? Where are you?"

"I'm walking over to the hospital. That's where everybody is.

President Humphries is having a press conference over there soon. But Brandon we need—."

Brandon hung up on Forrest before he could say anything else. He rushed down the hall to the bathroom, bushed his teeth, and got dressed. He felt like shit, but the call woke him.

He got to the press conference 15 minutes later and joined in with other *Hilltop* staff members who were crying outside of the emergency room. Forrest was there. So was Vicky, Ben's girlfriend. Vicky convinced Brandon to abandon every fear he held about Greg coming back for retribution, and he gave police officers Greg's cell phone number and Columbia Heights address. He couldn't mourn completely, because Forrest had put him on the big story and he would write it for Monday's paper. Forrest, in turn, was going to edit a story that Ben was working on and publish it.

Ten hours later, Ben and Forrest pulled up to the Metropolitan Third District Police Station and found a parking spot out front. Word on campus, through a source in the president's office that Forrest had been working, was that police had a suspect in custody.

"You coming in?" Brandon asked.

"I'll wait here. I can't afford another boot on my car and this spot is illegal," Forrest said.

Brandon swallowed hard and walked into the station. Pictures of fugitives hung on the wall inside, and Police Athletic League flyers with marker scribble on them stared back at him. Two female officers sat behind a glass window. Ben approached them.

"Hi can I help you, young man?"

"I'm from Howard University. I work for the student paper, *The Hilltop*. We heard that you guys had someone in custody for the murder on campus this morning," Ben said.

"Not quite," one woman said. "We had a suspect, but we're releasing him."

"Releasing him. Why?"

"Sir, I'm not allowed to release that information. You're going to have to call downtown to public relations."

Brandon was about to throw a fit when a door behind him opened and an officer pushed Greg through and unlocked his cuffs.

"Damn, man. You just gon' push me like that. I could sue y'all motherfuckers for that," Greg said.

"Keep it up and your little punk ass will be right back in here," the cop threatened before giving him one last push.

"Man, fuck you!" Greg proclaimed, garnering the attention of the two women behind the desk.

Greg turned around and saw Brandon looking at him. He nodded his head and walked out the door. Brandon started to follow him when someone else emerged from outside.

Falu Davis was dressed in a black wool coat, jeans and black sneakers, and makeup ran down her face from soggy eyes. A woman who was just as tall as her and looked like her, followed her in. A man that was even taller followed the older Falu lookalike.

"Officer, I called on the phone about the case at Howard. My daughter is turning herself in," the woman said.

Brandon should have been writing this down in his notepad, but he froze, staring into Falu's eyes, shaking his head, preparing to cry.

"I'm so sorry," Falu sobbed, pleading with Brandon. "I didn't mean to do it."

Brandon grabbed his notepad from his coat and started scribbling. Once Falu's mother saw this, she took over the situation.

"Young lady, shut your mouth, now!"

"But mom I didn't mean to do it. I want everyone to know that," Falu cried.

Her mother slapped her then, and asked the officer to escort them to an office where they could talk. The officer standing in the lobby opened the door he had just let Greg Harris out of, let them inside and asked Brandon to leave. While walking out, Brandon heard a shrieking sound from Falu in the distance.

"Hello, Ms. Davis. My name is Officer Culpepper. This is Sergeant Wilson," The officer said, after they had all sat down in a small interrogation room. Metallic gray and copper file cabinets lined the back wall, and a gray metal table sat in the middle of the floor. There were initially only two chairs inside, but Officer Culpepper rolled in three more. He let Sergeant Wilson, Falu and her parents sit.

Falu sobbed like a baby, using a tissue her mother gave her to wipe her eyes. She knew her mother wanted to slap her for showing so much emotion, so much weakness, but she didn't care. Her life was over, as far as she was concerned. No Harvard, no Supreme Court, she wasn't even going to graduate. There would be no marriage to Eric; instead she would be married to a prison cell for a very long time.

"Okay, Ms. Davis, we just want to be clear that you understand what you are doing," Officer Culpepper said, pulling out a notepad and tape recorder. "What you are about to do is give a confession of murder," he continued.

"More like manslaughter," her mother interjected. "I'm an attorney. I'm her attorney," her mother said, boldly.

"Well, now that we have her legal counsel settled, we can get along with this," Officer Culpepper said. He looked at Mr. Davis, who didn't speak much. He just sat and held his daughter's hand at the table.

"We can begin anytime you want," he said, nodding toward Falu.

Falu's father whispered something in her ear and squeezed her hand. She looked back at her father and nodded in agreement.

"I invited Ben over to my dorm Saturday night because I had some papers I needed to show him," she began.

"What papers?"

"Phone records," she sniffled. "Ben was the editor of the newspaper at school. He was working on a story about an exorbitant phone bill that my office had accrued."

"Your office?"

"Yes. I'm the student government president at Howard. I was the president last year, too."

"An overachiever, huh?" Officer Culpepper tried to joke. She was beautiful enough to make the hardest of cops flirt.

"Something like that. Well, last year, the staff and myself got carried away with making long distance and international phone calls. The bill came back this year and Ben found out about it."

"So, Ben was going to write a story about your staff?"

"Correct. We had multiple copies of the invoice circulating and I was unsure of the numbers, so I tabulated what I thought was a correct figure," Falu said, lying. She knew the figure Dean Thomas had was correct. "Ben and I talked on the phone, and I told him that he could come by and see the paperwork I had concerning who made what phone calls and how much the bill was. Oh, and I forgot to add that university phone codes were stolen to make some of those calls," she said.

"These codes were stolen by you and your staff?"

She hesitated and then said, "Yes."

"I see. Now tell me about last night. What happened when Ben came to your room?"

"He came to my room, we had tea, we talked and I showed him the paperwork."

"And that's it? Did he have to sign in and out of the dorm?"

"That was it, and yes, he signed in and out. I'm sure if you check, you'll see that," she said, conveniently leaving out the quasi-sexual encounter that she and Ben had.

She hadn't told her parents about that. She wanted to tell her mother, but her father was always present, and she feared judgment from him. Her mother was more cutthroat, Falu knew, so she was more likely to understand what Falu was trying to do by offering sex.

But if she had decided to tell Officer Culpepper about her tryst with Ben, she would have told him that she walked back over to her bed where Ben was holding himself, that she grabbed him and started caressing him. They kissed for a while longer, and just as she was tearing the condom wrapper, Ben grew a conscience and told her that he couldn't go through with it. He had a girlfriend, he said, and he was trying to be faithful. Falu tried to ignore him and began kissing him again, but he pushed her to the side and got dressed. He threatened to storm out of her suite if she didn't get dressed with him and walk him downstairs to sign him out, so he could get his student ID back.

Falu got dressed and made him one last offer out of desperate hope, but he declined. She walked him downstairs, signed him out, and walked him to the front door, where she hugged him and told him how sorry she was. Ben, being cool Ben, told her not to worry about it … but that he was still going to write the story.

"Then what happened?" Culpepper asked, oblivious to Falu's failed sexual bribery.

"I went back up to my room and realized that he left his knife," she said.

"A knife?" Officer Culpepper quizzed. "Why did he have a knife?"

"Greg Harris."

"The guy who just left here?"

"Yes. Greg and Ben have a history. In Friday's paper, Ben wrote a story about an illegal website Greg was running and how he was paying juveniles to pose naked. Ben was afraid that Greg and his friends would come looking for him, so he walked around with a knife."

"This is a crazy story. Well, where is the knife? Detectives didn't find one on the scene."

"I threw it in the dumpster behind the Engineering building," she said.

"I'll get someone over there," Sergeant Wilson said, standing up to leave the room.

"Ms. Davis, what happened when you caught up to Mr. Bishop?"

"I begged him not to write the article, but he said that he had to," she cried.

"And then what happened?"

"He walked away from me. So I ... So I followed him down the street. He saw me coming toward him and he started yelling. He grabbed my left arm and started shaking me, telling me to get away from him before I found out he wasn't so nice. I yanked myself free from him and I ... And I sta— ... I stabbed him a few times. Oh my God, I'm so sorry," she said. Now the tears flowed steadily. "He stumbled to the grass and fell. I heard a car screech in the background, so I ran," she said.

The part about her walking up to him and stabbing him was true. The screeching car that she heard, which was Greg and his crew, was true too, although she didn't know it was Greg. But Falu was lying about a couple of things. For one, Ben never approached her or shook her arm. And Ben did not leave the knife at her apartment; like an expert pickpocket, she had taken the knife from Ben when she hugged him goodbye. She contemplated what she had to do for three floors up on the elevator, before she decided that there was no other way.

She reversed the elevator and ran out after him. He waited for her at the light across the street, in front of WHU-TV, Howard's television station. Once face-to-face, she pleaded with Ben again, and offered him sex, but he declined. He turned his back and walked away from her, which was the wrong thing for him to do. She ran up on him and stabbed him twice in the back and repeatedly in the chest. The blade drove through his skin, shortening each breath he took. Traces of vapor billowed in the air from his short breaths. He looked afraid. The car screeched out of nowhere. Falu gathered herself, turned around and left. Holding out on those details would make it more prosecutable as manslaughter than murder. She told the story just the way her mother told her to.

"Is that the whole story?" Officer Culpepper said. He pushed a paper in front of her that had a line for her signature on it.

She wiped the corners of her eyes, sniffled, and looked up at him.

"That's everything."

About the author

Ira Porter is also the author of fiction novels, A Slow Accident Waiting to Happen and The Price. He is a graduate of Howard University. He lives in Delaware with his wife and son.

www.ingramcontent.com/pod-product-compliance
Lightning Source LLC
Chambersburg PA
CBHW071329250626
47159CB00004B/1523